THE GUILTY TEACHER

J. A. BAKER

First published as *The Face of Clara Morgan* in 2021. This edition published in Great Britain in 2024 by Boldwood Books Ltd.

Copyright © J. A. Baker, 2021

Cover Design by Head Design Ltd

Cover Illustration: iStock

The moral right of J. A. Baker to be identified as the author of this work has been asserted in accordance with the Copyright, Designs and Patents Act 1988.

All rights reserved. No part of this book may be reproduced in any form or by any electronic or mechanical means, including information storage and retrieval systems, without written permission from the author, except for the use of brief quotations in a book review.

This book is a work of fiction and, except in the case of historical fact, any resemblance to actual persons, living or dead, is purely coincidental.

Every effort has been made to obtain the necessary permissions with reference to copyright material, both illustrative and quoted. We apologise for any omissions in this respect and will be pleased to make the appropriate acknowledgements in any future edition.

A CIP catalogue record for this book is available from the British Library.

Paperback ISBN 978-1-83561-257-6

Large Print ISBN 978-1-83561-258-3

Hardback ISBN 978-1-83561-256-9

Ebook ISBN 978-1-83561-259-0

Kindle ISBN 978-1-83561-260-6

Audio CD ISBN 978-1-83561-251-4

MP3 CD ISBN 978-1-83561-252-1

Digital audio download ISBN 978-1-83561-255-2

Boldwood Books Ltd
23 Bowerdean Street
London SW6 3TN
www.boldwoodbooks.com

The face is a picture of the mind with the eyes as its interpreter.

— MARCUS TULLIUS CICERO

Nothing in the world can be compared to the human face. It is a land one can never tire of exploring.

— CARL THEODOR DREYER

PROLOGUE

The noise ricochets around the room, silencing everyone. Time passes. An endless stretch of nothingness, the world in a lull.

His heart thumps, a thick, resonant pounding, amplified a hundredfold in his head as it hammers away beneath his breastbone. His breathing roars in his ears, blood gushing through his veins, making him hot, restless, dizzy. The room spins. A scream from somewhere behind him cuts through the momentary hush, loud and visceral, followed by a collective gasp and the growing murmurs and whimpers of terrified teenagers. Blood pools beneath the writhing body at his feet.

Girls cluster in the corner, limbs hooked around one other in a protective ring, heads dipped, limbs rigid with fear. Sobs filter through the tight knot of bodies, low at first before building into a crescendo, each driving the other on. Distress fuelling distress.

'Fuck. Fuck!' His words echo, eerie and disembodied, cutting through the whispers and groans, cutting through the screams. It's not his voice, doesn't even sound like him. And yet it is. There is a distance between his actions and thoughts, a cognitive separation, his primeval reflexes kicking in as he goes through the motions. Some part of his brain is functioning, helping him though this, while his conscious self has backed into a corner, huddling there, numb and frightened, a whole gamut of emotions whirring inside his brain, slotting and spinning – terror, self-preservation, fear and disgust, colliding and crashing.

He drops the weapon, kicks it away toward the wall and stares at his hands as if they belong to somebody else. Maybe they do. He can't think straight. Everything is skewed, the world tilting on its axis, time expanding and contracting, reality a slippery thing, dancing away from him, hiding, putting itself out of reach. He tries to grasp at it but it floats and falls, like a stray feather, weightless, too delicate to catch, to be pinned down and held tight.

No energy. He is suddenly weak, every part of his body sapped of strength, his ability to breathe reflexively an onerous task. The floor sways, sloping and seesawing. He swallows, rubs at his eyes, takes a juddering breath, swallows again.

He didn't mean to do it. Or did he? It was an accident, that's what he keeps telling himself. Things got out of hand. He had no choice. Look what happened only seconds earlier. They needed to stop this, to get help in this room.

He needed to stop this.

A sob escapes. He stifles it with his fingers, the palm of his hand cold against his warm, wet mouth. She's dying. Dear God, she is dying. And now he is dying too, the twitching body at his feet. The bleeding, battered body, all life draining out of it as the pool of thick crimson spreads, creeping ever closer to him, almost touching his shoes. He pulls his feet away, revulsion and shock rippling through him. It wasn't his fault. He had no choice. Something had to be done. Somebody had to take charge.

The quivering body suddenly becomes still, arms and legs immobile. No more thrashing and squirming. No movement at all. It lies there – eyes closed, lines of fear and confusion etched into its features.

There's no escaping from this, no way out of this unholy mess. So many witnesses. So much blood. He can smell it – that metallic tang of damaged flesh. The cloying odour of near death. It's everywhere – clinging to his clothes, sticking to his skin. He can't shake it.

More screaming, a thunderous noise from outside; voices shouting, fists hammering on the door, demanding to be let in. The table and chairs jamming it shut rattle and shake; sharp, angular noises that cut through his thoughts, jarring his senses, forcing him into the moment. Then people inside throwing things aside, tables scraping, chairs toppling. The door handle being turned. A change of air pressure as the door is flung open.

The room takes on different dimensions. Fear pinballs through his veins, sparks of terror heating up his cold, clammy skin. His stomach roils as he stares down at the lifeless bodies, the spread of sticky blood congealing on the floor, a reminder of what he has done. What they both did.

He casts his eyes downwards, his gaze moving back to the shotgun. All around him has stilled, the world slowing to a stop as he shuffles forward and leans down, grabbing at the weapon with trembling hands. It's the only way. He can't go to prison for this. He wouldn't survive in there. He may as well be dead.

More screams from behind him, next to him, above him as he slumps to the floor and rests the gun against his body, the muzzle nestled under his chin. The cold metal is a release. He shivers and sighs, his eyes flickering as a sense of release pulses through him. This is how it has to be. It's his only option now. No other way. He's ready for it, welcomes it even. It's a way out, a journey to a place of darkness where nothing and nobody matters.

His vision blurs, his head pounds as he places his finger on the trigger, lets out a deep breath and closes his eyes.

PART I
THE BEGINNING OF THE END

1

Nina knew this was going to happen, could feel it coming. Ever since her baby boy slithered out of her body all those years ago, purple and bruised after a difficult, forty-eight-hour labour. Ever since she held his tiny body, swaddled in blankets, his diminutive features scrunched up as he let out an ear-splitting scream that could shatter glass, she knew.

As well as the all-encompassing love that settled on her like a warm glow as she sat in the delivery room, aching, exhausted, blood still trickling out from between her legs, she felt a twinge of doubt. That overwhelming sense that things were going to be tough, problematic. That the path ahead would be rocky. She was young, full of love for her new-born, yet also so full of fear, of apprehension.

Fatigue had settled into her bones. If she was allowed to sleep for a hundred years, she couldn't imagine ever feeling refreshed, back to how she used to be. Her body was different, her mind full of worry. Still is. She once read that a difficult birth is indicative of a difficult child, that one follows the other just as surely as night follows day. The words of that article never left her, always creeping back into her mind during the trying times, the dog-tired times, the days that left her wondering if it was all worth it. All that pain, the bone-aching exhaustion, the endless sleepless nights spent tossing and turning, worrying that something dreadful was going to happen, that he would make it happen. Her boy.

And now it has.

Or at least, she thinks it has. Her world is askew, out of sync, a dizzying, sickening shift from normality that only she can sense. She swallows, grips the receiver tightly, perspiration forming on her upper lip. She feels cold, needs to sit down. Just for a second, to rest her aching bones, her muscles that are knotted with worry. The floor is soft beneath her feet, spongy and unstable, the beat of her heart beneath her sweater a heavy pendulum that bangs against her sternum, *thump thump thump*. It makes her light-headed and queasy, forcing her to take stock and start thinking clearly. She can do that. Or at least she thinks she can.

'Nina? Are you still there?'

The voice is distant. Disconnected from her reality. She has slipped into another world. A world full of darkness and sharp edges. A world that is cold and unwelcoming.

She doesn't want to be here. She wants to turn back time, to not to listen to Sally's voice. She wishes she had never answered the phone. She could pretend that none of this is happening. That life is normal. As normal as it has ever been. Not Sally's type of normal. She could never achieve that. No, of course she couldn't, but the sort of normal that she is used to. The sort of normal where the laundry basket is permanently overflowing and her son's bedroom looks like a bomb has exploded in there. The sort of normal that they as a family have become accustomed to – a house full of noise and movement. A house full of loud voices and unanswered questions. She just wants that back. With all its worries and anxieties and disquietude, the most recent event worsening their lives even further and fragmenting things to shattering point, it is still better than this. Better than feeling sure and yet at the same time, unsure. Better than experiencing a tug of dread at not knowing what may lie ahead.

The iron sizzles, reminding her that it is still switched on. A drip of water pops out of a hole on the underside and runs down the metal plate, steam hissing as the trickle evaporates, leaving a tiny cloud of mist in its wake.

She leans forward, switches it off, feels the heat of the steel and closes her eyes, wishing she could rewind, be the person she was ten minutes ago. Even scrubbing the kitchen floor, disinfecting the sink, wading through the mountainous pile of ironing that never seems to lessen is better than this. Anything is better than feeling like this. The uncertainty. The certainty. The anxiety and trepidation. The release of so many years of pent-up worry about her child. It has all come to this point, this jagged knife edge that is dangling perilously close to her face, repeatedly jabbing at her, reminding her that heartache and terror are never far away.

'Nina, don't take my word for it. You need to ring the school. I just thought you should be informed, that's all. I'm trying to get in touch with as many parents as possible. The ones we know, that is. Our little friendship group. Dane might not be caught up in it. I just wanted to keep you in the loop.'

Might not be caught up in it.

Those words say it all. The possibility that he could somehow be involved looms large in Nina's mind. She knows it. Sally knows it. Dane is a law unto himself. Always has been. She has tried to combat his escalating behaviour, his non-conformist ways, but she has been a lone voice whistling in the wind, her wisdom and advice obliterated by the oncoming hurricane. And now it is here, ripping apart their fragile existence. The storm is finally upon them and there is nowhere to hide, no shelter in sight. If she thought yesterday and the day before was bad, this piece of news takes misery and desperation to a whole new level.

It's Rob that he listens to. Always has and probably always will. And therein lies the problem. She wonders how many of her so-called friends within that group of tight-knit parents will remain by her side when this all comes out, when it is over and the dust settles and the grisly truth of their tattered life emerges.

'Right,' she finds herself saying, her voice ethereal and without substance, a solitary sound that ricochets inside her head like a bullet bouncing off stone. 'I'll ring them. Ask what's going on.'

'They'll probably be busy. Be prepared for a long wait before you get through now that word is getting round.' Sally pauses, her voice dropping in volume. 'Nina, as I said, I only rang to keep you updated. I didn't want you hearing it from somebody else. Please don't worry. It's probably something and nothing. I'm your friend. I just thought you should know, that's all.'

She's right. Sally is always right. Always calm and measured. Always one step ahead of the game, able to control things, to keep her little household in order. Everything in ship-shape fashion. Her boy won't be involved in any of this. Sally with her perfect family and well-behaved children. Sally with her wonderful husband and argument-free house. She has never lain awake at night wondering where it all went wrong. How it all went wrong. Who her husband is with, where he is. With a family who toe the line, never questioning her methods or judgement, a quiet, peaceful home, a malleable husband and high-flying progeny, Sally has it all.

Nina sits, takes a deep breath, tells herself to stop it. Her thoughts are uncalled for: ill-timed and judgemental. Her imagination is in overdrive, her nerves frayed. Sally is a good person. A decent human being. Sally is her friend. Nina has a wonderful house, one that many of her friends could only ever dream of owning. But that all it is: a house, not a home. There is little else to draw people here except its size and sheer magnificence. The absence of love within these walls is a crushing sensation that she feels every single day. The last few days have proved how pointless it all is – the money and status, the widescreen TVs and sleek sports cars. Nina has nothing. She is an empty being, devoid of all the things other people keep stored inside. The things that give people momentum, pushing them forward, giving them the confidence to face each day with a smile on their faces – love, security, ambition. She has none of those.

'Thanks for letting me know. This is all a bit of a shock, isn't it?'

'It really is. Not what you expect to hear at all. Thing is, since this new head teacher came along, the kids don't have their phones with them, so it's not as if we can even ring them. All the mobiles get put in a locker until breaktime. Anyway, I'm sure the police have everything in hand.'

'I'm sure they do,' Nina says, chewing at the side of her mouth, tugging and nibbling until a sharp crack of pain causes her to stop, her vision misting over as an eye-watering ache sets in and a thin, oily streak of metallic-tasting fluid fills her mouth.

'I'll see you later then.' Sally sounds distant now.

Nina wonders if she is regretting her actions, wishing she had never made this call. It feels like a warning, a pre-emptive strike. What if Dane *is* involved? What then? She has no set script in her head, nothing prepared to help her deal with this scenario. She feels lost, alone on a choppy sea with no land in sight. She did this with her actions over the weekend. This is all her fault. She set this thing in motion and now look what has happened. Look what she has done.

'Yes. Thanks again, Sally. I'll see you soon.' Gravel has filled her throat, stopping her from speaking properly. Her gums are sore, her eyes heavy, her tongue thick and furry with the anxiety of not knowing. And yet at the same time, knowing.

She puts down the phone, leans her head under the tap and takes a long gulp of cold water, clearing her mouth, soothing her throat. Attempting to wash away her terrible thoughts.

Her hands are trembling; her knees are weak. Without a shred of evidence, she is already faltering, assuming the worst, picturing her life falling down around her, a wrecking ball battering against the crumbling walls that hold her life together. She visualises it smashing against the bricks, watching as they topple, too broken and fragmented to ever be rebuilt, turning to dust as they hit the ground. This is worse than what happened at the weekend. Much, much worse. And if Dane is involved, then she did this.

If he is involved.

There are almost one thousand pupils at that school. The odds are stacked in her favour.

And what if this person is wrong? What if this lady who spotted the armed police heading into the school has a vivid imagination and a loose tongue? What if she is no more than a conniving old gossip who doesn't care how much worry and anxiety she causes?

Word has spread rapidly. Parents are frightened, their senses heightened, every nerve ending shrieking at them, putting them on red alert as they wait for updates. And still no word from the school. Surely parents would have heard something by now? It would be remiss of them to not inform parents and carers. And yet, all those calls to make. The families of over one thousand pupils to contact and only a handful of office workers to do it. It could take them all day to get in touch with everyone. Nina's heartrate increases. She swallows, rubs at her eyes. She is exhausted. It is only 11 a.m. and already she is so incredibly weary, too tired to think clearly, her logic and lucidity in freefall.

Dark, unwelcome thoughts tumble and fight for space in her head. Dane and his new friend. Dane and his sullen behaviour. Dane and the events that took place in their house recently...

Then she thinks of the obvious and turns on the television. Armed police storming into a school will make the news. It has to, doesn't it? There will be some sort of attention for such an event. There has to be. Lesser stories have made the news. Surely an event of this magnitude will warrant major coverage?

Sky News and the BBC report on the usual mundane matters as she stands and waits, watching the scrolling updates at the bottom of the screen. Nothing. The weather, falling share prices, the usual bickering of MPs who bat comments back and forth like a ping-pong ball. Nothing about armed police entering a school. It feels conspicuous by its absence. It feels as if this woman has dreamt it up, set in motion a story that has gained speed and is now an unstoppable rock rolling down a hill, ready to crash into the lives of every parent in town while she sits, sated and replete, happy that her words have stirred up a whirling eddy of terror and uncertainty.

The wait continues, Nina's guts a mass of hot liquid. Theirs is a small town, tucked away in the remoteness of North Yorkshire. It will take time for word to filter through to the national news. That's what it is. This woman won't have lied. Why would she? What is to be gained from fabricating such an outlandish tale? Nobody is that stupid or thoughtless, are they?

Nina nibbles at her nails, wishing she hadn't read those notes in Dane's room, wishing she could be sitting here in blissful ignorance. Her insides shift and growl some more as she recalls those images, those words. She has done her best to blot them out, to pretend she didn't see them. Except she did. She has spent weeks and months and years making excuses for her boy. So many excuses, so many sleepless nights. He's an immature lad, still trying to work out the dynamics of the world at large. She knows that, she really does. Dear God, he barely understands his own emotions. He certainly doesn't have the capacity to climb inside the heads of those around him, the figures of authority who hem him in, force him to do things he doesn't want to do. He was lashing out when he wrote those notes, drew those images, that's all it was. A kickback against the adults in his life.

She has lost count of the number of times he has told her to shut up, calling her a stupid cow and telling her she has ruined his life, this boy, this lad who is almost a man. Her baby. And then with things turning sour at home, it may well have pushed him over the edge. They did this to him – his parents, her and Rob. They created the perfect storm for their boy and then cut him adrift, left him to flounder, watching as he splutters and drowns, sinking to the bottom of the ocean.

For so long now, she has buried the feeling that something is wrong, told herself he cannot process his emotions in the usual fashion, that it is simply a phase he is going through – a long, drawn-out phase that seems to have no end – but a phase borne out of teenage angst and anger nonetheless. She is his mother and despite her deep-rooted sensation that all is not right in his world, she still feels the need to protect him, to provide a rational explanation for his actions and conduct. But now that sensation is rising to the surface, threatening to drag her under. She struggles to breathe, her head swimming as she stands and makes her way upstairs, her legs carrying her towards his bedroom. His sanctuary. The place where he hides away from everybody and everything. Including his own mother.

It is everything she expects it to be – untidy, smelly, his personal possessions strewn far and wide. Wires snake over the floor, trailing a path to a pile of unfathomable machines that take up so much of his time. She has no idea what they are, these machines and computers, and admittedly has long since stopped monitoring what he watches or who he interacts with. Which parents do? Even the ones who claim to be vigilant and responsible let things slide. It's a minefield, this technology thing, a bloody minefield and she wouldn't have the first clue how to work out what sort of content he views. Christ, he could be watching porn or murder videos or any kind of shit that undoubtedly fascinates and repulses many teenagers in equal measure.

Telling herself he's no different to any other fifteen-year-old out there,

Nina slumps down onto his unmade bed, idly smoothing out the covers with her palm, breathing in the scent of him, questioning her parenting techniques. Wishing, wishing, wishing. What exactly is she wishing for? A different life? A different child? She shakes her head, tears falling freely now. Maybe she has it all wrong. Maybe Dane is at school, working hard, oblivious to what is happening around him. Maybe this is all one big, fucking nightmare. He's her son. She needs to quell her niggling fears, have a little faith in her boy. He's not a bad lad, just slow to develop.

If she hadn't found those notes, she wouldn't be having these doubts. If things hadn't escalated so badly at home over the past few days, she wouldn't be so nervous about his mental state. She would be concerned for his welfare, worried he may be in danger. It wouldn't be this. Definitely not this. She wouldn't be having these bad thoughts. Thoughts that he is the one behind all of this. She wants them to go away, to leave her be, let her think clearly, not clutter up her mind, drip feeding her bits of toxic information that poison her brain, turning her against her own child. For all she knows, he could be crouched behind a desk, cowering from an unknown assailant, praying to be saved. Thinking about his mum. Wishing she was there to help him.

A sob escapes. She searches for the drawings, her hands quivering as she sifts through his things, moving socks and underwear out of the way, opening books, tipping them upside down, hoping for those incriminating pieces of paper to flutter out and miraculously land at her feet.

God, this is terrible. She stops, her hand pressed to her breastbone in despair. What is she thinking? This isn't some American high school shooting. This is a small town in North Yorkshire. It's all in her head – an imaginary scenario. She is losing control, letting her imagination run riot, letting her worst fears take over.

Her footfall is loud and clumsy as she heads back downstairs and grapples with her phone. The school will have the answers she needs. No point in wild guesses and suppositions until she has all the facts. That's what her dad would say – get all your facts sorted and in line before you start firing your weapon. A bad analogy given the circumstances, she thinks.

She punches in the number, the one she knows off by heart, and waits, a thousand unimaginably horrible visions filling her head. She is greeted by an answer machine that tries to direct her to different departments and in her confusion, she presses the wrong key and ends the call.

Shit!

A visit to the school website and Facebook page proves fruitless. No news there. No updates, no pleas for parents to remain calm. No notifications to reassure them that everything is in hand and that it is a regular occurrence for armed police to visit the school. Nothing to see here. It's another normal day at a normal school in an average town.

Just as she begins to think that perhaps this is all a big mistake, a terrible misunderstanding by a witness who has alerted the entire neighbourhood over a false alarm, the phone rings. It stills her blood, makes her feel weighted to the ground, as if she has been encased in concrete, the ringing a shrill echo in her ears.

Her palms are slippery, her brain, her skin, her entire body burning with fear and anticipation. She wants to know. She doesn't want to know. She snatches up the phone, hardly able to breathe, her heart a caged bird banging against her ribs, desperate to be free, its wings fluttering manically. She sits, her legs too weak to hold her upright, clears her throat and speaks.

2

The house seems to shrink around her, the walls moving closer and closer, squashing Kate into a tiny, compacted being. This is how it is now. This is how she is expected to live – as a housewife in a small property that is identical to every other house on the street, living the life of a nobody. Complaining or voicing her concerns feels pointless. It simply riles Anthony into a state of apoplexy. Besides, there isn't enough space for private conversations and disagreements in this place. The house is too tiny for big voices. Any shouting or arguing rattles the windowpanes, shaking the very foundations on which they stand. So she hisses at him instead, her deteriorating mood conveyed by her lowered, tight voice and even tighter expression.

Time is a piece of elastic, stretching out ahead of her with no beginning or endpoint. She once asked Anthony when it would all be over, when her nightmare existence in this house, in this town, would ever end, to which he replied, 'Maybe tomorrow. Maybe never.'

Maybe never is her thinking. She cannot see any changes ahead, not as things stand and the thought that this is it, that this is her life forevermore, turns her stomach, twisting it into a tight, painful knot.

Her recent actions have backfired spectacularly, serving only to exacerbate their problems. She isn't sure they can survive this latest catastrophe.

The one that she caused. She and Anthony are now treading a fine line, the already thin strands of their marriage now hanging by an almost invisible thread. Maybe it's a good thing, them coming apart and unspooling. Maybe Anthony had his chance and blew it, ignoring her wishes, ignoring the needs of his family. Ignoring her.

Control and routine were the things that kept her going. She lost control when Anthony lost his job and as for routine – how can anybody be expected to have routine and order living somewhere like this? In this pinprick of a house on a new estate full of faceless, hapless families who think their success is measured by the extra foot they have gained in their living room or the fact they now have a fourth bedroom and, in some cases, a double driveway. Working-class people who think they've made it big, making their mark in society by upgrading to a bigger, better property, that's all they are. And now she is one of them.

She keeps telling herself that she doesn't blame Anthony, but deep down, she feels such anger that there are times when she can barely bring herself to look at him. She sometimes visualises herself slapping him, hitting and punching him. Inflicting so much damage, he no longer resembles himself at all but a wounded soldier, a war victim. Their war. Their own personal, ongoing battle. White-hot fury rages inside her, an unstoppable furnace, its flames scorching her insides, and the longer she contains it, the hotter and angrier it becomes.

Outside, a car passes by. It is so close, it feels as if it's about to drive straight into their living room. The rumble of a tractor, the screech of a bus, the inane chatter of passers-by, they penetrate her thoughts, disturb her musings, invading her personal space. Not that her musings are anything of value anymore. There was a time she felt able to paint, to attend the local choir, to do something creative, but just lately, she feels stripped of ideas, her artistic tendencies turned to dust along with their bank balance.

It could be worse. That's what she keeps telling herself. It could be a whole lot worse. It could also be a whole lot better. Still, at least they are all healthy. At least they have that fact to cling onto. She tries to stay positive, to remain upbeat and fight the tsunami of misery that regularly engulfs her, but she fails every single time.

How else is she supposed to get through this? She has Jocelyn and

Alexander to think of. They need her. She needs them. Soon they'll grow up and leave, start lives of their own, independent of their parents. She shudders. The very idea of just her and Anthony alone together in this house chills her blood.

None of this is how she envisioned it all those years ago when she married him. She pictured an easy life together, a large family home, a decent car, a couple of holidays a year and hopefully some leisure time – badminton club, art classes, shopping, eating in exclusive restaurants – that was what she hoped for. She certainly didn't bank on this – sitting in this bland, newly built house, surrounded by strangers, fearing for their future, wondering where they will all be in ten years' time. Wondering whether or not their finances will ever recover from this catastrophic downturn.

She loves him. Of course she does. He is her husband. It goes with the territory. Whether or not she likes him is another matter entirely.

The picture on the wall screams at her, its presence suddenly ugly and unwanted. A photograph of the four of them taken when they were happy, when they gelled together as a family. Taken before everything became unglued and fell apart.

Prior to the recent telephone call from Nina, Anthony didn't seem to think they had hit any sort of disaster. In fact, he seemed frighteningly happy with their situation, revelling in the fact that he no longer has to take on any heavy responsibilities. He appears to have settled nicely into his new role – too nicely. It won't last. It can't. She nibbles at her recently painted nails. This sort of life isn't him. She knows him better than he knows himself. It's not who he is. His ego will need a massage at some point. He will become bored, unused to being left out of making major decisions, pissed off at being ignored by his senior colleagues. Anthony is used to being top of the pile, not squashed underfoot by people with half his experience who are young enough to be his children.

It can't come soon enough, him reaching that boredom threshold. She isn't being uncharitable. She isn't being anything. He is the one who has changed, lowering his standards, being only too ready to accept less than his worth. He certainly isn't the man she married.

And they have the children to think of. What about them? It isn't snobbery to want the best for them, is it? It's common sense. That's what parents do – they look after their offspring and care for them, give them the best opportunities, protect them from the blows of the world. Right now, their children are attending the local comprehensive school, mingling with what she is sure is a fair sprinkling of decent children whilst also sitting elbow to elbow with a goodly number of undesirables. She has seen them in town – youngsters milling about on bikes, wearing hoodies, leering and shouting at passers-by, cigarettes dangling from the corners of their mouths, profanities swilling about in the air above their heads. And that's how they act in public. God only knows what they get up to in the privacy of their own homes.

She wants better than that for her children. What is so wrong with that? The fees at the school they used to attend now feel astronomical given Anthony's current salary. That sort of money used to seem like chickenfeed. Now the thought of forking out those staggering sums of cash makes her eyes water. What have they become? She blinks back tears. How far they have fallen in recent months.

She worries about the children. They're young, impressionable. They have been forced to start their lives all over again, to move schools, move house, leave old friends behind, make new ones. It's a traumatic time for them. And they're sensitive too. The confidence they exude is a thin veneer. Behind it are two frightened youngsters who have had their lives torn apart. They had no say in this move. It was thrust upon them by Anthony's mistakes and inertia. He had become lazy and inept in certain areas. Being a hedge fund manager requires a razor-sharp mind and dynamism. In recent years, he has let things lapse, blaming his age and younger colleagues who lack his ethics and integrity. He said he didn't care for their methods, the way they aggressively managed the funds. His sensitivities got in the way of his need to keep a decent salary coming in for his family and he was 'let go' earlier in the year.

Damn Anthony and his soft edges. Damn his sudden inability to develop a tougher side so they can all go back to how things were before everything tumbled and crashed around them. From hedge fund manager to financial adviser within the space of a couple of months. He now spends his days advising elderly couples where to shift their measly pensions to ensure they can afford their yearly cruise and still be able to buy their grandchildren half decent presents every Christmas.

More tears sting at her eyes. She suppresses them. They threaten to flow almost daily. Rather than sit here maudlin, wishing for something better, wishing her recent plans had paid off, she tries to do something, anything, but even the most basic of tasks feel so incredibly draining.

She thinks of their old life and wonders if Anthony misses any of it. And where are their old friends and Anthony's colleagues when you need them? God knows he used to have plenty. Funny how their acquaintances have all dropped away now they are no longer on an equal financial footing. Is that what bound them all together? Their large houses and healthy bank balances? It seems sad if that is the case but then who can blame them for abandoning people who happily settle for less? It's a cut-throat environment out there and everyone has to work hard to fulfil their ambitions. She and Anthony would no longer be able to keep up with the financial demands of the parties and social gatherings that they used to attend. It would be embarrassing for everyone concerned. Probably better that they have been dropped to save face.

She doesn't think she could stand it – mingling and chatting with the other wives who would be decked out in the latest designer dresses and expensive jewellery, while she stands, awkward and conspicuous with her cheap haircut and inferior clothing. There would be no proper holidays to speak of, no new cars to discuss, no chatter about the children and how they were all getting on at school. She doesn't think she could bear to talk about Jocelyn and Alexander and how they were settling in at the local comprehensive. Eyes would dip, people would make excuses to leave and they would all gradually shuffle away, her humiliation a tangible barrier between them all, setting her apart from people who used to be her equal.

The thought of being pitied makes her queasy. She would rather be forgotten than that. Pity is for the weak and the vulnerable and she is neither. What she is, is a victim of Anthony's incompetence, the entire family caught up in the slipstream of his slapdash ways. She deserves better. They all do.

Her fingers hover over the phone. Fiona was always a good friend to her. She could possibly call again, ask her to put out more feelers, see if

Gavin has heard of any more vacancies. Anthony and Gavin always got on well. Not close friends but they rubbed along together nicely. She thinks of how Anthony reacted the last time she did this, meddling in his affairs, begging for help behind his back. He was insulted, claiming it hurt his pride, but what about *her* pride? What about *her* needs and desires? Surely she is entitled to a say in how their lives should be? Their current trajectory is way off from its desired location. They are all heading in the wrong direction, about to become cut off from everything and everyone they know and she isn't prepared to just sit here and let it happen.

The longer she waits, the greater the distance. At some point, everything will be too far behind them, the miles between them and their friends too great to ever reconnect the broken link in their chain. She has to act now, to try again.

She punches in Fiona's number, her breathing erratic and heavy as she waits, every ring vibrating through her body.

'Hello?'

She sucks in her breath, tries to stop the tremble coursing through her veins. Her skin feels hot and cold at the same time, goosebumps prickling her flesh as her temperature fluctuates wildly.

'Kate, is that you? Are you there?'

She wants to reply, to speak to Fiona, to tell her that her life is coming apart at the seams and that she desperately needs her help but the words won't come. She wants to tell her friend that she has done something terrible to try to make things better, something unforgiveable in a desperate bid to improve their circumstances and now she has ruined everything but still the words refuse to formulate. They are there in her head but whenever she tries to speak, they stick in her throat, dry and ill-fitting, like jagged pebbles. This isn't the first time she has done this, called Fiona without saying anything. It feels so demeaning, so damn mortifying. They were once peers and now look at her, sitting here, phone in hand, too tongue-tied to speak, her life, her marriage an unrecognisable, sodden mess.

Holding the phone away from her face as if it is somehow contaminated, she ends the call, a wave of humiliation washing over her, its riptide pulling her under. Is this what her life has come to? Begging for help from people who used to be her friend? She doesn't think she can stomach this.

It's insulting, degrading. She will have none of it. She only hopes that Fiona doesn't tell anybody about the calls. She can hear them all now, chatting about her misfortune, viewing her family like bacteria under a microscope:

You spoke to her?

Poor Kate. Fancy having to live like that.

And Anthony, what a shame him losing his job like he did. Rumour has it, he just lost his edge, couldn't do what was required anymore. Got soft in his old age.

Those poor children. How on earth are they ever going to be able to make anything of their lives now?

Her scalp tightens, shrivelling and crinkling over her skull, each hair follicle sending a bolt of electricity through her. She places the phone down at her feet, kicks it under the table out of view and tries to see some positives in all of this. At least Jocelyn and Alexander have made some friends, not like the close pals they had at Searton School – but a friend is a friend and they seem happy enough. Happier than she feels.

Jocelyn has talked about a girl whose name she can't remember, and Alexander has Dane. She met him shortly after they moved here. How long ago is that? Two months, maybe three. Everything has been such a blur since leaving their real home behind. She has struggled to process it, unable to connect time to their everyday existence in this house, in this shabby excuse of a town, this Ormston that is so nondescript and forgettable, she often struggles to remember its name.

Dane has his rough edges for sure but then, don't all boys of that age? He is probably the best of a bad bunch. She visited their house shortly after Alexander met him. He had been invited over after school and she felt duty bound to let him go even though every nerve, every muscle in her body told her to say no. She had no idea who these people were, who her son was mingling with. But of course, Anthony had told her to loosen up, let the boy live, allow him to make new friends and because she had no real reason to not allow him to go, she was forced to say yes, so in a way, Anthony is partly to blame for what has happened. She was forced to mingle, to meet with the Bowrons. What happened after that isn't completely her fault.

The Bowrons' property was an exceptionally large and expensive-looking house – certainly a lot bigger than the one they are holed up in – and Kate wasn't sure what to expect as she stepped inside. The mother seemed like a nice enough woman, a little mousy perhaps. It was the father who took her by surprise. Loud and superficial were the only words she could think of to describe him. He met her at the door and shook her hand vigorously – a little too vigorously. It unnerved her, that show of affection and false joviality. She isn't used to it, preferring a more reserved approach when greeting strangers. Within the first few minutes, he had offered to show her around the house, telling her how he had built it himself, how he had an extensive portfolio of properties and that they were his retirement plan. 'Not that I have any immediate plans to retire, but you have to think of these things, don't you?' he had said, his words coming out in a flurry of excitement as if she was somebody he needed to impress.

And all the while, Kate had thought and thought about how his wealth could be used to their advantage. She had wanted to ask whether or not he needed any financial advice, figuring this could be a chance for Anthony to step in, to broaden his own portfolio. It irked her, this nouveau riche family who flaunted their wealth, spending it on frightfully ostentatious pieces of art that were neither well painted nor easy on the eye while she and Anthony had lost it all, forced to live in a tacky, characterless house surrounded by similarly characterless people. People who spent their spare time having barbecues in their gardens and drinking themselves into a stupor while ghastly pop music blared out in the background, polluting their airwaves and shattering their peace and quiet.

She had been desperate to salvage something from the meeting, desperate for the few crumbs that could be thrown their way. She tried, she really did, but of course it all got out of hand. She ruined everything. And now look at them, at what they have become. Her initial idea got bent out of shape and she has no idea how to straighten it back to its original form.

Her phone buzzes, rattling and vibrating under the table, rupturing her thoughts. She ignores it, unable to face speaking to anybody. Perhaps it's Fiona returning the call. She hopes not. The thought of Fiona sitting there in her luxurious home with her recently styled hair and flawless make-up, forcing herself to speak to a friend who has dropped to the bottom rung of the ladder, is more than Kate can bear. She doesn't want her pity. All she wants is for her life to return to how it was before everything curdled and turned sour.

The ringing stops, accentuating the sudden silence in the room. Kate can hear her own ragged breathing, feels the creeping distress building up inside her like a snake uncoiling itself as it stalks its prey, poised and ready to attack.

More noises from outside. Damn their proximity to the main road. Damn their tiny front garden and miniscule patch of lawn that separates them from the passing traffic. Engines roaring, doors slamming, footsteps coming closer and closer. Her ears become attuned to every little noise, every whisper of wind that passes through the treetops.

Then a knock at the door – a hard, relentless hammering that fills her with unease. More than unease. *Dread*. It sits in the base of her belly, a thick, tar-like substance, swirling and bubbling.

It comes again. Such a loud knock, so much strength and ferocity behind it. She shivers, wraps her arms around herself for protection. Something is wrong. She can feel it. Nobody ever calls here. This is a soulless house – no visitors, nobody ever calling around unexpectedly. She can see their shadows in her peripheral vision, the two dark figures standing outside her house. Two ominous, unmoving silhouettes. Two strangers. Right here on her doorstep. A memory pierces her thoughts – Anthony's colleagues arriving at their house after his dismissal, demanding his laptop, asking for all paperwork to be handed over to them as if he were a criminal. She had watched in horror as they gave her a nod of acknowledgement before marching past into Anthony's study and rifling through his desk, removing box after box of documents and then striding out of the house, slamming the door behind them.

The knock comes again – loud, demanding, insisting on an answer. Kate rises, her legs suddenly incredibly weak, her head swimming. Stars burst behind her eyes. A blackness threatens to overwhelm her, her vision attenuating as she shuffles towards the door, fear and anxiety weighing her down.

She pulls it ajar and peers around the jamb, her eyes narrowing at the sight of the two people standing there – a tall, willowy man, a smaller, soft-faced woman. *Kind eyes. She has kind eyes.* That's the one thing Kate focuses on as she listens to them speak, making no sense of the jumble of words that come out of their mouths.

She sees the badge however, the ID that tells her all she needs to know, and steps aside to let them in, everything dreamlike and severed from reality. She has no memory of walking back through to the living room, no recollection of asking them to take a seat.

Everything is out of kilter as she sits, clutching her knees, wondering, worrying, wishing she was somewhere else. Anywhere but here. What would happen if she were to stand up and leave the room, not be present to hear what it is they are about to say? It's bad. She knows it, can tell by their demeanour and expressions. She's had a gutful of bad news lately, just about as much as she can take. She pictures their old home – her safe place, her sanctuary – their friends, the children happy at their other school, and wishes she could turn back time, be the person she used to be all those months ago, not the woman she is now. Not the vacuous, desperate creature she has become of late.

Then she thinks of Anthony, wondering if this is about him. Has his jocular manner when he's around others been a cover up for something darker that was festering underneath? Should she have been less sharp, more sympathetic? What has she missed?

What exactly is going on in her life that has brought these people to her door with their pristine suits and probing gazes?

Is it her children? Or her parents? What if something has happened to them: a fall, perhaps? Or God forbid, a car accident. Her father's driving skills are less than adequate at the best of times. She has heard of elderly people who have a stroke or a heart attack behind the wheel of their vehicle. *What if...* She stops herself from going down that route. Why torture herself with unnecessary assumptions when these people can give her the answers she needs?

The woman clears her throat, leans over to Kate and catches her eye. 'The children, Mrs Winston-D'Allandrio. We were talking about your children – Alexander and Jocelyn.'

Blood rushes to her head. *Oh God. It's the children.* She knew it. She just knew it as any mother would. Her face burns. The floor opens up under her. She grips the seat to stop herself from slipping into the abyss that is beckoning beneath. *The children.* Her children. She doesn't want to hear this. And yet she needs to hear this. Something has happened to her children. Alexander and Jocelyn. She catches fragments of the words that these people are saying, small, indecipherable morphemes that float past her through the air, saying nothing at all and yet at the same time, saying just enough, telling her everything she needs to know.

Lockdown situation at the school.

Reason to believe that Jocelyn and Alexander are involved.

A shot fired.

A search of Alexander's bedroom.

It's not happening. It can't be. She's not prepared for this. It's wrong. They are mistaken, these people. They don't know her family, her children. She wants to tell them to leave, to get out of her house and never return, but isn't able to speak. She opens her mouth. Nothing comes out. She can't breathe, can't think properly. Somebody takes her hand, speaks softly to her. Words. Just a jumble of words. Nothing more. It doesn't make sense. She tries to stand up, stumbles, feels the ground coming up to meet her, hears the crack of her kneecaps as she hits the wooden floor, feels the jarring sensation in her bones as a wave of pain travels up through her body. Then a numbness. An emptiness. Everything slipping away from her.

Arms lifting her, placing her back onto the sofa. A soft hand brushing strands of hair out of her face, whispering that everything is under control and that she needs to concentrate and answer their questions as best she can.

Questions about Alexander and his friendship with Dane Bowron. Questions about Jocelyn and how well she knows Mr Rose, the English teacher. Kate doesn't know anything about any of this, tells them that she has no idea what is going on, although she can't be sure they heard her or that she even said the words out loud. She may have just thought them, sentences echoing around her head. No way of knowing. No way of being certain that she spoke and that they heard her. There is a definite disconnect between her brain and her mouth. They smile, nod and question her some more, their voices ghost-like, incorporeal sounds floating past her.

Does Alexander keep a diary? Can we look in his bedroom? So many questions. She can't think, is unable to snatch at any answers.

Everything is in slow motion: her thoughts, their movements, her ability to process what is really going on here, to sift through the formalities and work out what is happening. She needs to unpick it all and extricate reality from fantasy. *Not fantasy.* That word suggests a world of wild yet wonderful imaginings. *Nightmare. That word is more fitting,* she thinks, more suited to what is taking place right here in her living room.

'Does your husband own a gun, Mrs Winston-D'Allandrio?'

The question cuts her in two, slicing through to her very core, yanking her back to the here and now, forcing her to sit up and take notice. 'A gun?' Her mind is a kaleidoscope of thoughts, slotting and spinning out of place. 'Why do you need to know whether or not Anthony owns a gun? Of course he doesn't own a bloody gun! What do you think we are, terrorists or gangland members?'

'Can we ask you to contact him, please? Or could we have his number?'

She hears their words now, loud and clear, but is too confused to comprehend them, to pick up on the subtleties in their police language, the implied meanings. Everything is spinning out of control, her sensibilities and ability to think logically suddenly absent. The walls lean in drunkenly, the air is thick and muggy, the floor soft and pliable under her feet. She thinks of guns and Alexander and Jocelyn and feels the softness of the sofa falling away from her body and the floor rushing up to meet her.

PART II
BEFORE THE END

3

4 MAY 1978

My Dearest Clara,

    I'm sitting here looking out at the cobalt sky, willing summer on, thinking how beautiful it will be to spend it with you, our bodies side by side on the riverbank, our minds occupied and melded together as you recite your lines of prose, the words flowing like warm honey, each iambic pentameter making my skin tingle with delight and deep appreciation. I can visualise you shuffling closer to me, every movement infinitesimal and barely perceived as a movement at all until we are so close, we are almost as one.

    I hope that as you are reading this, my dear Clara, you are aware of how much I'm missing you, how much my body and mind ache in your absence, how my soul is entrenched in hopelessness and misery, my brain unable to function properly. I miss your face, the softness of your hair, the way you glance at me from beneath your lashes. I miss the sound of your voice, the light tinkling of your laughter and feel keenly the coldness of my bed without you in it. Being apart like this is a grieving process. Even losing my father doesn't register in my senses the way your absence does in my life. There is a person-sized hole in me that can be filled by only one individual, and that individual, my dearest Clara, is undoubtedly you.

A goldfinch has just landed outside my window, its startling colours so vivid that it causes me to stop awhile, to cease my writing and stare at it in awe, the vibrancy of its red face and yellow wings reminding me of a warm summer's day, the type that seems to go on forever, the heat making everyone languorous and indifferent, the landscape cracked and dry as the sun sucks every last drop of moisture from the earth, leaving it hard and unyielding beneath our feet.

Do you remember last summer, Clara? That day when we talked about spending the rest of our lives together? It was, and still is, one of the happiest days of my life. You spoke of love and commitment and how we knew each other intimately: every nuance of thought, every inch of skin, every breath that left our lungs, a shared action, a collective gathering of existential occurrences. I could almost hear my own blood as it pulsed around my body, felt the thud of my heart like a metronome – solid and steady within my chest. The innocent glassiness in your eyes told me everything I needed to know – that we were meant to be together. You are the other half of me, dear Clara. Without you, I am nothing. An empty husk, a shell of a man, lost and rudderless.

Which brings me to my next question – when can I expect you back, my darling? Time drags without you by my side. Every second is a minute, every minute an hour. I realise that it is right and proper that you must spend time with your gran as her illness progresses. Time spent with her is precious, as is our time together, but know this – I am counting every second until you return.

I am willing to bet that it is remarkably quiet up there in the wilds of Scotland. Good for the soul, I should imagine, although the sadness of seeing your gran's health failing will possibly be more than you can bear and will detract from any pleasures you may gain from your surroundings. I wish I was there with you, my darling, to reassure you and provide a crumb of comfort to you in this trying time. Were it not for my job, I would drive up there and keep you company but unfortunately, I am rather mired down in marking and the many other duties that come with my teaching position so will have to stay put, but rest assured, you are never far from my thoughts. If I am being perfectly honest, you are always in my thoughts, some of them bordering on sensual and erotic.

Your last letter left me wondering what is going through your mind up there in your grandparents' bothy. I didn't know how to feel after reading your words, the words that left me wondering whether or not you still harboured the same strong feelings for me that I feel for you. I am hoping that the stress of caring for your gran and the isolation all played a part in your terse missive.

Forgive me, I think 'terse' is too strong a word. You are too gentle, too caring a person to ever be described as such. I did, however, detect a note of weariness in your letter. I hope it is not directed towards me, but rather a generality of your current circumstances.

I realise I am rather old-fashioned in many respects and would do well to lay aside my crusty ways and sometimes grumpy demeanour. It's a veneer I use, a protective suit of armour to keep the rest of the world at bay but I think that perhaps in doing so, I have also inadvertently pushed you away. I hope this is not the case. I would never knowingly do such a thing. You do know that, don't you, my dear girl? I am hoping that by the time this letter reaches you, you will have changed your mind about extending your stay and will maybe give some thought to returning home in time for summer. Our summer. The time we could spend together. You do remember last summer, don't you, my darling? It will be forever emblazoned in my memory as the best time of my life. Each and every second spent with you is memorable and to be cherished. Every time I hear the rush of the river or the rustle of the breeze through the treetops, I am reminded of you, of our time together, the tender moments we shared in the past and the time we will hopefully spend with one another in the future.

Anyway, I am rambling. I began this letter in the hope of cheering you up and here I am, being morose and acting like a petulant child who is being denied his own way.

I miss you, my dear Clara, and look forward to hearing from you. Please give my love to your gran and grandpa.

All my love,
Dominic.

4

PRESENT DAY

Her silence says more than words ever could. Dominic pulls up the covers and tucks them under her chin. He wonders where her bulk has gone. Where is the large, buxom woman that once stood her ground and refused to back down or cower in the face of adversity? Before him lies a shrivelled husk of a person, cheeks shrunken, eyes set deep into her skull. He reaches out, his hand hovering over her face, wanting to touch her, yet not wanting to feel her parchment-dry skin, not wanting to be subjected to the coolness of her sun-deprived flesh. He can't remember the last time she was well enough to come downstairs, let alone go outside and raise her face to the sky, and feel the gentle warmth of a soft, spring day that would inject some life into her grey, pallid flesh.

So much lost. All that life and vigour and strength now reduced to this – this tiny, shrunken being lying before him in her bed. Is this what she would have wanted for herself? Is this how anybody should spend their lives, holed up in a dank bedroom, the curtains permanently drawn because of her sensitivity to light, a variety of creams and potions piled high on the bedside cabinet to help alleviate bedsores, a commode stuffed away in the corner of the room because she is no longer able to manage her own toileting needs? This isn't a life. It isn't even an existence. It's a nightmare from which there is no escape.

There are days when being by her side soothes him, makes him feel anchored to this house, to his life. And then there are days when the very sight of her makes him want to shout and cry at the unfairness of it all. It's an exhausting process, being here for her, looking after her day after day, making sure her needs are met, that she is fed and clean and cared for. And then there is the guilt that weighs him down for harbouring those feelings. She deserves to be looked after, to have somebody by her side who will hold her hand as her body shrinks and her brain shuts down. All those thoughts and memories that used to run through her head. Where are they now? It was those very thoughts and memories that made her who she was, brought her to life, gave her that spark. And now look at her. Look at their lives and what they have been reduced to.

He sits by her side, watching her, wondering how it all came to this. Where did the years go? Time is his enemy as it rushes past, ravaging the remnants of his life, shredding it into tiny little pieces. The sight of his own face in the nearby mirror cuts through his thoughts. He can see his mother's features in his own – the shape of his eyes, the slightly downward slope of his mouth and the fine lines that sit across his forehead, deepening with each passing year. It is hard to comprehend that he is twice the age that his father was when he died. So many difficult years to live through, although not as difficult as that other period in his life. The one he would sooner forget. He closes his eyes, blots out those thoughts then opens his eyes again, the lids heavy, his thin lashes fluttering as he stares down at her, a flood of ancient memories threatening to overwhelm him.

She's sleeping now. Her expression is peaceful, her frail body succumbing to the calming effects of a deep slumber. Reaching out, he trails his fingers over her face, trying not to shiver at the dryness of her skin, the sparseness of her carefully combed hair, the slight odour that wafts up from under the sheets. The odour of an unkempt body. He does his best to care for her, to make sure her personal hygiene is as good as it can be, but it's not an easy task nor is it a palatable one. Many men would shudder at the thought of it, but not him. He has kept at it all these years even though there are days when it all feels too much, as if the light at the end of the tunnel has been turned off, leaving him stumbling about in the darkness, crashing into barriers and losing impetus at the thought of making it through another lonely day.

He stands, his body feeling twice its usual weight. Everything will seem better after a shower and a glass of the good stuff. Just the one. He limits himself during the week, needing to stay alert for the following day, reasoning that one glass of whiskey is for medicinal purposes, calming him just enough to aid a solid night's sleep, blurring the edges and helping him to forget the things that keep him awake at night if he abstains.

The shower is hot, the armchair a welcoming sensation as he lowers himself into it, his body weary after another arduous week spent teaching youngsters who are impervious to his methods and dead set against any type of learning. They all seem to know better, their minds angled in other directions. Perhaps he has lost the knack of knowing what is required to delve inside their heads and stoke up some excitement, his methods now antiquated and no longer of use to anybody. Perhaps it's time to think about retirement.

He reaches over to the bottle, its heft and amber hue a reassuring sight in the dimness of the room, and pours himself a long slug, the gentle trickle of the liquid the only noise in the surrounding silence. The thrum of his heartbeat slows down from a racing pulse to a gentle tick inside his abdomen as he raises the glass to his lips and lets the whiskey do its job, allowing him to forget, allowing him to push everything away and focus only on the peaty flavour as it hits the back of his throat with a welcome punch. No more classroom worries, no more caring duties. No more of anything except being his own person and savouring the moment, his mind slowing down, his senses in harmony with his immediate environment.

This is where he is happiest. This is where everything feels just right, where it all makes sense. Not out there in society, amidst the bustling crowds and the constantly moving swathe of bodies that cross his path. This is his safe haven, somewhere he escapes to when it all becomes too much. Nobody can bother him when he is here, in his own little bubble of happiness. He is immune to everyone and everything.

He swallows and rubs at his eyes. Happiness is too strong a word. Contentment seems more fitting. Happiness suggests gaiety and merriment and he can't remember the last time he felt either of those emotions or partook in any activity that lent itself to such sentiments. He is content here in this place. For now.

The glass is empty. He stares at it, tempted to pour another, the will to finish the bottle so strong, he has to stand up and pace around the room to quell it. Two is too many. Two will make him tired and irritable in the morning. Tonight, it will numb and quieten his thoughts but in the morning, the effects will linger, leaving him fatigued, and that is the last thing he needs.

It's the emptiness of this house that gets to him. The quiet and the calm he welcomes; the lack of company is something different. It weighs heavily on him, pushing him deep into the ground, his feet slowly sinking into the loam. Another drink would help dampen those thoughts.

Another drink could also exacerbate them.

He snatches up the newspaper and sits down on a hard chair at the table, the solid surface beneath his backside forcing him into a less relaxed state of mind, his eyes blandly scanning the headlines, his mind unable to properly read and digest any of the news articles.

A noise from behind stirs him, cutting into his thoughts. He turns around, listening again. He could have sworn he heard his name being called. His senses now sharpened, he stands up, ready to rush upstairs. There is a part of him that is ever vigilant, aware always of the slightest of sounds, his body and mind ready to jump to attention when required. He has forgotten how to be fully relaxed. While his body grows older and begins to sag, his brain remains alert, prepared for every little movement, every murmur she makes. It's a skill he has learnt over the years, something he needs to do to care for her.

Going out during the day and leaving her here on her own is the hardest part. Living not so far from the school has made it easier. He calls home every lunchtime, leaving the noise and the mayhem behind for a short while to sit at her side and make sure she is happy and safe, to hold her hand and remind her that she isn't alone. He is here for her. Always here.

Does he wish he had a better life, an easier one, free from her demands? Free from the guilt? Of course. But it is what it is and nothing is going to change that. No amount of wishing or praying or moments of anger and angst will alter this situation. He has to accept it and get on with his life, not waste time carping about things he cannot change.

He listens again for her voice calling from upstairs but there is nothing. Just an endless silence that stretches on and on and on.

A heaviness settles within him, ploughing a furrow deep in the marrow of his bones. He stifles a yawn, then feels a frisson of apprehension as it comes again. Another noise, but this time it is different. Not his name being called but a rattling sound coming from nearby. Not a sound he recognises, but then again, his hearing isn't what it used to be. It is dulled by years of neglect and the regular, prolonged ringing of the school bell next to his desk.

The stairs groan, a discordant series of sharp thuds and creaks as he makes his way up to her bedroom. He pushes at the door and slips into the darkness of her room, his footfall now muted by the carpeted flooring. His palms are slippery with perspiration as he grips at the handle and peers into the greyness, bracing himself for what he may find there. Days with her are often long and unpredictable. She is sometimes prone to violent outbursts that are difficult to contain, her mind on another tangent and almost impossible to direct or distract. She was always predisposed to such behaviour, her temper a physical force in the house when he was a boy. Her emaciated figure now stops her from carrying out anything too forceful or damaging but he remains attentive at all times, just in case.

Relief blooms within his chest as he stares down at her unmoving body, the tiny mound under the bedsheets deathly still. She is asleep. Some evenings, she attempts to get out of bed, her legs flailing uselessly, her walking cane a weapon as she wields it in the air, her anger at her inability to walk unaided consuming her. But not this time. Tonight, she is sleeping peacefully. He heaves a sigh of gratitude and backs out of the room, closing it with a quiet, careful click.

Downstairs, he checks each room, looking for open windows, anything that may lead him to the source of the noise, but finds nothing. A loud rap comes again, clearly this time. A deep, dull thump. The sound of somebody using the brass doorknocker. He rarely receives visitors and is unused to hearing the sound of it as it echoes around the hallway. It's late and dark out. A chill skids over his flesh, prickling his arms and the back of his neck.

Hands clasped as if in prayer, he strides across to the hallway and unlocks the door, waiting a second or two before pulling it open and peering around the doorframe, only to be greeted by a blast of cold air and little else. He leans farther out, squinting into the darkness, waiting for his eyes to adjust, then glances both ways but sees nothing except a dim outline of nearby shrubbery and hedgerows, hears nothing but the distant rumble of traffic carried by the prevailing winds that rush over the fields towards his house.

Slamming the door in frustration would ordinarily be his choice of response but he is keen to keep the noise down, not needlessly drag his poor mother from a deep and soundless slumber. So instead, he closes it as silently as he can, muttering under his breath about local children and their idiotic pranks and how parents should ensure their offspring are accounted for. Because that's who it will be, prowling around here in the dark, knocking on his door then scarpering before he can discover who it is. Living out here in the woods almost a mile away from the rest of the neighbourhood has often made him a target. A solitary house is easier to spot. It's an incongruous sight, his home, with its dimly lit windows amidst the trees, and its tall chimney that spouts a spiralling trail of smoke from his open fire. He's heard it all before, had to listen to every derogatory term imaginable used about it – a witch's house, a haunted cottage, the house of horrors – by pupils past and present. He is perpetually torn between feeling insulted and caring so little that he finds it marginally amusing.

They should have moved after the death of his father, found somewhere more alluring, a modern property with all the latest mod cons, but the time never seemed to be right. And then with his mother's subsequent health issues, it became too difficult to consider. A smallholding had always been his father's dream and he worked hard to buy this place. Leaving would feel like an affront to his life's work even though the surrounding land is now barren. It's all too late now anyway. Moving his mother in her current state of health is unthinkable. They are both here to stay.

He drops down into his armchair, thinking that perhaps he is too old for everything. Too old to be a carer, too old to teach. Just too bloody old to give a damn about the things he once delighted in – flowers, the changing seasons, poetry and of course his study of physiognomy – the things that once held such great fascination for him are now the very things that leave him cold. No matter how hard he tries, he simply cannot drum up any enthusiasm for such pastimes, his energy sapped, his mind devoid of curiosity and passion.

His eyes stray to the corner of the room, to an area that has remained untouched for so many years now that he cannot recall exactly when it was that he made the decision to lock everything away. He shuts his eyes against the fear and nausea that rise. No, he won't go down that route. Not tonight. Maybe not ever. It's too painful, still too raw and besides, he has neither the energy nor the gumption for it. What is the point? Why put himself through it when nothing can be gained from such a venture? That box of things, the only keepsake he has, will remain untouched. It stirs up too many bad memories, dredging up things he would rather remain submerged and hidden.

What will happen to its contents, he wonders, when he finally shuffles off this mortal coil? Perhaps it would be best to take a match to the box and everything within it, help rid himself of those lingering memories, that time in his life when everything seemed shiny and new. When life held such promise before it became blackened and charred, an unrecognisable pile of ash that crumbled through his fingers, dusty fragments of a part of his life he would sooner forget.

The room feels smaller as he stands, walls moving towards him, the floor spongy under his feet. He's tired. No, not tired. That's not it at all. Jaded. That's what he is. He is jaded and disaffected. Tonight, he will sleep, and in the morning, everything will seem brighter and life will go on as it always does. He isn't one for trite, motivational idioms, but he does know that the darkest hour is just before dawn. Tomorrow, a shiny new day beckons. He can either embrace it or eschew it. The choice is his and his alone.

5

'So basically, you're here because your old man can't be arsed to be a cut-throat hedge fund manager anymore?'

Alex tries to smile, shrugs and stares off into the distance. He doesn't know why they're here. Not really. He only knows the basics, picking up on snippets of what Kate spits out, telling them that their dad has given up, has lost his edge and would rather be a second-rate financial adviser than a top-rate hedge fund manager. Not that he should believe anything that comes out of his mother's mouth. She is on a downward spiral, rapidly turning into a bitter and twisted woman with no focus and little compassion. They used to be friends, he and his mum. They would sit and chat, swap stories about their day, reeling off anecdotes while they sat at the kitchen table eating biscuits and drinking foaming mugs of hot chocolate. That's all in the past. He no longer knows her or recognises the person she has become. She thrived on glamour and money and now she has neither of those things, has turned into somebody that people don't want to be around. Including her own son.

'There's a party round Bobby's house tonight.' Dane's eyes dart around the room, his pupils small and bottomless, as if the thoughts inside his head are things he struggles to process. 'His parents have a huge, fuck-off summerhouse and a massive garden. They left us to it last time we were there.' He dips his head, turns away from Alex, his thinking already angled elsewhere, his gaze focused on the ground. He reminds Alex of a meerkat, always twisting and turning, watching and waiting for the next big event, something that will turn his head and draw him in.

'A party in a summerhouse?'

'Yeah. Bring your own booze but make sure you stash it under your hoodie. Bobby's mum and dad turn a blind eye to the drinking but they don't wanna be seen to be encouraging it either.' Dane suddenly springs to life again, his attention once more focused on Alex. He hops from one foot to another as if he is stepping over hot coals, unable to stand still for even one second. Alex is mesmerised by this lad, the way his moods oscillate so wildly, how his body follows suit, ranging from static and downbeat one second to dancing about as if on fire the next.

'So, what you're telling me is, we're going round to Bobby's house to have a party in his shed with his parents who are a pair of old swingers?' Alex allows himself a small smile. Dane has been a good friend to him since he started at this school. He won't push it too far. He's seen how Dane reacts to others around him, seen his dark, brooding look, his defensive manner and wonders what he is actually capable of.

'Fuck off, Alexander Winston-D'Allandrio, you posh twat.'

Alex throws his head back and laughs, gives his pal a playful punch on the arm. 'Just messing with you, buddy. What time does this thing kick off, then?'

Dane shrugs and juts out his bottom lip, his top teeth slowly nibbling at the inside of his mouth. 'Eight o'clock. Not that anybody I like is going. Most people in this dump are fucking idiots. I tolerate them. But with access to booze and maybe some skirt, who am I to refuse?'

The outdated, sexist phrase makes Alex cringe. He is unused to hearing it but suppresses any outward reaction, thinking of his mother's expression if she was around, listening to Dane's outwardly misogynistic outbursts. If there's one thing he has learned since starting at Ingleton Secondary School, it's how to keep his head down and not stand out. Posh kids like him don't belong in a place like this. That said, it's not half as bad as he expected it to be. He misses his mates from his other school and given the choice would go back there in a heartbeat, but it doesn't look like that's going to happen anytime soon, so he has mastered the art of mingling and keeping his mouth shut, not giving anybody any reason to single him out. Turn up, do his work and leave. That's his mantra.

'So, I'll meet you there then, shall I?' The thought of going doesn't fill him with the level of dread he expected it to. It's an excuse to get out of the house, to avoid the arguments and ice-filled conversations that take place every fucking day in their new home. It's endless – the constant rounds of acrimony and resentment and blame. His mother doesn't seem to know when to stop. She loads up her sling and fires missiles indiscriminately as soon as his dad steps foot in the door. It's not the sort of arguments that involve raised voices: more a case of hissed accusations, sarcastic comments and an atmosphere so thick, you can grasp it with both hands and tear it apart.

'You know where he lives?' Dane's voice is a murmur, a deep rumble of vowels and consonants with little emotion or inflection.

'Yeah. I walked home with him last week. Big, white house on the corner of Pendleton Avenue?' Alex recalls the conversation he and Bobby had. Bobby's dad runs a chain of restaurants and his mum is a primary school teacher.

My parents could afford to send me to private school if they wanted but Mum said she doesn't want to. She wants me to stay grounded, to get an idea of what it's like to mix with people who don't have loads of money and aren't aloof.

Alex had bristled at his words, his face burning, the usual need to defend himself rising up from his gut. His old school wasn't a place full of moneyed people who thought themselves superior, but trying to justify and explain it to anybody who has never been there was pointless. People have an idea in their heads and rarely budge from it. He wasn't about to waste his time and energy trying to persuade Bobby otherwise. Some things are best left unsaid.

'Right. Well, you can buy some cider from the off-licence on Brompton Street if you haven't got any. The owner couldn't give a shit about age restrictions. All he cares about is the ching-ching of his till.' Dane glances behind him then stares down at his watch, his features darkening with disdain. 'Fucking marvellous. Geography next then English with Dommy Rose. Fucking wanker that he is.'

The scowl on Dane's face reminds Alex of the time their old poor old dog chewed a dead fly before spitting it out in disgust. He refrains from laughing and won't engage in a conversation with him about his Geography lesson or Mr Rose. Not worth the effort of a reprimand for not comprehending Dane's dislike of the man.

Stuffing his empty sandwich wrapper into a nearby bin, Alex stands and stares at his recently acquired friend, studying the expression on his face, suspicion ever present in his eyes: his narrowed lids, the way his pupils dance about as if keeping watch for possible attackers.

'Will your sister be there tonight?' Dane's voice is distant, his attention already elsewhere, his thoughts moving onto somebody or something else before Alex has even had a chance to reply.

'Not sure. Has it been mentioned to her?' But before the words are out of his mouth, he feels sure he already knows the answer to his own question. Of course Joss will be going. She can sniff out a party at fifty paces, like a predator tracking its prey. She will have heard about it before he did. It's always been this way, his younger sister leading the pack with effortless poise while he trails behind in her wake like a hapless puppy. He'd like to say he doesn't mind, that it doesn't affect him, but that would be a lie. He feels it every day: the hurt, the rejection. To everyone around him, he appears confident, easy in his own skin. He has become adept at covering up his real feelings, knowing that saying the right things at the right time is the path of least resistance. Always the peacekeeper, Alex is the polar opposite of Joss, who is without exception the lively one of their family, the feisty one who turns heads and attracts all the attention. She only has to breathe for people to fall at her feet while she stares down at her adoring fans, enjoying every single second in the limelight.

Is he bitter about it? Perhaps. Is he jealous? Absolutely not. He has seen how his sister operates over the years, how she weaves her wicked magic. She manipulates every situation to make it all about her. Who would want to be like that? Why would anybody make it their life's mission to emulate somebody who cares only about themselves?

'I can ask her if you like?' Dane says, his lips parting slightly, revealing a row of small, crooked teeth. He smiles briefly then rearranges his features back into their usual sullen countenance, his dark eyes lowered and framed by even darker lashes that sit against his pale skin.

'Mate, I'm not even sure she knows who you are.' The words leave Alex's mouth before he has a chance to stop them. He studies his friend's face for any changes that might signify a sudden spurt of anger taking hold, travelling at breakneck speed from his brain to his fists. He is surprised to see Dane's expression remain neutral, his face its usual pallid colour. The complexion of old putty.

'Well, whatever. Mention it to her if you like. I'm easy.'

Alex doesn't laugh at Dane's words, doesn't even smile. He's seen it all before, can recognise the signs of yet another lad who has a crush on Joss. There have been so many over the past few years, he has lost count. It is both sad and laughable. Even if she does go to the party, she will barely register Dane's presence.

* * *

The day passes in a haze of movements and actions, one lesson rolling into another, words and phrases that are meant to fire his imagination and further his knowledge sailing over his head, leaving no lasting impression. He is impervious to everything today, his mind focused on getting home, seeing how his mother is functioning, trying to gauge the mood in the house as he slinks through the door. It's so difficult to tell lately, with her unpredictable emotions and bouts of misery and hopelessness. Some days are better than others and some days are just atrocious, his parents giving one another dour, hostile glances across the dinner table, then having protracted arguments when they think he and his sister are out of earshot. It's all about money. Money and status.

His dad isn't bothered about any of it anymore and his mum is. That's all it comes down to. It has to be. And it's so stupid, so pointless, but she can't seem to stop it. It's killing her living like this, having to be a normal person in a normal house. Alex sighs and stares out of the window.

Living like this.

She uses that phrase a lot. They're not paupers, for Christ's sake, but neither are they rich. Not the sort of rich they were used to. And it doesn't matter to him. He couldn't care less about the money. He misses his friends but more than anything, he misses the peace and quiet they had with their other life. No fights, no crazy arguments. No harsh words spat out when they both think the children aren't listening.

What is it with adults and their need to constantly vent their spleen about issues that aren't that important? Actually, it's not his dad. He is continually backed into a corner by his mum and is forced to defend himself, his words always calm and logical while she harangues and hisses at him, her rage a relentless force.

A rush of heat spreads over Alex's skin as the bell rings and everybody rises from their seats. Part of him would rather not go tonight and another part of him wants to be out of the house, away from the atmosphere, far away from the tension between his parents and that sickening sensation that it brings, twisting beneath his skin and churning about in his belly. It might be good to meet some new people, establish himself properly instead of constantly standing out as the newcomer in town. He's not sure whether or not to sneak some of his dad's beers out of the house or take his chances at the shop. Either way, he can't turn up empty handed. A drink will help him unwind, give him some confidence. Confidence people assume comes naturally to him when nothing could be further from the truth. Joss got his share of the exuberance gene and he has spent most of his life masking his insecurities with a false joviality that is both exhausting and tiresome.

'Change of plan.' The tug on his arm sends him reeling, pulling him backwards.

Dane is standing next to him almost smiling, his grin fixed as if it is an unnatural state, something he has to practise to fit in with those around him. He leans into Alex conspiratorially, whispers in his ear. 'Got hold of my phone at lunchtime and sent a text to the old man. He said he'll give us some of his beers to take tonight provided we say nothing to my mum.'

Alex shrugs, manages a wry smile. 'Sounds perfect.'

'So if you come to mine first, we'll pick up the booze and then head over to Bobby's together, yeah?'

They part, Alex watching as Dane disappears into the throng of teenagers, a moving collective of bodies that bends and sways through the school gates, spilling out onto the sprawl of asphalt beyond.

* * *

The moment between opening the front door and stepping into the cloying atmosphere of disgruntlement, annoyance and boredom that exudes from his mother is one Alex savours. He stops awhile, sniffing at the air, looking around at the curling tendrils of the honeysuckle, at the conical lilac blooms that line the driveway. It's similar to their old house, this new place they call home, on a smaller scale admittedly, but still appealing. Less imposing. No stone pillars, no sleeping lions atop the gateposts. Entering their old home felt like walking into a colosseum. This is a gentler way to live, a softer, less defined way to exist. Apart from the arguments, that is. They grow exponentially, his mother's dissatisfaction at her predicament a constant source of unhappiness and bitterness.

As he steps inside and closes the door, he hears the music that emanates from his sister's bedroom above, a series of sharps and flats accompanied by a deep thrumming bass beat that echoes through the hallway.

He throws his bag on the floor. It skids across the tiles and lies slumped next to a statue of a naked black woman, a baby clutched to her breast. He steps out of his shoes, a habit he can't seem to break even though his mother no longer seems to care about the trails of dirt that they trample in. The things that used to irk her, such as untidiness and unmade beds and mud being dragged in, have taken a back seat. Her attentions are focused on their dad's misdemeanours or moreover, his lack of drive and ambition, and his general apathy.

Alex doesn't see it as apathy, more a slow winding down from a hectic occupation that left no room for family life or anything resembling happiness and contentment. His dad smiles now, has time for meaningful conversations with his children, is a different person altogether. Until Kate rears her head, that is. Then everything changes. Then a black cloud sails overhead, lowering the air pressure, depressing everyone in close vicinity, emptying its heavy, rain-filled belly over them and whipping up a great tempest.

She is sitting at the kitchen table as he walks in, her expression sullen, sadness tattooed into the grooves that sit around her eyes.

In the sink lies an empty goblet, remnants of red wine clinging to the side of the crystal, like tiny droplets of blood. He doesn't say anything about it, is too tired to engage in this particular conversation. 'I've been invited out to a party tonight. I'll be leaving in a couple of hours.'

She doesn't respond. He sees her in his peripheral vision, observes how she is watching his movements as he makes a sandwich and pours himself a glass of milk. Ordinarily, he would sit at the table, eat, chat, tell her about his day, but it all seems too much, too tiresome an endeavour with her sharp quips and putdowns, her relentless tirade about their new house and substandard lifestyle. He can sense her mood, the unbearable weight of it. It's too much and he hasn't the stomach for it. Not today.

Instead, he takes a bite and carries the snack upstairs, trying to decide whether to mention tonight's party to Joss, working out whether or not she will curl her lip at him and sneer as she tells him she already knows about it or whether she will smile at him, show genuine interest and talk about who might be going. There's no telling with her, no predicting her responses or mood. *Like mother, like daughter,* he thinks as he heads into his bedroom and closes the door.

He won't ask her. He's not in the right frame of mind for pointless quarrels that go nowhere. Far easier to do his own thing, not become embroiled in any of Joss's needless questions or opinions where she dominates the conversation and doesn't give him a chance to interject with his thoughts and ideas. It's not as if she even knows Bobby or Dane. And anyway, the thought of her being at the party makes his toes curl. With her flamboyant behaviour, he would rather she stayed at home. Just for once, he will be able to relax, be his own person, not have his own character obliterated by her presence.

Lying back on his bed, he takes another bite of the sandwich and a long glug of the milk, wondering how they came to this, how their lives diverged so badly. Three members of the same family, sitting apart, living apart.

All together and yet very much alone.

6

Somewhere in between the moments of chaos and silence, Nina realises that it is a sense of loyalty is keeping her here. Loyalty and a deep fear of being alone, starting her life all over again with a troubled past and an uncertain future.

She looks around the kitchen – at its gleaming surfaces and precisely placed furniture, at the AGA she used to adore, the picture window that affords her a view of the large garden – and thinks how little it all means to her. The trappings of wealth now act as her prison, reminding her of how far she has come and how far she could fall. How very different her life could be should she choose to leave. A thread of unease is interlaced through her veins, becoming knotted and tangled, knocking her off balance.

She bats all those thoughts away. Thoughts of Rob and a life without him in it. It's stupid. Unfeasible. And then there's Dane to think about. He needs her. He needs his family. A young lad going through a difficult patch. To uproot him is unthinkable. What sort of a mother would that make her? To drag her boy away from everything he knows – away from his father, his home, his friends. She couldn't do it. The thought repulses her almost as much as Rob's philandering. It's all about balance, weighing up the good against the bad. She will sit this one out, wait for it to blow over, just like the others. This woman, this latest episode, will mean no more or no less to him than any of the others. In a few months, possibly even a few weeks, it will all be a thing of the past. Another notch on her husband's bedpost is all it will amount to.

She swallows and lowers her eyes, blinking back tears. The floor needs cleaning. Others wouldn't see it but to her, it is unmissable, the flecks of grime incongruous against the smart, white flooring. In the corners of the tiles, set deep in the grooves of the grouting, are fragments of dirt. If she can focus on removing them, on washing and scrubbing until everything gleams, it restores some of the control back into her life, allowing her to feel as if some things are within her grasp, not spiralling downwards, taking her and everything she knows with it.

She is reminded of the words her mother regularly recited that related to her years spent teaching in a challenging school. The key to dealing with behavioural issues and for sure the easiest way to end what is going on, is to pick off the peripherals, the children who tag along, sitting beside the central offender. Take care of the small stuff, she used to say, and the big problems will sort themselves out. That's what she is doing here. Sometimes, the bigger issues are too much of a headache to tackle. She will busy herself with the smaller stuff, ignoring what is right in front of her nose until it disappears and everything goes back to how it was.

Until next time, that is. She's no fool. And she knows her husband. She knows him better than she knows herself, having studied him and his undesirable behaviour for so many years, trying to please him, to anticipate his moves, always preparing herself for his next misdemeanour. She is practically an expert. So why does she dread it so, these episodes? Why does it always leave her feeling hollowed out and utterly miserable? She should be inured to it by now, hardened to his ways and able to shake it all off with a shrug. Except she can't. Each time it happens, it flattens her that little bit further, squashing her emotions deep inside her abdomen until she is hardly able to breathe. Each new woman he beds pushes her mood lower and lower until she is almost at ground level and feels as if she is being buried alive.

And yet here she is, letting it happen again. History repeating itself because the other options are too unpleasant to consider – living alone, fighting Rob in the courts for her share of the house. Dane deciding he no longer wants to live with his mother and that he would rather spend his days with his dad. His loud, insensitive, brash father. The idea of it makes her feel faint.

Nina thinks back to last night, to the smell of Rob's aftershave as he splashed it around his face, to the lustful glint in his eye as he gave her a quick, dismissive peck on the cheek, telling her he was going out for a few beers with the boys. 'Somewhere different tonight,' he had said. 'Billy said we should try The Kings Head for a change.'

She listened to him laying out the groundwork, covering his tracks, him unaware she had already seen the thinly disguised message on his phone as he showered, a short missive from somebody named *Buzzy*.

She knew the signs, recognised his modus operandi. He had done it before, given them random pseudonyms, his flings, then after getting caught, after much questioning, capitulated, begged for forgiveness, told her he would never do it again, the worry of having to hand over half of his house so apparent, it was laughable. Until the next time.

Until now.

> I'll be there at 8. Xx

An innocuous message. Short and to the point. With kisses at the end.

She had waved goodbye to him as he left, trying to keep her manner distant, trying to appear disinterested as he headed off for a night of passion, then spent the evening curled up on her bed, whiling away the hours with a book she couldn't read and a programme on the television that didn't hold her interest.

By the time Rob staggered home, still reeking of aftershave, his own scent combined with an undertone of something softer, something sweeter and more fragrant that lingered in the air for longer than she would have liked, it was after midnight and her skin was on fire, her rage barely hidden beneath the surface of her burning flesh. Sleeping was impossible. She was still laid there rigid many hours later, staring at the ceiling while he slept beside her, his breathing deep and regular interspersed with the occasional snore, his lustful needs sated, his ego massaged and smoothed out.

She should be used to it by now, these dark but brief affairs. That's what she tells herself, but each time it happens, it becomes that little bit more insulting, cuts that little bit deeper, stripping away another layer of her dignity until one day, there will be nothing left of her but muscle, sinew and bone.

Her hands are red and sore as she scrubs at the tiles, digging her nails into the cracks, picking at flecks of dirt that refuse to budge, adding hot water to the bucket and cursing as it sloshes over the sides, wetting her clothes.

The therapeutic easing of stress that she hoped for doesn't occur and she is left instead with an aching back and burning hands, her fingers pink and tender, her nails broken and ragged. A greater sense of relief rips through her as she throws the scrubbing brush across the floor. It bounces and land with a thud on the other side of the kitchen, water and soap suds spreading out over the floor.

She sits for a while, seconds ticking by, those seconds turning into minutes until the click of the door drags her out of her near trance-like state, shaking her back into the moment.

In her head is a scenario, a vision of her son shouting through to her that he is home, his voice light, his mood even lighter. He will walk towards her with a grin, perhaps even give her a hug. She will ask him if he is hungry and he will nod, enthusiasm oozing out of him. He will sit, waiting for his snack, and they will chat about his day as she makes him a sandwich, him recalling the odd humorous event, telling her with a half-smile about how much he hates school while deep down, she knows this is not true, something he says because it fits the stereotype of difficult, sullen teenagers. He will tell her about his PE lesson where he scored the winning goal and how wonderful it is to have so many friends and then she will smile as she butters the bread, a warm glow settling in her chest, spreading through her body as she listens to his soft, velvety voice.

Then the true picture of her son punches its way into her brain and her throat constricts as she braces herself, listening to his heavy footfall on the wooden flooring, the way he stomps through to the kitchen like a morose, sulky toddler where she sits in a state of nervous readiness, her skin prickling, her muscles flexed and ready, her muscles stretched and taut.

'Fuck sake! The fucking floor is soaking wet.' Dane kicks at the bucket of water, sending it sailing across the floor. It rocks from side to side before coming to a standstill. Nina waits for it to tip over and for the water to spill over the recently cleaned tiles. It remains upright. She silently heaves a sigh of relief, lowering her shoulders. Exhaustion swamps her. She is too tired, too immersed in misery to clean up any more mess.

'Would you like a snack before I make our evening meal?' She tries to keep the tremble out of her voice, attempting to muster up a smile and appear relaxed and at ease when she is anything but.

'I'll do it myself. I'm going out later. Don't want a meal.'

He turns away and rummages in the fridge, pulling out items, throwing packets and cartons to one side. She is at a loss as to what to say or do next. This should be easy, this type of conversation. It should happen naturally, without any forethought or planning, without worry of retribution for fear of saying or doing the wrong thing. Why is it so damn hard? This is her baby, her boy. It should be as easy as breathing, being around him, having a conversation. It should be a reflex action, not this stilted, awkward procedure where she has to overthink and analyse every damn thing that comes out of her mouth. Perhaps it's her. Maybe it is all her doing, this inability to connect and make small talk. She is tense. He is still a child. She is the adult here and needs to say and do the right thing. Always. It's her job as a mother to guide him, to show him what is expected of him in these situations. And if she isn't willing to do it, then who will?

'I'll pour you some juice.' She is on her feet, her tone playful and easy. 'How is Alex getting on? Must be tricky for him being the new lad at school. I was saying to Sally that you've helped him along, made him feel really welcome.'

The rummaging stops. She picks up on his abrupt cessation but chooses to ignore it, grabbing a tumbler and filling it with ice from the fridge door. Their bodies are close now, almost touching. The body that she used to snuggle to her chest, the same child that she fed from her breast, his small fists curled into tight balls, his small, bright eyes gazing into hers as he suckled contentedly.

'You told her what? Fuck sake, he's just another kid at school. I'm not his fucking minder!'

Electricity bolts through her, sharp and painful, making her woolly-headed and woozy. Tears mist her vision. She blinks them away, determined to get through this, not to be browbeaten by her own child. 'Well, I'm glad you're doing the right thing. I've heard that some of the other kids have singled him out because of the school he used to go to.' She turns and moves away before he can reply, her spine rigid, her movements stiff and laboured.

'Where's all the cheese gone?' Dane holds up a small block of orange Cheddar wrapped into a clear roll of plastic and surveys it, his brow wrinkled into a deep frown, the expression in his eyes hidden by a row of dark lashes. 'Why haven't you bought any more cheese?'

'It's behind the eggs.' A sing-song voice. Again. Her heart is hammering now. She can feel his simmering anger and has no idea why he is always this furious, always on the cusp of telling her how much he hates her. How useless she is. What a terrible mother she is.

'*Behind the eggs.*' His voice is a whine as he attempts to imitate her. 'Well maybe next time, try moving it to the front so we can find it. It's not as if you've got anything else to do all day, is it?'

Their eyes meet for a brief second but that is all it takes for her to see the darkness there. The smouldering anger. And she wishes she hadn't. That look, the look of a stranger, turns her cold whilst simultaneously coating her neck and top lip in tiny, iridescent pearls of perspiration.

As much as she tries to slink away, to get out of his line of sight, every movement, every single step she takes feels heavy and cumbersome, as if she is made of concrete. As if she has no right to be here at all, here alongside her child in her own home.

The chair is cool under her legs. She perches on it, doing her best to stay in the background, away from his words, away his obvious anger and fury.

A memory comes back to her unbidden – the three of them on a family day out. Rob being his usual noisy, gregarious self, chatting to locals as they made their way to the fishing farm, and she and Dane linking arms, her other hand carrying the small picnic basket they had prepared.

They entered, paid the required fee and collected their equipment then sat themselves by the lake while Rob prepared everything. The sun was hot on their backs and everything felt perfect.

'Come on, son. I'll show you how it's done.' Nina had listened and watched as Rob demonstrated to a young Dane how to throw food into the lake and then hold out the small net, placing it in the water to catch a trout. It only took a couple of seconds for the net to suddenly spring to life with a squirming fish, the handle swaying from side to side as their catch tried to escape. She remembers Dane's face, how his eyes had sparkled with delight, the giggle that came spilling out of his throat as he and Rob lifted it out of the water and tipped the contents onto the grass.

A silvery trout flapped about on the ground, its eyes grey and wide, its mouth opening and closing as it gasped for breath, its small, rubbery lips leaving a lasting impression in Nina's memory. She had wanted Rob to throw it back, not keep it. It was the fun of catching it, she had argued later. It was always about the catching, not what came next. Not the ending of a life. Never that.

Dane's voice had cracked through the stillness, his small, reedy tones filling the air around them. 'Kill it, Dad! Kill it!'

Nina had watched in horror as Rob handed the small wooden mallet over to Dane who gleefully brought it down on the fish's head over and over and over until the squirming and flapping ceased and the poor creature lay motionless, those wide, grey eyes staring up at her, filling her with deep shame and remorse.

'I've killed it!' Dane cried, holding the mallet up and swinging it around. 'I've killed it. Let's kill another one, Dad. Let's do it again.'

A shaft of repugnance shot through her, growing and multiplying until she could stand it no more and she jumped up, snatching the mallet out of her son's small hands. 'I think one is enough. Let's get you cleaned up and have some lunch.'

Leaving Rob to gather up the dead fish and the equipment, Nina grabbed Dane's hand and whisked him away, their bag of food firmly tucked under her other arm.

She pushes away other thoughts that crowd her head – the jar of mini-beasts they collected together that Dane emptied and stood on, trampling them with his feet, clapping his hands and laughing as a spider tried to hide only for him to chase it and stamp on it repeatedly. The shrieks of delight as he watched a lion stalk and catch its prey on a nature documentary, his eyes fixated on it, and then the subsequent tantrum when she turned the TV over to another channel. She cannot think about any of it any longer. It's all too much. It causes her stomach to clench, her innards to roil with fear and disgust.

It's a phase. That's what she has told herself over the years, a chant she plays out in her head over and over to protect her sanity. A phase that has lasted almost fifteen years.

Swallowing and rubbing at her eyes, Nina stands up, a headache building behind her eyes, the sort of headache that lasts all day, refusing to be erased by even the strongest of painkillers. She goes into the living room, not glancing back, too drained, too anxious and too bloody unnerved by her own child's presence and unpredictable behaviour to risk looking his way.

7

'Alex, my boy. Come in. Come in. Dane said you were calling round for some supplies before you head off.' Dane's dad winks at Alex and nudges him as Alex steps into the expansive hallway and takes off his shoes.

'Leave 'em on. The missus won't mind. She loves a bit of cleaning anyway. Nothing else to keep her occupied.' Rob glances upstairs and cups his hands around his mouth as he hollers through the hallway, his voice echoing and bouncing off the cream tiles and bare walls. 'Dane! Come on, get a move on, lad. You're going to be late. I need to sort you out before you head off.' He turns and gives Alex another conspiratorial wink, his grin a mile wide.

'Yeah, all right. On my way down now.' The contrast between Rob's bright, raucous voice and Dane's dour, croaky timbre is stark. Alex wonders how they are even related, these two people – Dane with dark crop of hair and even darker eyes and then his dad with his bald head and bright, chirpy demeanour.

Alex's eyes roam around the house. He twists his body to one side so he can peer into the living room at the tapestry that stretches across the entire wall, the sprawling, white, leather couch and the huge, curved TV screen that looks bigger than his bedroom at their new house. This place reeks of money and yet Dane is the one who claims that Alex is posh. Sometimes, he just can't work people out. His dad claims that when he was younger, societal structures were more clearly defined between the haves and the have-nots but nowadays, things are more complicated, the structure more closely interwoven and almost impossible to tease and pick apart.

Not that it bothers him. Alex couldn't care less where Dane lives – a castle or a garden shed – it's all the same to him. He's just glad to have a friend in the overcrowded building that is his new school. Their other school was much smaller; everybody knew one another and some of the teachers were known to the pupils by their first names. It had a relaxed feel about it, an ethos of calm and equality which is a far cry from the picture most people have in their heads of an elite establishment that excludes outsiders and looks down on those who are less well off than those who are privileged enough to attend.

'Right lads. Come with me.' Dane's dad claps a hand across their shoulders. His son's head is dipped as he stumbles down the last few stairs and stands next to Alex. 'I'll show where I keep my stash.'

The garage is almost as big as the house itself. Alex is led into it via a door from the utility room. His eyes sweep over the white, concrete floor that has been cleaned and brushed to within an inch of its life and land upon the two low-slung sports cars that are parked over in the corner of the room.

'My two toy cars,' Rob says casually as he opens the door of a beer fridge and wrestles with an armful of bottles. 'I take them out at the weekends. Not Nina's style, though. She prefers her everyday car, the Suzuki that's parked out there on the drive, but we love 'em, don't we, Dane?' He gives his son a slap between the shoulder blades after placing the bottles of lager down on the floor at their feet, and lets out another raucous round of laughter. 'Will that lot do you, or do want a few extra? Plenty more where they came from.'

Alex wonders what Dane's mum thinks of all this and then turns his thoughts to his own parents and how they will react to him rolling in later, drunk and clumsy; him trying to hide it from them, especially his dad, then creeping upstairs, the walls and floor swaying as he blindly staggers into bed with a crash. Upsetting his mum doesn't trouble him so much these days but the thought of disappointing his dad makes his head fuzzy. The old man deserves better. He's had a rough couple of months and with his mum's moods and perpetual need to pick fights, he is reluctant to make things worse. Somebody needs to be on his dad's side.

'This is great, thanks, Mr Bowron.'

'Rob. For God's sake lad, you make me feel ancient calling me Mr Bowron.' Once again that loud tone, his voice full of gusto and confidence as he leans towards Alex and hands him a bottle. 'Here you go. One for the road, eh? Get stuck in, lads. The party starts here.'

The cold liquid is bitter as he snaps off the top and guzzles it down. It leaves a sour taste in his mouth and he tries not to grimace. He's had alcohol before at Christmas parties and once before a school disco but doesn't remember it tasting like this stuff. It feels powerful. A quick route to oblivion.

'6 per cent proof. Get it down your neck, boys. Give one to the girls and it'll work as a knicker dropper. This stuff is potent.'

Alex feels his face grow hot, certain that it's visible to both Dane and his dad. He turns away, pretending to glance around at the cars.

'Beauties, aren't they?' Rob walks over to the red Mitsubishi parked at an angle in the corner of the garage and runs his hand over the sleek paintwork, stopping as he reaches the roof. His fingers rest there, caressing the scarlet metal like it is the most precious thing he has ever touched. 'This is my summer car. She comes out when the sun does.'

Alex thinks of his dad's old Triumph Spitfire Mk IV and the everyday car that he uses for work – a run-of-the-mill Ford. Even before they moved here, when he was a hedge fund manager and earning megabucks, he still owned the same car and would spend his weekends tinkering with the Spitfire, occasionally going out for a spin in it. Unlike some of their friends, his dad was never one for ostentatiousness, preferring instead reliability and perhaps a bit of speed. The Spitfire is a throwback to his youth, a hobby, not something he purchased to turn heads or as a way of flaunting his wealth. It's part of who he is, an insight into the workings of his soul.

Innumerable thoughts run through Alex's head as he gazes around; thoughts about how strange it is that because he used to go to private school, and because of his double-barrelled surname, people assume he is the snob, the upper-class one, and yet here Dane is, surrounded by items that cost unfeasibly large amounts of money, yet he is the one who is thought of as working class. It defies all logic and the harder Alex tries, the less able he is to work it all out. He has never understood why he has been made to feel guilty about his purported privileged existence. Here he has a friend who is swimming in cash and surrounded by expensive stuff and yet the same lad dares to jeer at Alex and his upbringing and obvious posh accent. How does that even work?

He takes another swig of the amber liquid, now enjoying the bitterness as it coats his mouth and trails an icy path down his throat, thinking what a divisive thing money is, how it can drive a wedge between the strongest of families and friendships. Seeing his parents' marriage begin to fragment has taught him that much; watching his mother's once buoyant mood slowly sink and slip away out of view. Listening to Dane's thinly disguised jibes about his previous school have only cemented that belief.

'Right, come on. You ready?' Dane glowers at Alex, that look from beneath his lashes that Alex is rapidly becoming accustomed to.

They leave Dane's dad in the garage, the two of them strolling back into the house and through to the kitchen where his mum is busy at the sink. She seems so small compared to his dad's bulky, solid frame, her arms and legs like that of a young girl. She is less made-up than his mum ever is, her face pale and free of any cosmetics, unlike Kate, who he feels certain was born wearing thick foundation and crimson lipstick.

'Bye, Mrs Bowron.' Alex is prepared for a scowl from Dane, is more than prepared to put up with it because saying goodbye feels like the right thing to do. She seems like a nice woman, Dane's mum, and ignoring her feels wrong.

'Call me Nina. Have a great time, lads. And try not to be too late back, Dane.'

'Yeah,' he mutters as they leave the room and make their way into the hallway. 'Whatever,' then closely followed by 'bitch' when he is out of earshot.

Alex doesn't ask what his friend's problem is with his mum. He has enough of his own issues at home to contend with. Every family has their share of feuds and simmering tensions. Perhaps, he thinks, it's the lager doing its thing, or perhaps it's because it's been decontextualised, this particular scenario, but he doesn't question Dane's behaviour. The thought of calling his own mum names despite her often appalling behaviour makes his skin crawl, yet somehow Dane doing it in this place at this point in time seems perfectly normal and perhaps even acceptable.

A sliver of guilt tugs at him for thinking such a thing. Maybe this is what happens when you spend too long in the company of abrasive people – you eventually become one, your own values merging with theirs until your own standards and morals are obliterated by their more forceful ways. Or maybe it's this house and its sleek, emotionless decor. It isn't the most restful or warmest of homes despite its size and splendour.

They step out into the road, the bottles rattling and clinking as they lug them along in a flimsy carrier bag. Conversation is sparse, Dane focused on making sure the bag doesn't split; Alex wondering if he should have told Joss about this party. Too late now. He left the house without informing her where he was going and what's done is done.

The walk to Bobby's house doesn't take too long. Their exchanges are monosyllabic, which suits Alex just fine. Sometimes, prising words out of Dane is like squeezing blood out of a stone – why bother when the whole exercise is pointless and exhausting? Besides, he enjoys the near silence, save for the faraway hiss of traffic and the occasional chatter of passers-by.

They hear the deep thrum of the music before they reach the house, its ground-shaking bass beat loud enough to upset a whole host of neighbours. In the distance, Alex sees Bobby, his tall, willowy frame an unmissable sight. He is standing in the middle of the pavement looking out for people, waving in groups of teenagers with his long arms and wide smile, his perfectly white teeth a contrast against his caramel-coloured skin. Groups of bodies disappear around the side of the house and as he and Dane get nearer, Alex can hear their voices, a murmur, incomprehensible and barely audible to begin with then growing in volume until the noise reaches a crescendo; shouts and whoops interspersed with the odd shriek of laughter that makes him think of nails being dragged down a chalkboard.

'Come on in, you two,' Bobby shouts, his voice breaking slightly. 'Food and drink around the back. Glad you made it, mate,' he says to Alex, who acknowledges his words with a shrug to indicate his ignorance. 'Your sister said you were ill and that you weren't coming. Said you had the shits and couldn't get off the toilet?'

Alex feels his diaphragm concertina into a small, fist-sized configuration and squeezes his eyes shut for a brief second before opening them again and smiling at Bobby. 'Nah. Joss is a born liar. I wouldn't trust her to tell me what day it is.'

'Ah well.' Bobby slaps his shoulder and half pushes him inside the gate. 'She's in there somewhere, mate. She was already well pissed that last time I saw her so she might need a lift back to yours later on. Or a piggyback. That is if you don't mind a ton of puke down your back while you do it.' His laugh echoes halfway down the street as he pushes Alex and Dane into the garden and turns to speak to another gaggle of teenagers who are sauntering up the street behind them.

Alex sags. Joss is here. He should have known, really. And to think he pondered over whether or not he should ask her to come along and actually felt guilty for not doing it.

'You ready for another one?' Dane hands him a bottle, his eyes scanning the crowds then dipping away again to stare at the ground. 'Sasha's over there with your sister.'

'Sasha?' Alex takes a long gulp of the lager and wipes his mouth with the back of his hand.

'Yeah. She's a real bitch. Thinks she's God's gift.'

Alex sees a girl who looks more like a twenty-five-year-old than a teenager. Tall, slim and sassy, she commandeers the room, her long, blonde hair framing her face and curling around her shoulders, falling in great, long, silken waves, her low-cut top revealing a healthy expanse of pert breasts and her white jeans so tight, they look as if they have been spray painted onto her skin. Joss stands beside her, not quite as attractive but with enough confidence to cover up the lack of glamour. Hers is a more rugged look yet still she conveys an air of sureness coupled with an unmistakable charisma that he can see is turning heads and magnetising people to her. She sees him looking at her and gives him a wink before blowing a kiss his way. He returns the gesture by showing her the finger and turning away. Maybe later, he will speak to her about spreading stupid, childish rumours, telling everyone he wasn't coming – or maybe he won't. It's too exhausting to even attempt speaking to her. Reasoning with Joss is like repeatedly slamming his head into a brick wall. He would rather conserve his energy and try to enjoy his night here. He will do his best to avoid her. Fewer headaches. Fewer bruises.

'Like I said earlier,' Dane whispers, 'all losers, each and every fucking one of them.'

Alex suspects that Dane actually fantasises over Sasha but knows she is out of his league so uses a defence mechanism as a way of preserving his own wellbeing and dignity. Alex knows this because he has done it himself on more than one occasion with girls that he liked. Girls he knew would never have thought of him in the same way. Easier to pretend hatred and dislike than to mask sentiments of love and lust by acting nonchalant and neutral in their presence. Love and adoration always have a way of seeping out and making themselves known. Better to show disdain than run the risk of being caught out and humiliated as they publicly reject you.

'Come on,' Dane growls, pushing Alex ahead of him. 'Let's go and mingle with the arseholes. See what's going down.'

8

It was average. That's the best Alex can say about it. An average party surrounded by a few fairly average people, although if he is being perfectly honest, the bulk of them were less than average – loud, brash, superficial.

The floor of the summerhouse was swimming in vomit by the time they left, the smell still even now continuing to invade his olfactory senses as they make their way home with Joss teetering behind them in her ragged jeans and high heels. She stops every now and then, leans into some poor unsuspecting resident's shrubbery and throws up, the contents of her stomach splashing into the flowerbeds.

Alex doesn't step in to assist her. Instead, he waits. That's all he can bring himself to do, to be passively helpful by not leaving her to collapse in the middle of the street, face down in a pile of her own vomit. He will make sure she gets home safely, try to shield her from their parents and their questions and anger and obvious disappointment by shoving her in the back door and trundling her upstairs into her bedroom. That's where his allegiance ends. After that, she's on her own.

'Oh, look over there,' Dane says, his voice a low drawl. 'Can you see what I can see?'

Alex heaves a sigh, unwilling to get dragged into whatever his friend has in mind. He's tired, his sister is so drunk she can hardly stand, and now Dane wants him to stop and take part in what he is certain will be some stupid prank that will piss him off and finish the night off on a sour note.

'I spy a Rose house.' Dane has stopped walking and is staring at an average-looking house barely discernible from all the other houses that flank it.

'So what? It's a house. Come on, I need to get her back.' Alex flicks his thumb over his shoulder. Behind them, Joss stumbles about blindly, her legs buckling and bending like a new-born calf. She staggers to one side, is about to careen into a brick wall before righting herself, bending double and throwing up, a hand clutched at her stomach as she retches and heaves. The gurgling reminds him of a wild animal being slain, the splatter of her vomit akin to the spilling of the blood. Alex sighs, closes his eyes and wishes himself elsewhere.

'Not there.' Dane stands on his tiptoes and points. 'Look, over there, above the rooftops.'

Alex sees nothing but a swathe of black sky punctuated with a scattering of stars. He grits his teeth, tries to suppress his growing anger. Two drunken idiots. He is stuck out here with two drunken idiots who seem hellbent on cruising around town instead of going home where it is warm and light and there is a soft, welcoming bed waiting for him. The atmosphere may not be the warmest but at least he can climb under the quilt where it is quiet and comfortable and he doesn't have to babysit his younger sister, who has drunk her bodyweight in gin and vodka and is now exhibiting the base behaviours and reactions of a spoilt toddler in the throes of a candy-ingested sugar rush.

'Come with me. Come on.' Without waiting for a response, Dane crosses the road, hands shoved deep in his pockets, head dipped and shoulders rounded.

Alex could stay here, refuse to follow him. He's got Joss to think of. He has to get her home or his parents will kill him. He may not be close mates with Joss but leaving her here to fend for herself isn't something he would ever consider doing. He could, however, leave Dane on his own. He has no good reason to follow him, except for the fact that he is his friend. From day one, Dane was there for him, helping him through those first few weeks at school, showing him the ropes, pointing out the good guys, helping Alex maintain a healthy distance from the bad ones.

'Right, come on. Up.' Alex hooks his arms around Joss's waist and hauls her upright from her crouched position. She lets out a groan, a trail of saliva landing on Alex's arm. He winces and grits his teeth, averting his eyes and focusing on keeping her on her feet. 'Stand up. Follow him.' He points, forcing Joss's face around to the direction in which Dane is heading. 'Keep going, and no more throwing up or I'll kill you.'

They stagger along together, her body colliding with his, her legs bending beneath her like rubber. Only as they pick up their pace does she regain some semblance of normality, her slightly less inebriated self slowly returning.

'Where are we going?' The voice of a small child, whiny and desperate.

'Fuck knows. To hell and back.'

Ahead, Alex can see the top of Dane's head, his hunched, wiry figure as he wends his way through a small cut between the row of houses. Following, Alex hangs onto Joss, feeling her initial resistance wane. Leading them up a small, gravel track, Dane turns, checks they're in pursuit, then continues.

'Dane! Where the hell are we going?' He tries to keep his voice to a whisper but exasperation gets the better of him, squeezing his patience to a thin, wiry strand. The words come out as a near roar.

'Keep your voice down, for Christ's sake. We're almost there.'

The gravel track leads them uphill, through a small field and onto the edge of the woods. Shrouded in darkness, there is no light pollution, no streetlights, no dim reflections from neighbouring properties. They are very much alone. Except for one property – a small house shielded beneath a canopy of trees. It's surrounded on all sides by a ragged stretch of shrubbery. Alex shivers. Joss moves away from him. She strides over to a large oak tree and rests against the wide trunk, her body still wobbling, her head nodding as she tries to give off an air of confidence and poise.

All Alex can see is Dane's shadow and the small building beyond and even that is partially obscured by a tangle of tall weeds. Dane stops and turns, his finger outstretched. He is sporting a smile that has split through his usual dour expression, giving him the look of somebody slightly unhinged. 'Fancy a bit of fun?'

'I fancy going home.' Tiredness and a lack of tolerance is edging its way into Alex's timbre, his usually reserved tone now absent.

'Aw, fuck off Winston-D'Allandrio. Let's stay and have a bit of a laugh for a change.'

'I wanna have fun as well.' Joss's shrill voice comes from behind them. 'Let me join in.' Her speech is slurred and as she shifts into view, Alex supresses a wave of laughter, placing his hand over his face and shaking his head in despair.

Vomit is matted into her hair, mascara streaked down her face in long, oily rivulets. She has abandoned her heels and is staggering towards Alex and Dane in bare feet, her shoes held out in front of her at arm's length.

Alex turns, expects Dane to be repulsed by the sight before them, but is shocked to see his friend's face lighten with interest and lust, his usual dark countenance lifting, replaced by something even uglier. Dane eyes Joss up and down, his mouth twisted into a lopsided, expectant grin. An iron fist grips at Alex's insides, grasping, pulling and twisting. Dane and Joss stand side by side, their heads dipped together conspiratorially. He watches with growing impatience as they gaze at the isolated property, wondering what comes next. You never know with Dane. That's the major flaw in his friend's character. You just never know.

'Joss. It's time to go. Now.' Alex's voice is carried away by the breeze. She is impervious to his requests to leave, her interests now honed in on this stupid house that sits on its own in the middle of the woods.

'This, ladies and gentlemen,' Dane says as he takes a faux bow, 'is the home of none other than Mr Dominic Rose, English teacher extraordinaire.'

'And?' Alex begins to walk away, his tolerance levels now close to zero.

'Ugh.' Joss turns to one side and pretends to spit on the ground. A thin line of drool hangs from her lip. She stands, unaware of its existence until Dane reaches over and wipes it away with the tip of his finger. Alex's stomach roils. Not here. Not now. Not these two. Definitely not these two.

'He's a perv.' Joss's tone is one of contempt.

Dane steps back then moves closer again when she raises her finger and points at the house. 'Him, over there. He's a total perv. He tried to touch me up last week in class.'

Alex's eyes droop. He's tired. He wants all of this to go away, to just disappear. Joss is drunk, Dane is both lustful and angry. A dangerous combination.

'What?' Dane moves ever closer to Joss while Alex takes another step away.

'It's true!' Her eyes are glassy, her voice as shrill as a whistle. Alex imagines that her breath will smell like the bowels of hell. 'Last week, he asked to see me and Sasha after class, told us both to stop back so he could speak to us, said we were talking during the lesson and that we needed to stop it and that we have to start knuckling down. When I tried to leave, he moved past and pressed himself up against me.'

In his peripheral vision, Alex watches Dane attempt to put his arm around Joss's shoulders. She slumps under the weight and ends up sprawled on the floor, her hair fanning out around her, skinny legs jutting out at awkward angles.

'Tell you what we need to do,' Dane murmurs as he heaves her back up and places his arm around her waist. 'We need to teach him a lesson. Let him know we're onto him, the sick old fucker.'

Before Alex can say or do anything to stop him, Dane picks up a small stone and throws it at the house. It skims past the front window and lands in the shrubbery with a thud. Alex's heart hammers out a sickly, solid beat under his shirt. His neck pulses in a synchronised rhythm. This is what fear and anticipation of an unpredictable scenario feels like, he thinks, wishing all the while that he could spirit himself away, be elsewhere. Wishing he could be at home in bed, far away from here.

This is what happens when you hang around with Dane Bowron. Things happen that you can't always control. Dane has a way of stringing him along, making sure he is witness to each and every event.

'Come on. I need to get her home. Jocelyn, let's go.' He starts to walk away, his footsteps the only ones to be heard as Joss and Dane stay put, their bodies angled in eagerness while Dane finds another handful of stones and hurls them at the window. This time they hit, an explosion of gravel that rattles the glass.

The burst of noise causes Alex's skin to prickle. 'For Christ's sake, Dane! What the hell?' He strides over to Joss and tugs at her arm. She yanks it free, pulling her hand up in the air and waving it about aimlessly.

'Piss off, Alex. I'm staying here with Dane. We're going to do stuff together, aren't we, Dane?' She nudges him and bends down to pick up another handful of small stones. 'Here, chuck this lot at the old codger's window till he wakes up and sees us. No more than he deserves. Filthy old bastard. He's completely rank.'

They giggle, their voices a crack in the silence. Alex thinks about Mr Rose peering out of his window, calling the police and the ensuing chaos that would follow. He thinks of his mum and her permanent state of anger, then his dad and the disappointment on his face that would crush Alex more than any scathing words or fits of fury ever could.

Dane leans over to Joss, takes the stones and throws them, a worrying amount of strength in his trajectory. This time, they hit the front door and Alex hears the immediately recognisable sound of glass breaking and shattering. He sucks in his breath and feels a rage flare up inside him, building in his chest, bubbling up into his throat like lava. He turns and walks away, only to be pulled back by Dane; his fingers clasped tightly around Alex's forearm.

'Where you off to?' Dane's eyes are like tiny flecks of coal set deep in his skull, dark and menacing. Even in the pitch black of the evening, Alex can recognise the intent that lies behind them, that unmistakable craving for friction and unrest. 'Come on, man. It's only a bit of fun. And anyway, don't you think the old bastard deserves it for what he did to your sister? Are you really going to let him get away with touching her up?'

Alex's stuttering heartbeat increases, jumping about his chest, making him feel faint and queasy. He thinks about walking home, leaving this behind. Then he wonders if Joss's story is really true. She may well be a manipulator but is she really devious enough to think up such a damaging narrative, knowing this man could lose his job if he is reported?

Crippled by confusion and anxiety, Alex stands, unable to move. A lone voice drags him out of his stupor like the clap of thunder overhead.

'Hey! I can see who you are!' Mr Rose is there, standing on his doorstep, silhouetted, his finger pointing at them as they dive for cover amongst a clump of shrubbery. His tall, stooped outline stands dead centre of the doorframe, the light behind casting him in an eerie glow. A caricature of himself. That's what springs into Alex's head. Mr Rose is like an exaggerated version of himself with his flyaway, candyfloss hair, bent posture and long, skinny legs.

Joss's inane giggle makes the hairs on the back of Alex's neck stand on end. So far, they have remained hidden in the shadows but once they move, which they will have to, he will spot them. He needs to stop her, to shut her up, or they will all be done for.

Alex grabs for his sister but misses, staggers and falls onto his knees with a clatter, twigs snapping, branches breaking beneath him, the carpet of rotting leaves breaking his fall but not absorbing the noise. Hands grab at his shoulders, Dane attempting to pull him up out of the way, but it's too late. The beam of a torch lands on his face, blinding him, a spread of pale yellow illuminating his shocked expression.

'You!'

Alarm spears through him, piercing his temporary frozen stance. Scrambling to his feet, Alex turns away from the light, his feet struggling for purchase on the soft, damp ground, alcohol and fear making him clumsy, his movements ungainly and cumbersome.

'I can see who you are! It's Alexander, isn't it? Who's that with you? Is that Dane Bowron?'

A sudden silence descends, an atmosphere of tension surrounding them as they wait, wondering what he is going to do next, this teacher whose window they have smashed. This teacher who has identified them and caught them red-handed. An imaginary wail of sirens booms in Alex's head, blue flashing lights stopping close by while a trail of uniformed officers creep up behind them, pushing Alex, Joss and Dane to the ground before cuffing them and throwing the three of them in the back of the van. He swallows, rubs at his eyes. Is unable to see a way out of this stupid, fucking mess.

'Get away from here. If I see you around here again, I'll call the police!'

A bang echoes into the thickets and tall trees as Mr Rose slams the door and turns out the light, plunging them once again into darkness.

'Ha!' Dane spins around, spluttering with excitement. 'We did it! We fucking did it. We got old Rosey.'

Whilst Dane and Joss celebrate, whooping and cheering, chattering and dancing around, Alex turns and heads back over the field towards town. If Joss doesn't want to follow him, she can make her own way back home. He's done here. He has had enough. He is well and truly done.

9

Dominic pads upstairs, wondering if it was the same lot that knocked at his door yesterday. Weary acceptance settles on him, coupled with a strong streak of disappointment. He should be used to this by now, being bothered by pupils. There was a time they would knock on his door asking for help with homework but now their appearance is usually coupled with abuse – throwing stones, shouting through his windows, making idle threats. He's witnessed them all, the juvenile activities they get up to, and each time, it chips away at him, lowering his resistance, pushing him one step closer to retirement.

Seeing Alexander there, knowing he was one of the baying mob, has left Dominic flattened and marginally depressed. He had high hopes for that lad, thought him better than that. Thought that such childish pastimes were beneath him. Just goes to show that his judgement is skewed, that he is losing his touch. Even the most intelligent and thoughtful of pupils have a darker side, demons that lurk somewhere deep in their souls.

Given their immaturity and lack of worldly knowledge, he would, at one time, give all students a second chance. But lately, his feelings have changed, his perspective shifting in another direction due by and large to age, lethargy and general disinterest. He will bide his time, do the best he can to teach those who want to learn and then leave it all behind him. Gone are the days of enthusiastic debates, a need to pump as much knowledge into their brains as he can. Nowadays, he considers it a successful day if he can make it through without buckling under the strain.

Heading back downstairs, Dominic checks the door again, tugging at it, making sure the chain is in place. Chances are they will be halfway home by now, those miscreants, but he's not prepared to take any risks. Dane Bowron is a strange lad, his thoughts hidden and unreachable, his behaviour predictably unpredictable. Scowling and muttering seems to be his default stance. Getting him to engage and interact in lessons is exhausting, like shovelling snow while it's still snowing. And Dane isn't the worst of them. Not by a long shot. There are others who will sink lower, take more risks, do very little to get by, knowing that a safety net will catch them, help them through life even though they have done nothing to deserve it.

Dominic heads back up to his room, taking the stairs two at a time, surprised and pleased at his own agility. He thinks back to those days, to long before Dane was born, when Dominic taught his father, Robert Bowron. The father is louder and more forceful, but they are both still cut from the same cloth, their core values plain for all to see. Dane's recent essay showed elements of misogyny: his dislike of women and a deep hatred for figures of authority. It sent a shudder through him reading it, knowing that nothing he could ever do or say would shift the boy's attitude. It's too deep rooted, too embedded in his psyche.

There was a point in his career when he would have put aside some time, spoken to Dane, put another side of the argument across to further the boy's thinking skills, show him how to reflect on situations critically. But not anymore. Not when the boy has the likes of Robert Bowron behind him, that influential father figure pushing him on, whispering in his ear, installing his own warped ideas into the head of his son. It's a losing battle and one for which Dominic simply doesn't have the vigour or willingness. Soon he will step away from it all, leave it to his younger counterparts, and spend his days at home, whiling away the houses in this ramshackle old place.

A stone sits at the base of his belly at the thought of spending more time with his mother. A serrated rock of resentment. She has good days and bad days and then there are those days that are long and drawn out with no end in sight.

Teaching gives him some respite. Without it, his life will feel shaky and out of balance with no sense of direction. He will have to recalibrate his free time, find a new hobby, muster up interests in other areas. Tending to his mother's needs cannot take up every minute of his day. It's not healthy. Not good for his soul.

She is sleeping as he peers around the door. The same familiar smell pervades every corner of the room, that musty aroma that no matter how hard he tries, he simply cannot remove.

He tiptoes in and sits by her bed, watching the rise and fall of her chest, listening to her breathing, low and soft. Shallow gasps of air. Dominic glances beyond the shadows, casting his mind back.

This used to be his room when he was a young lad. This was where he spent his evenings, studying for exams, playing his music, perusing his stamp collection, and when he thought he was alone and there was no chance of being disturbed by either of his parents, looking at girlie magazines: that insubstantial stash he kept hidden at the back of his wardrobe.

This was also the place where he first made love to Clara. Blood rushes through his ears, clogging up his veins as he thinks about it, that day, that hot, summer's day when he slowly peeled away her layers of clothing, caressed her skin, his fingers trailing down over her body, treating her as if she were a porcelain doll while she sighed softly and responded to his touch.

Dominic shifts in his chair. There is a stirring in his groin, something he hasn't felt for quite some time. Even now, all these years later, thinking about her still sends a rush of blood whirling through his system, reaching parts of his body that haven't seen any signs of life for so long that he had forgotten what they were truly capable of.

A low groan slips from his lips as he leans back and closes his eyes, his hand finding its way beneath his clothes and resting just below his navel before trailing lower and lower.

No.

Not here, in this bedroom. Not now. Maybe not ever.

He stands, the arousal exiting his body in a sudden, cold rush, and strides towards the door. He needs to leave this room and the many memories it holds. Sometimes, thoughts of that period of his life provide him with comfort, make him feel at ease, and then other times – other times, it stabs at him, piercing his heart and skewering his emotions. He isn't in the right frame of mind to deal with the past tonight. Tomorrow, things may look brighter, less gloomy and fraught, but tonight, he would rather leave things alone, let the past rest, not stir up a host of unwelcome sensations that make him feel like he is plummeting through a dark, starless sky with nothing beneath him to break his fall.

His own bedroom is cool, the bed soft and welcoming. He slips between the sheets, allowing sleep to embrace him almost immediately, whisking him off to a place of impenetrable darkness and safety.

* * *

Despite it being a Saturday, he is up bright and early. Last night feels like a hundred years ago. His mind is clear of cobwebs and the sluggishness he felt sure would linger. He dresses and heads downstairs to make breakfast. The darkness is always the hardest time, small problems multiplying exponentially, exploding, firing off bits of shrapnel into his brain. But now the lightness is here. Dawn has broken. The sky is a deep, cerulean blue, the sun lingering somewhere behind a lone, grey cloud, its heat already introducing itself as the breeze pushes the spread of white away, leaving a clear patch of cobalt above him. The world feels like a happier place to be.

His singing fills the house, bouncing off walls and travelling through each room as he moves about, tidying and putting things back in place, arranging items just how he likes them. With his mother bedridden, he is the only one in this house and yet by the end of his working week, it feels as if an army of people have trampled through it. Newspapers are strewn about the floor, blankets lie crumpled on the sofa, dirty cups stand in a line on the coffee table; one for every day of the week.

I need to do better, try harder at this housework malarkey, thinks Dominic, enjoying his use of educational terms applied to his own chaotic existence. He smiles. Sometimes it's the small stuff, the inane, the mundane and the downright absurd that helps him through, injecting levity back into his life.

He enjoys the task, ridding himself of the clutter and detritus, stopping only to make a coffee. He stands, sipping at it, staring around at the kitchen, thinking that even when clean and tidy, it still looks dated, having not been modernised for as long as he can remember. The cracked, laminate surfaces feel dry and porous as he runs his fingers across them, his nails catching on the small grooves that run the length of the worktop. Years of use, of cutting, of placing hot cups on it. Years of neglect.

He thinks how little has been done to this place. Not even how little. Nothing has been done at all. Everything is still as it was when his father was alive, the fixtures and fittings the same as when they first moved into it. Not a lick of paint or a strip of wallpaper has ever been applied. He could have done something about it, turned his hand to it, even paid somebody to refurbish it, but the time never seemed to be right. Life got in the way.

Is there ever a right time for ripping the heart and soul out of a house to replace it with things that are not associated with the people who inhabit it? It seems unnatural and superficial to replace things just to keep up with the latest fashions and trends. What is to be gained from such endeavours? Memories are what make a house a home, not designer units and expensive fabrics and unremarkable and yet ludicrously expensive pieces of art. Sometimes, it feels good to stand still, to slow down time and be anachronistic in his approaches and methods. Following the latest trends has never been his thing. It's not always easy, pushing against the oncoming crowd, heading away from current leanings and forging his own path, but he knows no other way of existing. It's just how he is.

Dominic closes his eyes, thinks about time, the passing of years. Thinks about Clara. How different everything could have been, how life seemed to turn on him, tipping his world upside down leaving him with nothing but the dregs. For so many years now, he has had to put up with what was left, wading through the aftermath, making do and yet never quite getting used to not having her in his life.

Sipping at his coffee, he tunes back in to the present, dismissing any fleeting ideas he had about decorating or changing this old place. It's fine as it is. Stripping away at the layers of paint and wallpaper would take with it his many memories and he cannot contemplate doing such a thing. They are all he has.

A sound cuts through his thoughts. He spins around, looking for obvious sources, checking the gas taps on the cooker, leaning towards the window, his head cocked to one side as he listens out again.

It comes once more, muted, dulled yet definitely audible. A scratching. He stares down at the floor, his senses now heightened. It's in the cellar. The noise is coming from the cellar, drifting up through the floorboards. Mice perhaps, and yet it feels too loud. They're small creatures who scurry at night, making little or no noise during the day. Mice in the cellar is a given. They cause him no trouble. Whatever is down there is large enough to make itself heard. He thinks of rats and takes a long, shaky breath before pushing his feet into his mud-encrusted wellies and unlocking the back door.

When his dad was alive, the old man used to use the cellar as a workshop, somewhere he would go to carry out any maintenance work – sawing, fixing, mending the bits of farm machinery he had, but to Dominic, it is a dark, dank place, somewhere for storage of things he no longer uses but can't bring himself to throw away. Perhaps he should have put it to a better use, turning it into another living area. It was an idea that occasionally rumbled about in his mind but somehow, he never quite got around to doing anything about it. Like so many other things in his life, it got pushed away and neglected, left to rot.

The ground is soft under his feet, wet and slippery after a downpour during the night. He pulls the key out of his pocket and slides it into the lock. It turns, the small door opening a crack, a shaft of low light spreading into the darkness, incrementally illuminating the small space. It's still dim down there, the door set too low to allow in enough daylight even when fully open. His hand slaps at the wall, his fingers trying to locate the light switch. He misses, slips slightly and stumbles forward into the murkiness, the surface under his feet now dry and hard as he rights himself and looks around.

In the far the corner, he sees a glint of something, a swift movement then a sensation against his legs that freezes his blood. Hands splayed out, he tries again for the light switch, flicks at it with fumbling fingers and lets out a half laugh, half cry as a cat stands there next to him, its eyes fixed on his before it pushes past and slides out of the door and back into the open.

At his feet sits the half-chewed carcass of a mouse, its head missing, its small body littered with scratches where the cat has mauled at it.

The small well built for catching water, which should be almost overflowing, is only half full. The last time he was down here was two days ago. That must have been when the cat made its way in. It has been down here all that time, feeding on mice, drinking rainwater and doing its messy business. He will have to seek out the offending filth and clean it up. He isn't averse to dirty jobs; it's the thought that if he doesn't find anything in the main part of the cellar, he will have to slither his way into the crawl space that runs beneath the front part of the house. Heaving himself through a tiny space on his belly in the dark searching for cat shit wasn't how he planned on spending his weekend. He has a new book he is looking forward to reading, perhaps even a little light gardening. Maybe even some cooking, but not this. Definitely not this.

Closing the door behind him to stop any more unwanted visitors from slinking their way in, Dominic glances around, hoping to spot anything untoward, anything obvious. He sniffs the air, hoping to catch a scent of anything nasty lurking, but all he can smell is dank, musty air and perhaps the odd musty whiff of dead mice.

He picks up a torch, aware that the overhead bulb isn't bright enough to highlight the whole of the cellar, switches it on and blinks as the room is suddenly flooded with a yellow beam of light. He swings the heavy torch around, aiming it in all four corners before trailing it along the edges of the room and across the dusty, concrete floor. Nothing. No cat shit. No more dead rodents. Nothing at all.

Striding past his father's piles of old tools and defunct farming equipment, he drops to his knees and takes a deep breath, bracing himself for what comes next. Crawling into that space is something he did regularly when he was a youngster, when his body was leaner, smaller, his fears less prominent in his mind, but nowadays, it makes his guts swirl and his skin pucker with dread.

The gap in the bricks that leads to the crawl space looks smaller than he remembers – smaller and darker and everything beyond the aperture a damn sight more cramped. The thought of having to creep and slither his way through it is bad enough but then what if he gets stuck and can't turn around? He will have to shuffle his way back out on his belly, using only his hands and his feet to feel his way, never knowing if he is heading in the right direction or whether he will hit a brick wall and end up jammed in there, unable to manoeuvre his way back into the relatively wider space of the cellar.

He lies down, his heart hammering wildly, and shines the torch through, scanning the darkest corners, hoping the offending article is within grabbing distance.

The smell attacks his nostrils, his gag reflex going into overdrive; small, curling fronds of foulness reaching down into his throat and curdling his guts. The light lands upon a small pile of excrement over in the farthest corner of the crawl space. Unpalatable images lodge themselves in his head; sliding through to retrieve it and getting jammed in there; or leaving it where it is and allowing it to fester until the smell becomes so bad, rising through the floorboards into the living room, that he is forced to come back down here to clean it up anyway.

There's little to be gained from leaving it where it is. At some point, it will have to be removed. Dominic pokes his head in, propels himself forward and snakes his way through the hole on his stomach, the torch jutting out in front of him, his body writhing and wriggling along the cold concrete. It's only as he approaches that he realises he has nothing in which to put the damn stuff. With not enough room to turn and reach into his pocket for a tissue or anything he can use to pick it up, he feels helpless. He has been so focused on his fears that he has forgotten about the practicalities. He almost laughs out loud. Forgetfulness, ill-thought out manoeuvres. The story of his life.

Body rigid, he sweeps his arms out wide, hoping to land upon something that will do the job. The elongated arc of light lands upon an array of discarded objects that have been down here for decades – old roof tiles, spare bricks, broken plant pots. Any of those would suffice. He could scoop up the mess and carry it outside.

Shuffling farther forward, his fingers brush over what feels like a roll of plastic. He swallows and recoils, removing his hand and sweeping it sideways, the sensation of that old plastic sheeting still attached to his nerve endings, making them shrivel and tingle. He continues feeling, searching, grasping. Within seconds, his fingers touch something soft that doesn't feel suspiciously like a dead animal. Dragging it closer, he realises that it's a piece of fabric, one of his mother's dresses that has been turned into an old rag. He recognises it, grasps it tightly, scrunching the fabric between his fingers and inhaling the scent. Traces of her perfume still lingers, woven deep into the strands, years and years of accumulated oils that have saturated the cotton, leaving an indelible mark. He holds it close to his face, the aroma of the material preferable to the stink of cat faeces.

With one swift movement, he slides himself forward, rag in hand, and scoops up the pile of shit, a fist clenching at his stomach. He swallows, wriggles back, exiting the same way he entered, feeling his way out as best he can, one hand clutching the torch, the other holding the fabric. His elbows aid his movement, pushing himself backwards. Only when he feels the temperature change, a cooler breeze hitting his feet and legs, does he let out the breath he has been holding in. With one last shove, he pushes himself out of the hole and back into the main part of the cellar, his fingers still curled around the patterned fabric, his panic dissipating, relief ballooning in his chest.

He pulls himself upright and flicks off the torch and the main light. One last glance around then he backs out and shuts the door, locking it and slipping the key into his pocket. The offending article nipped tightly between his thumb and forefinger, Dominic carries it to the back step where he drops it before going into the kitchen to locate a bag.

It takes him just seconds to place the material inside a plastic carrier and tie it up. He drops it in the main bin and stands at the old sink in the ancient lean-to, washing his hands repeatedly. He shudders, feeling contaminated; his skin, his pores, every inch of him reeking of dust and decay and an earthy smell that he can't seem to shake no matter how hard he scrubs.

Were it not for the well that needs emptying after heavy rainfall, he would seal up the cellar completely, ignoring its vacuous, dark presence beneath him. Even as a child, he didn't particularly care for the place, only going down there to assist his father with jobs. It's a grimy, miserable place that holds nothing but bad memories. Turning it into a usable living space was only ever a pipe dream. It's better left untouched.

Drying his hands, Dominic heads back into the kitchen wishing it was later in the day so he could have a glass of something stronger than coffee. Something that would take his mind off things and obliterate the memories that are bouncing around his brain. They vie for his attention, muscling their way in like the bully boys that they are.

He shuts his eyes, takes a long breath and shakes his head. *Not today.* Those thoughts and feelings and dark, desperate recollections can go to hell. *Not today. Not any day.*

He fills the kettle, makes his coffee and takes it into the living room where the daily papers await him. Today will be a peaceful one. He'll make sure of it.

10

1 JUNE 1978

Dear Clara,

I thought of you today while I was out on my early-morning walk. That doesn't actually sound quite right, does it? I think of you all the time but what I meant to say was, you were on my mind more than usual. I didn't sleep too well and had to get out of the house for a while.

Your grandparents are in my thoughts too, please know that and send them my best wishes.

My stomach is folded into a tight knot as I pen this letter, the words too difficult to say but I will do my best. Even as I am writing it, I am finding it hard to stay focused because of what I am about to ask, but ask it I will – my dearest, darling Clara, have you fallen out of love with me?

There, I've said it. I only hope that as you are reading this, you are smiling and shaking your head, a glassy, loving expression in your eyes. I like to think that you have a perfectly valid reason for not replying to my last letter and that my worries are unfounded. A million things have run through my mind, so many excuses as to why you haven't written to me – the postal service is erratic to the point of being non-existent up there in the back of beyond, the health of your gran has deteriorated to the point she now needs round-the-clock care from you.

And then of course, the final worst scenario that I can hardly bring myself to even think about – you no longer want to be with me. You no longer love me. Actually writing those words feels like a punch to my solar plexus, making me dizzy and robbing me of the ability to breathe properly.

I decided before I set to writing this, that I would pen it with the idea in mind that things haven't changed between us at all, that we are still the same loving couple parted only by miles but very much still together, our hearts still fused as one. It's easier that way, otherwise it would feel as if I were writing to a stranger and not to you, my dearest Clara, the person who is the other half of me. I couldn't bear that you may be reading this whilst rolling your eyes and working out a way to tell me that we are over. So I will continue on as if nothing has changed, because for me, it hasn't. I only pray that you feel the same way.

Yesterday, I saw another of your favourite birds and am convinced it's a sign that you are coming back to me very soon. I was driving home from work and parked up by the field where we took a photograph last year. Do you remember that day, Clara? The time when the entire area looked as if it was flooded with water when it was, in fact, filled with cornflowers? A sea of blue was how you described it. An ocean of beauty. Sitting on the fence next to that field was a bullfinch. I immediately thought of you, my darling, and sat for a while, contemplating our future together. I pictured you in a wedding gown, a delicately stitched, white veil covering your beautiful, porcelain-like features, the train of your dress trailing behind, everything about you framed to absolute perfection. Is that too presumptuous of me? To want you for my wife? For us to spend the rest of our lives together as loving spouses?

Perhaps it is. Perhaps I am being overly dramatic and possibly even maudlin, wishing my life away, hankering after something that may never happen, and so I will move on and speak of other things for fear of embarrassing you.

Work is still proving to be interesting. There is so much to do and I still have a lot to learn. I thought that when I completed my college training, I would be a fully rounded, clued-up teacher but it appears there are many, many strands and skills required to penetrate and guide young minds, to steer them along the right path and make sure they leave my classroom, their heads stuffed full of knowledge, ready to enter into the world as fledgling adults.

How is your writing going? I'm guessing your book is nearing completion and hope that the solace up there in Loch Rannoch has provided you with enough peace and tranquillity to produce the next bestseller! You deserve every success, my darling, and more.

I would love to visit you but as I said in my last letter, work is all-encompassing at the moment. Perhaps if you are still there during the summer break, I can drive up and we can spend some time together? I'm hoping you will have returned home by then and we can pass the long, hazy days wrapped in one another's arms but in case you're not, how does a visit from me sound? I don't want to crowd you or make you feel uncomfortable but am missing you so much, it's like a physical ache. I wake every morning with an image of your face in my mind, its perfectly sculpted features and rosebud lips, and I'm not sure how much longer I can go on without hearing from you. If only you had access to a phone, I could speak to you and hear your voice. Then I would know. I would be able to tell from the lilt of your timbre, from the modulation in your tone, whether or not you want out from this relationship.

Sitting in front of me on my desk is a photograph of you: the one where you are sitting staring up at the sky on that day when we visited York. Do you remember it, darling Clara? With hindsight, I think perhaps that was the day that things had begun to change. The obvious angling of your body away from me, the slight wrinkle on your brow that at the time I mistook for dreaminess and satisfaction now looks to me like restlessness and perhaps even disdain. Yesterday, I looked at more photographs of you, studying them closely, using my knowledge to try and work out more about you, because for all we are a couple, I realise that I actually know very little about you. I am aware that you will deny this, will want to tell me that my strange interest in an antiquated and often castigated hobby is a ridiculous waste of time and that I am seeing things that aren't there. But it isn't a waste of time, you see. Physiognomy is very much a valued discipline and skill. It may have gone out of fashion and been rejected by many modern scientists but this is mainly *because of its links in the late nineteenth century to phrenology, which is indeed worthy of being rejected and discredited, but physiognomy on its own still has its own merits and its use will one day be required as a way to study the human mind and all its complexities. Of that I am sure.*

So anyway, as I was saying, my studies of your features have led me to some unsavoury and unpalatable conclusions. For now, I will reserve judgement and keep my thoughts to myself, but if I don't hear from you soon, I may be unable to hold back my thoughts and it will all come spilling out – my deepest fears and worries about you, dear Clara. They are all stored up in my head and your lack of communication is doing nothing to alleviate them.

Please write back, my darling. I fear I am going mad here without you. I'm feeling extremely low and, possibly even a little depressed. My world is definitely a lesser place without you in it. You are my ray of sunshine, the warmth on my face. My reason for living.

Mother sends her best wishes, as do I.

I am sending you all of my love and will wait with bated breath for your reply.

Goodbye for now, my dearest Clara.

Dominic xx

11

PRESENT DAY

It feels wrong, and yet so very right. It's a mask Kate wears to blot out the wretchedness and the loneliness and the humiliation. Sitting here putting on lipstick, applying perfume, dressing in the designer clothes she no longer wears because she doesn't attend social functions, does little to lift her spirits but it's better than sitting here doing nothing, wallowing in her own misfortune. It's exhausting feeling so low all the time. Draining. She needs a bit of happiness. Deserves it. It's like trying to catch butterflies, snatching at fragments of joy, often missing but sometimes capturing a few fleeting moments of unadulterated bliss.

Anthony has taken to his study and is reading the *Financial Times*, his eyes lowered away from the comings and goings of their family life. There was a time he would have asked her where she was going, perhaps even offered to drop her off and pick her up, but those days are behind them. Perhaps it's for the best. The less time they spend in each other's company, the less stressful everything seems to be. Distance is what keeps them together.

A small frisson of excitement pulses through her at the thought of tonight. It's wrong, she knows that, but there is so much about it that feels right that she is compelled to go, to say yes to something that could end her marriage, irreparably breaking apart her already damaged little world.

There would be no going back from what she is about to do, no escape route to happier times.

Her heart stutters about beneath her breastbone, its staccato rhythm an uncomfortable sensation in her chest as she applies more perfume, its oily scent coating her skin, filling the room: delicate yet overpowering, musky yet sweet. She has to get it right. Coming across as brassy and overbearing will put an end to things before they have even begun. It's all about balance.

In the room next to hers, she hears Jocelyn moving about, still groggy after coming home inebriated from that party last night. While Anthony slept soundly, Kate had listened as Alexander had tried to guide his sister upstairs, her shouting at him that he left her, him claiming he went back for so she had better stop complaining and why did she drink so much anyway?

She had left them to it. Jocelyn would have only batted away her attempts to help and anyway, Alexander managed to get his sister home safely so what else was there to do? He appeared to have everything in hand. Jocelyn had made it to the bathroom to be sick, leaving behind her an instantly recognisable stench that reminded Kate of her own student flat when her evenings were spent in a drunken haze, surrounded by friends, pizza and empty bottles of vodka. She thinks back to those halcyon days when her life was one long round of parties and the future held such promise. She graduated from Durham University and somehow managed to gain a 2:1 in English Literature despite missing more lectures than she cares to remember and handing in projects and essays that were well below the standards of which she was capable.

It had been a giggle, her days at university, a time in her life that she remembers with great fondness. She made friends, lost her virginity, had a string of boyfriends and one-night stands and on many evenings, drank herself senseless. Getting a degree was an incidental occurrence, something that happened along the way. And now here she is, trapped in a marriage that is deteriorating daily, living in a house that is beneath her aspirations, with few friends and little money. What was it all for? Going to university, making the effort to mix and mingle with Anthony's colleagues, all those years spent climbing the rungs of a ladder that has been pulled from under her, sending her back down to the bottom with a crash. Is this what she dreamed of when she was a student at Durham, or did she seek something bigger, something better? In truth, she can't remember making any real plans or having any particular dreams; she just remembers a pulsing sense of excitement at what the future might hold, a wonderful anticipation at the possibility of making something of her life.

And now look at her: a lonely housewife stuck in an average house in a less-than-average part of the suburbs of North Yorkshire. Her journey from student to grown woman has been condensed into an insignificant slice of nothingness. She has little to show for her life. A husband and two children. No major accomplishments, nothing of any import that marks her out as different or better than anybody else. Just another bland individual: a forgettable face in a crowd of thousands with little to offer.

She dabs on more perfume, applies another layer of lipstick and fluffs up her hair. Does it matter if what she is about to do goes against the grain of all that is deemed good and wholesome? Life has shit on her from a great height. She has nobody to turn to, no friends to call upon, no family to turn to. Her parents are elderly and live their own insular lives in Oxford. She has no siblings left. Her brother's nomadic lifestyle has put paid to that. The last time she heard from him was before he embarked on yet another soul-searching visit to Tibet just over a year ago. Even before that, contact had been sporadic. Now it is non-existent. She is completely alone, floundering in a sea of unhappiness, reaching out for help, waiting for somebody to breathe life into her slowly dying body.

And now that somebody has arrived.

The floor shifts like quicksand under Kate's feet as she makes her way over to the door, her heels clicking, the noise echoing in her head, reminding her of what it is she is about to do; reminding her of who she will hurt and what she is about to ruin.

Waiting for the bout of dizziness to pass, she shakes the thought away, glances once more in the mirror and steps out of the room, closing the door behind her.

* * *

The light is dim, the room small as Kate walks into the bar, watching out for him, tuned in to every single sound – the boom of laughter from a clutch of drinkers in the corner, the TV in the background, the clink of glasses emanating from behind the bar – they all ring in her head, her senses heightened, her skin on fire. She takes a seat, feeling incongruous in her tight clothing and high heels. Her knees tremble. She places her hands in her lap, presses down hard to stop the obvious involuntary movement there.

Over in the corner. There's a flicker of something, of somebody. A shadow in her peripheral vision. An approaching figure. Her heart speeds up; her mouth is suddenly as dry as sand. It moves towards her, the shadow, coming closer. She blinks, brushes away an imaginary hair from her face and rubs at her eyes, swallowing nervously as the shadow develops into a fully formed person and sits down next to her.

No! Please, not now!

'Kate! I thought it was you.' Gavin has his backside perched on the edge of the wooden stool, his lean body angled towards her. 'How the hell are you? Christ, it feels like forever since we've seen you!'

She is suddenly made of concrete, limbs solid and heavy, her rictus grin a manic split in her face, teeth bared, chin jutting forward. She stares down at her hands, the skin stretched across her knuckles taut and white, the sinews in her neck pulled tight like cat gut. Her nerves are in shreds. *Gavin, here, tonight, in this pub. Really?*

Her eye twitches. She blinks, flicks at it, leans forward and gives him a light peck on the cheek. He looks exactly how she expects him to look – fresh faced, dressed immaculately in high-end clothes and smelling divine, his skin recently splashed with expensive aftershave. And calm. He is so fucking predictably confident and calm, it enrages her.

'Oh, you know! We're fine, Gavin. Ticking along nicely as the saying goes.'

'Fiona said she's had a few calls from you. Is everything okay?'

The awkwardness between them is almost physical, a thick veil that has descended, separating them, pushing them in opposite directions. Two friends sitting close together and yet so very far apart. That's what they are now – discrete people with divergent lives. Nothing to hold them together. No common ground.

'It's fine. Really,' Kate says, attempting to inject an air of conviviality into her tone. 'We're absolutely fine.'

Gavin nods, seemingly pleased that she doesn't want to talk about anything of substance. The relief on his face that the moment has passed without incident is too obvious to disguise. No raking over their change in circumstances, no dredging up of any dirt. Just a stream of banal pleasantries. Easier that way. Less painful. Less embarrassing.

'Is Anthony here with you?' He turns and gazes around the pub, his eyes scanning the dark corners, moving over the crowds at the bar, his dark pupils searching for the man he left behind, the man who was once his friend but got pushed to one side and discarded because he wasn't hard working enough, wealthy enough. Ruthless enough.

'No. I'm meeting a friend. Anthony's at home tonight.' Kate hopes she has disguised the tremble in her tone, the slight warble that could betray her lies. No, not a lie. She *is* doing just that – meeting a friend, but not in the conventional sense. Not in the way Gavin imagines.

'Ah. That's a shame. Would have been good to have a catch up.' He shuffles closer and leans into his inside pocket. 'Look, I realise it's not the done thing to talk shop while out socially, but tell Anth to give me a call. There's a position come up at work and I think he may just be in with a chance. There are a few other candidates up for it as well, but nobody with his experience and nous.' He pushes a business card into Kate's palm and taps her knee playfully. 'Tell him…' Gavin looks away briefly then turns back, his eyes lowered. 'Tell him he's missed and to call me, okay?'

Tears blur her vision. She swallows, tries to compose herself, smoothing down her skirt and clearing her throat to speak. The words refuse to come, imprisoned deep inside her throat. Somebody cares. Gavin cares. He cares and understands.

She tries to speak again and instead nods and smiles at him. He holds her gaze then stands and winks before moving away, disappearing into the crowd of people at the far side of the bar.

Kate rummages in her bag, grabs at a tissue, dabs at her face before standing up and turning to leave. This is wrong. Everything is wrong and stupid and miscalculated. She has made a big mistake. She shouldn't be here. It was thoughtless and reckless to even consider this and she has come close to being spotted. Had Gavin come over a few minutes later, everything could have come tumbling down around her, and for all she is angry with Anthony and unhappy with her family life, is that really what she wants to happen? For talk of her purported affair to be bandied about amongst their old friends, her good name sullied, her reputation in shreds?

Weaving her way through the crowd of people standing close to the door, she steps outside, the fresh breeze that laps at her burning face, a welcome reprieve after sitting in that dark, cloistered place.

The car park is littered with potholes. She picks her way through them, staggering and stumbling, coming close to falling on more than one occasion, her eyes still misted over with unshed tears. Her hand buzzes and vibrates, the phone she is clutching sending small pulses through her skin. She stops and looks down at the message.

> You're leaving? I'm here sitting at the window.

Kate turns, her gaze locking with the eyes that stare out at her, his mouth set in a thin, firm line. He's angry. Upset. She can see that, understands why, but also had no other option. She had to leave. She shivers, suddenly cold, wants to reply, to explain her abrupt departure, but can't seem to summon up the energy. Everything is an effort, the world and its wily ways sucking every last drop of energy out of her.

Only when she has rounded the corner and is heading back into town to hail a taxi does she stop, resting by a wall while she formulates the right response.

> Sorry. Saw an old friend and couldn't risk it. Perhaps another time...

The reply comes immediately. She doesn't read it, instead deleting her original message. Deceitful is what this is. Her behaviour, she knows, is unacceptable and duplicitous and yet she can't seem to help herself. She has been edged into a corner and this is her way of lashing out.

She can't recall Anthony ever looking at her phone but she isn't willing to take any chances. Perhaps she will contact her new friend later. Perhaps she won't. Changes could be afoot after meeting Gavin. Changes that could rekindle her old life, the one she loved and misses beyond reason. The one she now knows she took for granted. Only when something is taken from you, do you realise how precious it really is. Her life was, still is, worth fighting for. Their family life, their friends, the things they had, were all exceptional and irreplaceable and she desperately wants them back. Getting Anthony to accept Gavin's offer could do just that. It could turn everything around, catapult them back to where they belong. Back to the place they should never have left.

The spring in her step isn't imagined as she heads back into town, pushing against the tide of people heading towards the pub. For the first time in months and months, everything feels lighter, rosier; the sky that little bit bluer, the colours around her no longer a wash of grey. She can do this. She can live through the present in order to step into a brighter future. All she needs to do is persuade Anthony to make this call. Already, she is formulating the words in her head, using all of her persuasive techniques to get him on side. He needs to listen to her, to be susceptible to her ideas about speaking to Gavin. Because if he isn't – well, that isn't something she is prepared to consider.

She wants her old life back and now that she knows it is within her reach, she will go to any lengths to make it happen.

12

'No.' Anthony's mouth is set in a tight line, his eyes not meeting Kate's. He keeps his head dipped, continuing to read the newspaper clasped firmly between his fingers. 'I will not call Gavin and that is my final answer.' As if to emphasise his point, he straightens out the paper, its crisp rattle an affront to Kate's ears.

She keeps her initial reaction of anger and disappointment under wraps, was prepared for this and refuses to let it throw her off track. Anthony is a stubborn man. This was never going to be an easy task. He might be resolute now but she can work on him, soften him. Make him see it from her point of view.

'Anyway,' he says, his tone inscrutable, 'you never did tell me who you were going out with. I thought you said you didn't have any friends here?' Without waiting for a reply, he looks up, a sudden realisation dawning in his eyes. 'And why are you back so early? Did the mysterious friend not turn up?' He lowers the paper, drums his fingers on the table, agitation building in his features. A second passes, two, three. Their low, controlled breathing fills the space between them.

He closes his eyes. Kate assesses his every move, every nuance of thought, every damn thing about him. Anthony is a cool customer, always has been: cool, calm, detached, keeping his deepest sentiments and feelings well hidden. She used to love that about him, that he wasn't overly emotional, that he wasn't given to bouts of uncontrolled anger or spells of turmoil as some of her friends' husbands were. Always composed and dignified, his reactions to situations were predictably polite and measured. It was one of his most attractive and defining features. Now it irritates her, makes her feel unspeakably frustrated. How long is she supposed to sit here, trying to work out what the hell is going on inside his head?

'I get it now,' he says, almost hissing at her. 'I see it all, what you've been up to.'

Kate's heart pounds. Perspiration springs out on her face, tiny, translucent beads coating her neck and top lip. She has been ultra-careful, deleting messages, making sure to speak when Anthony was out of the house. He can't know what she had planned. It's impossible. Her scalp prickles and tightens, her skin flashes hot and cold.

'I haven't been up to anything. I have no idea what you are going on about. I was going to have a drink with Sylvia that I used to go to yoga classes with. I met her in town the other day and we arranged to meet up. Or am I not allowed to do such things now?'

Sylvia is a safe bet. Anthony didn't know anybody from Kate's yoga classes. He wouldn't know Sylvia if he fell over her in the street.

'So you say.' More finger drumming, the sound of his nails hitting wood fills the room, an eerie echo. 'But I'm willing to bet that that is a lie.'

A wave of dizziness forces her to hold onto the edge of the desk for balance. He doesn't know about her real reason for going out. He can't. This is a wild guess, a way of knocking her off balance, making her think that he's one step ahead. He isn't. He is grasping at straws here, his judgement way off beam.

'It's not a lie. Why would you say such a thing? I know we've had our problems lately but do you really think so little of me that you're prepared to label me a liar?' She shakes her head, more to clear the woozy sensation that is taking hold than anything else, but is aware he will construe it as a rebuff, her way of processing his words as an insult.

'Because it's too much of a coincidence, that's why. You disappear for a night out with a friend I've never heard of and then all of a sudden out of the blue, Gavin appears with an offer of a new job. Don't insult my intelligence, Kate. Just be honest and tell me you contacted Gavin and met up with him on my behalf, begging him to find me a position back with the old firm.'

She tries to stop the laughter, the look on his face telling her that he isn't taking her response to his suggestion too well, but his summary of events is so far removed from the truth that it truly is laughable. To add to that, she is flooded with relief, euphoria at her secret remaining just that – secret. It almost amuses her, his ignorance, the way he is putting two and two together and coming up with five. Anthony knows nothing about her real reason for going out. He has completely misjudged her, scrambling about to make sense of it all and as a result, has tried to piece together two separate events, jamming them in place.

'Oh, Anthony. You are so funny sometimes.' She bends down and faces him, trying to catch his eye, to rekindle some sort of bond between the two of them, a bond they once shared, the same bond that is loosening and unravelling by the day. If she can grasp onto one last strand of the thin fabric that still connects them, there is a chance she can make this work, help weave together a new stronger net that will save their crumbling relationship. Because she *does* want to make this work. She wants them to be a happy family again with a cohesive approach to their everyday lives. Just not like this. Not here in this house or in this town. Not while their children attend a less than adequate school. She wants their old lives back and now it is suddenly possible. It is all within their reach. She just needs to persuade Anthony to call Gavin. She just needs to make him see that this is a good idea and holds such promise, that this one short call could actually help turn their lives back around and help them all to flourish. Her, Anthony, Alexander and Jocelyn, all of them right back where they belong.

'I was sitting there in the pub, waiting for Sylvia to arrive when Gavin spotted me. He came over and asked how we were.' Kate hands him the phone and places her palm on his knee, her touch light, undemanding. Affectionate even. 'Here. If you don't believe me, why don't you ring him? Ask him whatever you like but I can guarantee his story will be the same as mine. It was a chance encounter. Nothing more, nothing less.' She smiles, trying to keep her voice soft and amicable, not coarse or angry or any other emotion that will further rupture their fragile relationship. They are already miles apart. This new job opportunity is perfect for him, a chance to repair their broken marriage and give their children the best possible start in life.

As things stand, their prospects are bleak. Both Alexander and Jocelyn will have to fight for everything they get – exam results, university places, job offers. Having Searton School on their CV would afford them a greater chance in life. She isn't so stupid or selfish to think that everything would automatically get handed to them. They will have to work for it. Of course they will, but a private education gives them a leg up and doesn't everyone want that for their offspring? Why can Anthony not see that? For an intelligent man, sometimes her husband is obtuse to the point of being almost blind to what is going on around him.

He turns away from her, blinking rapidly, a sign she knows from old, a trait that tells her he is thinking, trying to work out his next move. A breath is suspended in her chest, a pocket of air that she cannot release until she knows what he is going to say or do next. Everything hinges on this moment, how he chooses to react.

Take the phone! Call him. please, Anthony, just call Gavin and make everything right.

Thoughts careen around her head, bashing into each other as she waits, silently praying he will do the right thing, that Anthony will put aside his pride and stubbornness and speak to Gavin, their friend, the man who is willing to help them out of their current hiatus.

A buzzing fills her ears as Anthony turns the phone over in his hand, inspecting it closely before placing it back down and standing up, his frame towering over her, his shadow spreading an ominous, grey mass over the floor.

'No. And don't ask me again. I have no desire to go begging to Gavin or anybody else for that matter. I have a job. It may not be the job you want it to be but it's a job that I enjoy and that I am happy with. A job that doesn't entail working every hour God sends with stress levels that were enough to fell a lesser man.' He bends down and catches Kate's eye.

She tries to turn away from him, to hide her glassy-eyed expression and stop the tears from falling.

'What price happiness and contentment, eh Kate? Money means

nothing to a dead man. Money means nothing to a lonely, widowed woman. Because that was the way we were heading. You just couldn't see it though, could you? You were so wrapped up in your little social circle, locked into the idea of having whatever you wanted whenever you wanted it that you were blind to everything else. Money was no object and now you simply cannot handle the idea of being like every other person who has to stop and think before they buy. You cannot handle the idea of not being top dog anymore. Ordinary doesn't sit well with you, does it, Kate? You see it as being beneath you. Well, I've got news for you; you had better get used to it because I am not going back to that lifestyle, to that type of cut-throat environment where I travelled to work every morning wondering whether that day would be the one when I would lose it all – take a gamble and lose everything – my money, my family, my sanity.' Anthony stops, looks around the room then back at her, his expression somewhere between gentleness and exasperation with a touch of fury thrown in for good measure. 'You have no idea, have you? You never did. Are you honestly telling me that you didn't know?'

She tries to stop her chin from trembling, thinking back to what she missed, what signs she didn't pick up on, those subliminal messages and signals that passed her by. 'Anthony, I—'

'No. Stop.' His hand is a barrier between them, held up to silence her. 'Whatever it is you're going to say, I don't want to hear it. I'm not in the mood for excuses or to hear you play some pathetic little guessing game as to what was going on in *my* world, the busier, bigger world that happened outside your paltry existence.' His voice is a low hiss, menacing, intimidating. 'Do you have any idea what it was like for me having to commute from York to London several times a week? How the hours got to me, the stress of possibly losing everything?'

She shivers, wishes she had handled this better, been a better listener in the past, provided him with a shoulder to cry on. But she didn't. She can see that now but of course, he never appeared to need it. Anthony, the strong, resilient leader. Anthony the stalwart who never buckled under the strain. She has no idea what it is she missed, what it is she should have been looking out for.

He is staring down at her, shaking his head, his brow furrowed. He looks old, as if he has aged ten years in ten minutes. She never considered herself a bad wife, a cold-hearted spouse who left her husband to cope on his own and yet here they are; Anthony claiming she was too wrapped up in her own little life to notice or care what was going on in his while she is left second guessing at what she could have done to help him. What she could have said to make his life easier.

'You never knew about my counselling sessions either, did you? Or my near breakdown? The day Ralph from accounts found me down by the river and coaxed me back into the office. I was ready to do it, Kate. I was ready to jump right in. And now here you are, begging me to go back to that environment, to that job, the one that was nearly the undoing of me.'

Kate closes her eyes; she can hear his voice, sharp and breathless, the urgency in it. The desperation. He is almost begging her, imploring her to see it from his point of view. And she should, she knows that. But there are barriers there, large blockades stopping her from being empathetic and sensitive to his needs. She didn't know about how down he was, how low he felt about his position at the firm, how the constant travelling and the long hours got to him. But that's because he didn't tell her. He hid it well, carrying on as if nothing was amiss.

She isn't the only one to blame here. If they are meant to be a partnership then why didn't he confide in her? Why didn't he speak up and ask for help? She isn't a mind reader and doesn't possess psychic powers. Anthony is a charmer, a master at it. Was that why didn't she see the cracks in his veneer? Because he is so adept at covering up and putting on a good show? Wearing his game face to work every day because that's what he excelled at. Or was it because she was too self-centred, too wrapped up in her own existence to see it? Kate chews at her lip, biting down hard and wincing as a line of pain slides across her mouth. Every inch of her stings with distress and irritation.

No, she won't have the narrative that she is the conniving, selfish wife who neglected her husband's welfare. She simply won't have it. She did everything she could for her family – made a lovely home, kept it clean and tidy, always ensuring their meals were on time, that their clothes were laundered, that they mingled and had lots of friends around. Theirs was a happy, contented house. A happy, contented family. She failed to notice his mental decline because he lied to her, covered up and pretended everything was perfect when it was not. She isn't the only selfish one here.

For all she was immersed in her activities and clique of friends, Anthony too, was totally submerged in his. Nights out with the boys, business trips away in swanky hotels doing God knows what with God knows who. She turned a blind eye to it all because it was what was expected of them. Those were the circles they moved in. And now look where it has left them: two people struggling to make sense of this situation. Two people cast adrift, directionless and bereft.

She wants a better life. He wants the one they have. She strives for more. He is happy to tread water here in this house for the remainder of their lives. She wants to swim the entire ocean.

'You didn't tell me, Anthony. You didn't tell me anything!' Tears start to flow. She is lashing out now. She knows it but can't seem to stop. 'How was I supposed to help a person who acted as if nothing was wrong?'

He doesn't reply, leaving her to gabble and sob, each utterance feeling as if it has been plucked from deep within her body, leaving a great, big void where her soul should be.

'Maybe,' he says, squatting down on his haunches to meet her gaze, his grey eyes steel-like, 'you should have tried harder, looked beyond the superficial, tried to see behind the mask I wore every fucking day.' He stands back up and stares down at her. 'It's not as if you had anything else to do, is it? No job, no real housework to do. We had a cleaner, for fuck's sake. You ran a duster around the place once a month and acted as if you'd cleaned the entire bloody street. Breaking a nail at one of your yoga classes was your idea of a bad day, Kate. Maybe you should have tried walking a mile in my shoes, put your neck on the line every fucking day. So, if you don't mind, I won't be ringing Gavin or any of his cronies. I won't be stepping back into that life. Not for you, not for me or the kids. Not for anybody. Not ever.'

His footfall as he passes her and the subsequent slam of the door makes her tremble, sending a spear of disquiet through her. She wraps her arms around herself, shivering despite the warmth of the room.

This isn't the end. Far from it. Kate may not consider herself the most skilled or qualified of people but if there is one facet of her personality of which she is proud, it is her tenacity. Anthony may believe that what he is doing now, taking this retrograde step, is the best route for him and his family, but he's wrong. With a renewed sense of purpose and Kate's support, he is capable of so much more. He just doesn't know it yet. But he will soon enough. And if he doesn't – well, the cracks and fissures in their little family unit may just become too wide to ever be repaired.

13

Alex lies on his bed, listening to his parents arguing downstairs. They don't think they're arguing. If he were to point it out to them that they are continually at each other's throats, they would wave him away, insisting they were simply having a discussion. A debate. That's what they would call it. A heated conversation.

We're just discussing a few things, son. We need to speak at length every now and again to clear the air.

It's a complete lie and he is sick of it: sick of the constant battles, sick of the snide remarks and the filthy looks. It's like living in a war zone.

Joss doesn't seem to notice or care. It slides over her head, the dark ambience about the place, the caustic exchange of words. She's too busy posting stuff on social media or dyeing her hair or chatting on the phone to people she barely knows who since getting to know her just a few months ago, now hang onto her every word. She is so wrapped up in her own little life, the pretend one she has created for herself since moving here, that she has failed to notice that her real life and her close family is slowly falling apart.

With his mum and dad warring downstairs and Joss engaged in a conversation that would make their mother's hair curl, Alex feels very much on his own.

He stares down at the message from Dane.

> Fancy meeting me at the end of Town Road? The part that leads into the woods. Got a plan.

Ordinarily, he would say no, politely decline using any excuse he can think of, knowing how Dane's plans always play out, but tonight, he reacts differently. The walls of his bedroom, of this house, are closing in on him. He sends a reply that he is on his way and jumps up off the bed, pulling on a hoodie and running his fingers through his tousled hair. He has no idea what Dane has in store, nor does he care. It's got to be better than sitting around this house, listening to Punch and Judy fighting it out downstairs.

Tonight, rather than be the sensible one who pshaws Dane's outlandish ideas, he will go along with them, break out of his routine as the sensible, well-behaved lad who never puts a foot wrong, and he will live a little. Constantly trying to do the right thing is wearing. Why shouldn't he allow himself to be carried away by the moment? And if his parents, who are purportedly the adults around here, can't behave themselves, then why the fuck should he? The time has come to loosen up a little, have some fun and be the teenager that he is, not walk around as if he has to keep the rest of the world in line.

Without telling anybody where is going or shouting any goodbyes, he leaves the house, the door closing behind him with a dull thud, and heads down the road, weaving his way through trees and parked cars, past people heading in the other direction and onto the street that leads to the park. If he cuts through it, he will make it in good time. He may even have enough minutes spare to call into the shop, buy a couple of cans of Coke.

Alex pushes back his shoulders. Empowerment throbs in his veins. Suddenly, he knows how his sister feels to not be constrained by the expectations of others, to just please herself and think about her own needs and nobody else's. It's liberating, shrugging off the shackles of sensibility and throwing caution to the wind. For so many years, he has always wanted to please those around him, never disappointing anybody, worrying that he didn't live up to the image that everybody had of him. Especially his parents. But since their move here, since his dad took a different job, everything seems to have spiralled downwards and the normal pigeonholes they all neatly slotted into have melded into a big, sticky mess. Everything has shifted. Their world is out of kilter and all the usual restrictions they adhered to have been abandoned in favour of something less rigid. Something more exciting. He can turn in a different direction, go wherever he pleases, be with whomever he likes. Do whatever he wants.

A frisson of anticipation and exhilaration surges through him. He enters the shop, delving in his pocket for a handful of change, stopping to scoop up two tins of Coca-Cola before marching to the counter, his heart thumping around his chest.

'A pack of Marlboro, please, and I'll take these as well.' He holds out the two cans and waits for the girl behind the counter to reply. She doesn't look much older than him, maybe eighteen or nineteen years old. His spine is locked solid as he sees her ice-cold glare, realising suddenly that she exudes the confidence of somebody much older than eighteen or nineteen, somebody who is much more experienced than he could ever hope to be.

'I'll need to see some ID.' Her voice is like granite. He can see now that he misjudged her. She is probably in her early twenties, with a harsh expression and a voice to match.

'Right. I don't have it on me, so—'

'No ID, no cigarettes.'

Torn between anger and humiliation, Alex passes her a handful of change and turns to leave, trying to stem the feelings that are rising in his gut, turning his face a deep shade of mauve.

'You need your change.'

He isn't imagining it. There is definitely sarcasm in her tone, perhaps even a touch of amusement at his predicament.

'Keep it.' He is shouting now. 'You look like you need it more than I do.'

He hears her sigh as he steps outside into the cool breeze. A small vortex of leaves swirls at his feet.

Stuffing the drinks into his pocket, he thinks about how long it will be before he can take control of his own life, not be viewed as a child but seen instead, as an adult, someone who is ready to spread his wings and take flight.

The wind pushes at his back, an invisible palm thrusting him forwards to the path that will lead him to Dane.

* * *

Alex spots him in the distance, is able to immediately recognise his friend's stooped, wiry figure. Dane is standing, silhouetted against the backdrop of a row of houses. Beyond the rooftops, Alex can see the sway of the trees, their tops bending and flexing as they are pushed back and forth by the growing gusts of wind. Maybe they are due a storm.

The figure in the distance sends a burst of contentment through Alex, small bubbles of happiness popping and exploding in his belly. Being stuck at home with the two warring factions only serves to dampen his mood and make him feel miserable. For all of Dane's faults and negativity, at the minute, he is the one static thing in Alex's life, somebody who regardless of everything, has stayed by Alex's side, introducing him to new people, making sure he found his way around school. Six months ago, he would have avoided somebody like Dane, given him and his stupid tricks and ideas a wide berth, but things have changed and now here they are, mates together. And it feels remarkably good. He is cool with it. It's all good.

He thinks that he might make a joke about Dane having the hots for his sister but decides against it, knowing how awkward Dane is around members of the opposite sex, pretending he doesn't see them or care about them when his adoration of them is written all over his face. Tonight, Alex just wants to relax and have some fun. He doesn't want to ruin it by overstepping the mark, making a jibe at somebody else's expense, especially Dane's. He's one of the good guys in this town. He deserves better.

'Now then, bro.' Dane raises his hand and they fist bump. 'Bobby said he might meet us later if he can escape his mother's clutches.'

Alex shakes his head, unaware of the joke.

'Ah, his old woman is a teacher, isn't she? Makes him sit and do all his homework, then checks it over with her beady eye before he can leave the house.'

'I thought his parents were really laid back? Y'know, with all the booze at the party and all that?'

Dane cocks his head and eyes Alex from under his brow. 'Yeah, they are but with her being a teacher and everything, she's always telling him how well he has to do at school. He gets shit-loads of extra work to do off his parents. That's why he always comes top in tests.'

Alex can't work out which is worst – having a mother like his who is oblivious to him and his life, or being saddled with somebody like Bobby's mum who breathes down his neck over his schoolwork, even giving him extra stuff just because she can. It's as if adults need lessons themselves on how to be decent parents. Sometimes, he just can't work it all out, this growing up shit and everything that goes with it. All the more reason to live in the moment, have a bit of fun and dispense with the usual conventions and sensible ways of going about things. Time to live a little, be a normal teenager. Time to chill the fuck out.

'Anyway,' Dane says, his finger outstretched, 'take a look at that place over there. It's Bennison's house.'

'Bennison?'

'The Maths teacher? Walks like she's got a pole up her arse? Wears eight inches of make-up?' Dane is scowling, his face scrunched up, eyes narrowed into tiny, suspicious slits.

'Ah.' Alex smiles and winks at his friend. '*That* Bennison. The one with the legs that go on forever. The same one who wears the tight skirts and even tighter sweaters? Nipples like fighter pilot's thumbs?'

'Fuck off, Winston-D'Allandrio. She's nothing but an old harridan. Here,' he says, pulling out a letter from his pocket. 'This shows you just how much of a bastard she is. Her and Dommy Rose. Pair of miserable fuckers together.'

Alex stares down at the letter, scanning each sentence, spotting the school letterhead at the top and wondering what misdemeanour Dane has committed this time that warrants a letter being sent home. He usually keeps all of his rule-breaking activities at a low level, just enough to sneak under the school's radar, not doing anything that is worthy of being sanctioned. But not this time.

'It says here you missed lessons even though you were registered as being in school.'

'I know what it says!' Dane grabs the tin of Coke from Alex and snaps it open with a crack, gulping down half the liquid in one swift movement. A cream foam moustache sits on his upper lip, tiny bubbles shifting and creeping over his skin.

'So?' Alex shakes his head, staring at Dane for answers.

'So I was hiding out behind the store cupboard having a fag and now they've caught me and they want a meeting with my folks. My dad's not so bothered, though. Dommy Rose taught him when my dad was a kid and he can't stand the guy so it's all good. My mum's pushing to go and speak to the pair of them but nobody takes any notice of anything she says anyway. I'm not worried.'

'So, what's your problem?' Alex drains his drink, tosses it to the ground and crushes the can underfoot. He likes the sensation of the metal shrinking beneath his heel. It folds and concertinas into a small, flat, circular shape.

'My problem? My problem is, Dommy Rose reckons I'm on target to get a fail.' Dane's voice is a growl, low and sinister. 'No qualifications. No college place. Nothing. Not that it matters. I've got other plans anyway. It's just the fucking cheek of it. Who does he think he is?'

Alex stares at his friend and is shocked to see that Dane's eyes are glassy, as if he is about to burst into tears, his skin pallid and drawn, small creases lining the edge of his mouth.

'Anyway.' Dane's voice is a tinny echo as he rubs at his face and laughs. 'Who cares, eh? Who fucking cares about any of them? Come on.' He nudges Alex, juts out his chin. 'Let's go and have a laugh at somebody else's expense. Let's show them all who's boss.'

Alex follows Dane as they head towards the small, terraced property of Miss Bennison, a small amount of anger building at the thought of his mate being punished and leaving school with nothing to show for it. How can that be fair? Dane may be surly but there are loads of kids at that school who are far more worthy of being singled out and humiliated and stripped of their exam results. What he has done, or more importantly, not done, does not warrant him being threatened like this or being branded a failure.

They move past the house and continue walking. 'I thought she lived at that one?' Alex is pointing to her small, terraced house, a nondescript property with a glossy, black door. He spots her car outside, a small, red Fiat with a dent in the passenger side wing.

'She does. We'll get her on the way back,' Dane shouts over his shoulder to Alex, his voice carried by the breeze.

'Why do all the teachers live so near the school anyway?' Alex is breathless as he runs to catch up. 'If I was a teacher there, I'd live miles away. I wouldn't want to be so near to the place where I work.'

'It's only these two. Maybe a couple more that I don't know about. I made a point of finding out where Bennison lived. I got lucky when I found out she was local. Dommy Rose has lived here for years. He's been in the same cottage since he taught my old man. What a saddo, eh?'

'He never married?' Alex stops and looks up at the dim, grey sky. Soon, it will be inky black save for a sprinkling of stars. Soon, they will be plunged into darkness.

'Ah,' Dane says, his expression brightening, a new playful bounce to his timbre. 'Now there's a story. My dad knows the ins and outs of that particular tale. It made the papers, apparently. I'll tell you all about it once we're done here.' Dane suddenly grins, his eyes dancing with happiness. It's a look that takes Alex by surprise. It's a rare occurrence to see his pal smile or display any emotion akin to happiness. His default character traits are gloom and near anguish. 'Come on,' he says, breathless. 'Let's shake old Dommy Rose up. Give him something to think about before he starts labelling me as a fucking failure.'

14

The silence is deafening. Perhaps even worse than the shouting. Worse than Rob and Dane yelling at her that she is wrong and that she needs to lighten up, not get so worked up about something so insignificant. Her son's qualifications, his future deemed insignificant. That's what they're talking about here and yet apparently, she is blowing it up out of proportion, turning it into something that it isn't. According to Rob, it's a trivial matter and not worthy of serious discussion.

Not worthy of serious discussion.

The words ring around her head. So much commotion and upset – Dane, Rob, her words drowned out by their anger at her suggestion they call the school, arrange a meeting, get their son back on track.

'Qualifications aren't the be-all and end-all. He can come and work for me, be a general labourer. Don't know what you're getting so worked up about. That's your problem, Nina. You're too bloody intense. Everything is a fucking problem with you.' Rob had turned away from her and given Dane a smile, tousling his hair, telling him to ignore any teachers that give him hassle in the future.

'Send 'em my way, son. I'll soon sort them out. And take no notice of your mother. She takes everything to heart, sees life as one big, bloody problem.'

Winking and nudging one another, the two men in her life had sauntered out of the kitchen, leaving her dizzy – her head reeling at how things had deteriorated so rapidly – and feeling marginalised, an inconsequential bystander in her own life. That's what she has become. Or has it always been this way? There was a time, even after Dane was born, when she saw Rob as a witty, charming individual, somebody she could rely on. Because that's all everybody wants in a partner, don't they? Reliability. Kindness. Not someone who continually lets them down and fails to deliver on promises. He worked hard, gave them a good home, made sure they had enough money in the bank. Always with a smile, he was a handyman, a comic, a perfect gentleman.

So when did it change? How did things get to this point? Or has it always been this way? Was she so blinded by his charms and charisma that she simply didn't see it – his darker side, the part of him that was possibly always present, lurking, just waiting for the shine of their relationship to dull so it could reveal itself.

Or maybe it's her. Perhaps she has altered in some imperceptible way: become less frivolous, unable to see the lighter side of life. They used to have such good times together, Rob's raucous laughter filling any room they were in. She can't remember the last time they smiled together, let alone laughed. Those days seem to be so far behind them, it's as if they never existed at all and are just a figment of her imagination – implanted memories she has dreamt up to keep herself sane. At some point, their lives diverged and went in opposite directions and now it's as if they are so far down different paths, they will never meet up, a family fractured and broken, the glue that once held them together, spoiled and damaged beyond repair.

Nina swallows down the lump that has risen in her throat, blinks back tears, and tells herself she is being overly dramatic, proving Rob right, that she *is* too intense, turning everything into a problem instead of just letting it be.

Some problems repair themselves. That's what he has said in the past. *Stop thinking you have to fix everything and everyone, Nina. You're not God.*

Will Dane's future and his school problems repair themselves without any intervention from her? Will her boy get fixed and set himself on the right path? She hopes so but fails to see how. Without any guidance or assistance, Dane is rudderless, a young boy lacking in experience and knowledge of how the world works. He cannot see the bigger picture. How many fifteen-year-olds can? He isn't alone in that respect. But with his immature ways and absence of foresight, he lacks more than many when it comes to functioning on a day-to-day basis amongst other people.

She thinks of her parents, of her dad and how he discreetly tried to warn her away from Rob, telling her how some mistakes can never be patched up and made good. She didn't understand the meaning behind his words, couldn't see it at the time, how he had done his best to be subtle, attempting to dodge the obvious topic of Rob's brashness and arrogance, using philosophical phrases, esoteric language to guide her thinking. She was blind to it all, unable to see beyond the initial attraction she felt towards her husband-to-be, was too enamoured by Rob's exuberance and confident manner to take a step back and analyse it in any great depth.

And now here she is all these years later, thinking about how those attributes that originally caught her eye, making her feel comforted and even aroused, now make her toes curl with embarrassment and revulsion. His loud voice that turns heads whenever they walk in the pub, his castiron opinions, his inability to stop and slow down and just think about what he is saying, they all serve to heighten her misery, making her feel trapped.

This isn't how she planned it. She entered this relationship dead-set on happiness and contentment and finds herself miserable and weighed down with thoughts of how it will all end. And then of course, there is Dane to think about. For all his brusqueness and surliness, deep down, he is fragile. Ending this marriage would stir up a hornet's nest, exacerbating his behavioural issues, making everything a thousand times worse.

Sometimes, it's not so bad. She has a lovely home. Rob has a thriving building business. She doesn't rise out of bed every morning utterly miserable but neither does she rise happy. She simply exists. Existing is a thing, isn't it? Surely that is enough? Many suffer far worse. There are men and women the length and breadth of the country who are trapped in abusive relationships, living in poverty, suffering beatings every single day. Rob has never hit her. He is careless with his words, cruel even, and then there is the matter of his affairs. But he has never kept her short of money or beaten her.

Nina slumps down onto the sofa, her legs weak, her head throbbing with the effort of trying to hold everything together, to reason with herself that things, although not great, could be a whole lot worse. Is anybody truly delighted all of the time? Surely such people don't exist? And yet there are times when she does feel so terribly lonely. She has never told anybody about her woes and thinks that perhaps keeping it all hidden is part of the problem. Maybe now, her cracks are starting to show, the pressure inside her too great to contain her misery. Soon, it will all come pouring out, a roaring, beastly thing.

She feels worn out, a hundred years old. It's exhausting having to cover up, trying to be jolly whenever she talks to any of the neighbours or the other parents at the school, especially Sally, whose faultless life oozes brilliance and charm. For years, she has consoled herself with the fact she isn't depressed but now all of a sudden, that doesn't feel as if it's enough. She doesn't want to be just okay. She wants to be happy.

She stares out of the window at their immaculate lawn and wonders how low things have to go before she acts, before she is able to catapult herself out of this loveless marriage and into a life that is worth living. Always lacking in confidence, she is happy to plaster over the cracks, too frightened to confront Rob and tell him how she feels. Striking out on her own scares her, the possibility of failing miserably, getting stuck in bottom gear with no way back up. And it's a distinct possibility. With only Rob's salary and her limited knowledge of how to make money, she would struggle on her own.

A sting takes hold on her lip as she bites at it, reminding herself that it isn't all about money. She has become indoctrinated in Rob's way of thinking, assuming that life is all about making heaps of cash and having the biggest and the best of everything. Rob knows the cost of everything and the value of nothing. He is stuck in a groove, motivated by financial incentives and very little else. Except other women. There is always room for other females in his life. Sex is what drives him, making him feel powerful.

The tears flow freely as Nina fights back a sob, placing her hand over her mouth to stop it from escaping. It's at times like this she misses her parents. Such wise, kind people. Why didn't she take notice of them? Why was she so blinded by love and carried away by a wave of euphoria that hinged only on Rob's good looks and his stream of humourless one-liners? Those awful, banal jokes that now make her skin crawl as he barks them out time and time again.

She wipes at her eyes and clears her throat, checking in the mirror to make sure her face isn't blotchy, that her cheeks aren't stained with mascara and her eyes red rimmed. Nobody likes a weeping woman, especially her husband.

Rob had caught her a few weeks ago crying quietly and was incredulous that she had anything to be upset about. 'Got a bloody huge house and a tonne of money in the bank. What you got to cry about, eh?' he had shouted as he grabbed himself another beer out of the fridge and held out the remote, scanning channels until he found the football, turning up the volume full blast. The roar of the crowd forced her to flee upstairs where she remained for the rest of the evening. When she eventually found the courage to go back downstairs, he was sprawled out on the sofa asleep, head flung back, an empty bottle dangling from his fingertips.

The thought that she could visit the school alone, speak to Dane's teacher and beg for confidentiality, crosses her mind. She is unaccustomed to taking such steps, to being wily and forthright and issuing demands. It doesn't come easily, but something is going to have to be done about Dane's education because although she is lacking in confidence when it comes to certain areas of her own life, she is damned if she is going to sit back and allow her son to miss out on getting some qualifications, to allow him to slip into working on a building site alongside his dad, who will manipulate and twist their offspring, moulding Dane into a younger version of himself.

Buoyed up by the thought, she wipes at her eyes and sniffs. It feels good to do something on her own – empowering and uplifting. Tomorrow morning, when she is at home with nobody else around, she will ring the school, ask for an appointment with the teachers in question and request that it is kept confidential from Dane or her husband. This is something she wants to do unassisted.

It's not as if Rob is even interested in Dane's education. She is the one who in the main, visits the school, she is the one who puts the effort into attending his consultation evenings, assuring them she will work with Dane to help him complete homework and achieve the best results he can for his end of year exams. Not Rob. He rarely has time for such stuff, stating repeatedly how much he hated school and what a waste of time it was and look how far he got in life without exams and grades, that it's all a load of bullshit and it's hard work and sheer graft that counts and gets you the big house and the flash cars. The one and only time Rob accompanied her still makes her toes curl every time she thinks about it – Rob's curt manner, his dismissal of any advice. She wanted to shrivel up and disappear on the spot.

Every time he mentions how healthy their bank balance is, she wants to add that yes, they have plenty of money but little or no culture in their lives. She doesn't consider herself to be a particularly learned person but is willing to pick up what she can as she goes through life. Rob has a gaping hole inside him where facts and knowledge should be. He picks up snippets and isn't willing to delve in for further details, to stetch his brain or try to expand his knowledge of the world around him. Football, fast cars, big houses – they are Rob's interests. The women are just an addition to the status he likes to project to the outside world, that he is one of the boys, a player, somebody who can have whatever he wants, whenever he wants it.

She knows her husband, knows him well. Probably better than he knows himself. Rob isn't a thinker or a people watcher. He is too wrapped up in his own little world to take any notice of anybody else and that is not the life she wants for their son.

Sitting by the window, Nina realises that there is hope, just a glimmer, but she at least feels mildly optimistic that all is not lost as she once feared. Anything is possible. Anything at all. She stands up and pulls back her hair into a ponytail, staring at her reflection in the window, at the tired, wan-faced woman looking right back at her, the woman who once was so full of happiness, convinced nothing could go wrong in her neat, predictable, little world. She smiles. She is older, her worries stamped into her face, showing in the small lines forming around her eyes, in the slight sag of her neck, but she is wiser too. It may have taken some time for her to wake up to what is necessary and what isn't but she is finally reaching the point where her sanity is more important than her status.

It may not be tomorrow or next month or even next year, but one day, she will leave this house, forge a better life for herself. But only when Dane is on an even keel. Only when she can truly say she has done her utmost to make him the best person he can be, not a surly teenager who lashes out with insults and hurtful, acerbic comments, but a kind, respectful human being who knows right from wrong and always chooses to do the correct thing. Until that point, she will remain here. She will endure the arguments, the lack of respect, and try to be a force for good. That is important to her, being helpful and kind and leaving people with a sense of positivity. Because if she can't even do that, then what is the point of it all?

15

30 JUNE 1978

You are everywhere, my dearest Clara. Everywhere and nowhere. I see your face as I travel to work, your smile is ever present in my head, the twinkle of your eyes in the sunlight, the scent of your perfumed body in the freshly opened flowers that I recently planted in the garden. You are everywhere, my dearest girl, and yet so very far away from me. My body aches for you. My body, my mind, they cry out for you – the lightness of your touch, the sound of your laughter – I crave them like an alcoholic craving for that first drink after they make a vow to abstain.

Nobody else exists in my world. Nobody. I only have room for you, dearest Clara. Only you.

Yesterday, the men with whom I work asked me to accompany them on a pub crawl, stating I looked down and in need of a friendly face. I turned them down. As I did it, I could hear your voice in my head, cajoling me, telling me I should take them up on their offer, get out and live a little, and yet nothing holds any appeal for me while you are not here. The beer is tasteless, their jokes witless and disagreeable. It's all pointless without you.

I'm writing this because I took the liberty of visiting your parents and was deeply saddened to hear that you have been writing to them on a regular basis. I apologise if you think this bold of me but your lack of *response left me with no other option. For so long now, I have told myself that you were too busy to write to me or that the postal service up there is erratic and unreliable. But of course, I now know that that isn't the case.*

You have made an active choice to ignore me.

Not only that but your parents also informed me that rather than feeling compelled to go there to care for your gran, you opted to do it, telling them you needed some time away from everything. I know now, that by 'everything', what you actually mean is me. You needed time away from me.

I tried to remain upbeat as I spoke with them. What else could I do? I put on a brave face, told them I wished you well, pretended I wasn't hurt by your actions. But I was. I am. Very hurt.

I am sitting here, trying to picture your face as you read my words, your downcast expression, the stoop of your spine as you now appreciate that I know. I am crushed, dear Clara. Crushed not just by your need to leave me in such a manner but by the fact you couldn't tell me face to face. I thought we had everything that any couple could ever want but I now discover that it was a one-sided affair. The feelings I have for you are unrequited and the devastation I now feel as a result of that is vast, a fathomless sea of hot emotions that swirl in the pit of my stomach day and night. There is no end to it, no reprieve. The misery I feel is crushing, a bottomless pit of despair.

Please come back, dear Clara. Please do something; write or call me. Anything at all. I will take whatever crumb of comfort you are willing to throw my way, such is my desperation, and I promise I hold no ill feelings toward you. I could never do that. You are still my whole world even though I now know that I am no longer a part of yours. I would love to hear from you, if only for you to explain why you felt a need to leave me like this. I feel as if my life has been ripped apart, my feelings ground underfoot.

What I wouldn't give to see you one last time. I know now that it's over between us. I accept that, I really do. I just wish you had told me yourself and saved me the indignity of hearing it from your parents in such an unexpected and, dare I say it, humiliating way.

I'm going to sign off now, knowing you are glad to not have to hear from me anymore. I'll never stop loving you, dear Clara. You are my moon, my sun, my stars. My reason for living. Your beautiful face will forever be embedded in my brain, etched into my heart, carved deep, deep into my soul.

Stay safe, dear girl and know that you are loved always.

Dominic xxx

16

PRESENT DAY

'It feels darker than last time: more trees, less light,' Alex says as they pick their way through the long grass, branches and twigs cracking underfoot, the whistling of the wind sending an eerie tingle down his spine. 'I mean, it's fine,' he says, correcting himself, standing up that little bit taller, pushing back his shoulders and taking a deep breath. 'It's all good. I'm just thinking that if we need to make a run for it or anything like that, then we're done for, y'know?'

Dane shoots him a knowing grin, his eyes, black as the night sky, twinkling with undisguised mischief. 'Yeah, like old Rosey is ever gonna catch us. As if he is gonna even give chase. Have a word with yourself, Winston-D'Allandrio. He's in his sixties. I bet he can't remember the last time he even broke into a fast walk, never mind a fucking run, especially one that has him galloping after a couple of teenagers!'

Alex lets out a hollow laugh, still unsure about this. Still unsure just how far Dane will actually go. All of a sudden, throwing stones at windows seems like a harmless pastime. Something in his gut tells him that Dane has something bigger planned. Something more destructive. A knife twists in Alex's stomach. He balls his fists together, his knuckles cracking, his nails digging into his palm. He tells himself to stop being so soft. This is the guy who tried to press himself up against his sister, the same guy who has threatened his mate with a U in his exams just because he skipped a couple of lessons. Whatever they do to him won't be half as bad as what he has tried to do to some of his pupils.

'My dad reckons Rosey has got it in for me just 'cos he remembers him from when he taught him, way back when.'

Alex thinks about that statement, wondering why anybody would hold a grudge for so long. It doesn't make sense to him but then, many things that adults do leave him scratching his head. For all he gets top marks in his schoolwork, life in general still baffles him.

'How come,' Alex says, feeling as if all barriers that once stood between them are now lowered, 'that you go to the local school and not a private one? Your parents are loaded. Didn't your mum want you to go to a school that...' Alex stops, stares down at the ground while choosing his next words with care and precision, 'that offered you a wider choice of lessons? At my old school, we had trips to America and Canada and loads of other places that our current school would probably never visit.'

Alex lets out a long breath as Dane shrugs and drags a stick through the long grass, seemingly unperturbed by his question. 'Dunno. Maybe she tried to get me in one and my dad said no. He's not one for schools or anything to do with education. Says it's a waste. He thinks you learn more once you leave and get a proper job. Anyway,' Dane says with a crooked smile, 'I don't think I'd fit in at a private school, do you?'

Alex laughs and shakes his head. 'I think you would but it doesn't matter, does it? Because we're in this one now and we've only got one more year and then that's it for us.'

'For me maybe, but not for you it isn't.' Dane kicks at a stone and shoves his hands in his pockets. 'You'll go onto college and then university and you'll get a degree in Advanced Mathematics or Physics or some other shit that I could never do. I'll leave and work for my dad on a building site, but that's fine.' He picks up a stone and skims it across the floor. It lands in a clump of grass with a thud. 'It made him a packet, building houses, so you never know, I might end up a millionaire.'

They laugh together and Alex feels soothed by the easiness between them. He moves closer and nudges Dane. 'Tell you what. Let's knock on his door and tell the old fart what we really think of him, eh?'

Dane's laughter is loud, raucous even. 'Nah. He'll probably call the police. We can have more fun by taunting the old bastard. Come on,' he says, 'let's put the creeps up him. You go around the back and I'll do the front of the house.'

'Wait! What? What are we going to do?' Alex says, panic slithering into his voice. He would rather stay with Dane, have safety in numbers, not do this alone. Whatever *this* is.

'Anything you like,' Dane shouts as he disappears amongst the towering foliage, his voice swallowed up by the dense gathering of trees.

Anything you like.

Alex swallows, rubs at his face with his sleeve and takes a deep breath. What does that even mean? *Anything you like.* Enough to scare the old guy but not enough to warrant him calling the police. Sometimes, trying to work out the tangle of Dane's thoughts is like foraging through a deep jungle, trying to pick out the salient points and discarding the rest.

Crunching his way through the waist-height, gnarled shrubbery, Alex winds his way around the back of the house, wondering why anybody would even consider living here. This place looks ready for demolition, the surrounding woods eerie and dense, the darkness making him shiver. The hoot of an owl in the distance accentuates his isolation. It echoes through the treetops, a shriek into the night, swallowed by the gloom.

He tries to imagine what Mr Rose's house looks like inside. He visualises dirty, tiled floors, sticks of broken furniture and an old, black-leaded fireplace covered with grime and soot. Alex shivers, his eyes lowered to the ground as he concentrates on his footing, trying to not fall down one of the many rabbit holes that are littered across the uneven ground.

A moss-covered fence lies in pieces around the perimeter of the house, its wooden slats rotten. Alex bends down and brushes his fingers over the rough surface of the wood. He picks up a piece and heads around the back of the house, thinking that he must be mad, wondering how he let himself end up in such a juvenile situation. All of a sudden, he feels silly. Childlike. This whole thing is horribly predictable. Here he is playing the stereotypical, angst-ridden teenager role, and yet... and yet for once, it feels good to be rebellious and not always be the lad who worries on behalf of other people. Not be the sensible one who curbs his own feelings to spare the feelings of those around him. It is mind-numbingly boring being good all the time, being moral and upright and virtuous. Having a conscience is tiresome. It's time to have some fun.

Moving nearer to the house, he shakes off any residual negative feelings, feelings that he shouldn't be doing this, that it is silly and pointless and infantile. Instead, he is consumed by a sudden surge of excitement, remembering that this is the man who got too close to his sister, much closer than he should have. Maybe this is what the old guy needs. Perhaps shaking him up and scaring him a little might get the message across. They could let him know that they are onto him. Joss is no angel but she is also still a child and Mr Rose is a grown man and he should know better. He is in a position of authority and needs to be held to account.

Without missing a beat or giving himself any time to change his mind, Alex takes the stick and drags it along the wall of the house, across the crumbling brickwork, over the windows, stopping only when he reaches a small door at the bottom of a set of stone steps. Intrigue pulls him in, forcing him to look closer. The small, pale-green, wooden door is partly obscured by ivy. He tries the handle and gives it a yank. It doesn't budge. He expected as much. He tries again, giving it one more firm tug, then turns and heads towards the back of the house. A door to a cellar. He spots it straightaway. It would be interesting to get in there and have a poke around, see what he can find. Maybe another time. If there is another time.

He holds up the stick and once more drags it over the external walls of the house until he comes to a window, whereupon he taps it against the glass, quickly ducking back out of view and panting hard. He wonders what Dane is up to around the front. It's quiet round there. No cracking of twigs, no rustling of leaves. No noise at all. Alex shivers, pulls his hoodie tighter around his body.

The wind picks up, roaring through the treetops like the howl of a wounded animal, before dying down again to a low moan. A stone sits at his feet. He bends and picks it up, turning it over and over in his palm, the smooth, cold surface soothing against his hot palm. Then he stands back and throws it up on the roof. It lands with a clatter before rolling down over the tiles, stopping as it hits the guttering. It rocks back and forth, the cracking noise filling the near silence. It stops. Alex waits. Another hoot of an owl. The murmuring of the wind. The susurrus whisper of leaves.

Then next to him, a square of pale-yellow cutting into the darkness as a light is switched on inside the house. He ducks, instinctively crouching down out of view, his heart hammering against his ribcage with a heady combination of fear and excitement. Adrenaline courses through him. Saliva floods his mouth.

A voice shouts out above his head. 'Who's there?'

Unable to move, crippled by anxiety married with a level of exhilaration he has never before experienced, Alex covers his mouth with his hand to stem the laughter that is clawing to be free.

The light goes out. His breath escapes in small gasps as he stands, raises the stick and rattles it again, tapping against the window. The light is switched back on. A series of muffled thumps as the window is flung open. Above him, Alex can see a face looming out into the near darkness. He huddles down amongst the foliage, hidden from view.

'I'll call the police if you don't clear off! Do you hear me?'

A couple more seconds pass; the window is slammed shut. Alex waits, thinking he could hammer on the back door then salt himself away in the snarl of weeds and bushes that surround the property. His thoughts are disturbed by a loud bang in the distance. It rings through the woods, filtering through the blackness. Alex's skin prickles as he hears a roar of protest and the sound of a scuffle nearby. In his peripheral vision, he sees the outline of Dane appearing from around the front of the house, a manic grin plastered across his face. In close pursuit is Mr Rose, hands flailing wildly as he tries to reach out and grab at the lad, missing and stumbling then falling onto his knees with a crash.

Alex gasps, the sound drowned out by another thunderous cry as Mr Rose stands and hollers into the darkness, his fists raised into the air. Alex wants to laugh at this man who looks like a parody of himself. 'I know who you are, Dane Bowron! And I suppose Alexander is here with you, isn't he?'

Alex is unsure whether to remain silent and do nothing or stand up and run after Dane. If Dominic Rose decides to do a tour of the immediate perimeter of his house looking for suspects, or more specifically, looking for him, then Alex is done for. The old guy might grab him, hang onto him, call the police.

Scenarios fill his head, none of them pleasant – his dad having to collect him from the local police station; his mum screaming that she knew this would happen, that it was only a matter of time before her son descended into the gutter with the other lowlife scum from the local comprehensive school. It was bound to happen just as surely as night follows day, she would shriek, now that her children are hanging around with the miscreants from the local estate and that it is all his father's fault for being a lazy bastard and not bringing in enough money to look after his family and allow them to go to a better school. The repercussions would be excruciating, an endless round of blame and accusations, their family pushed even further into the darkest of corners. And it would all be because of him.

Alex crawls backwards, feeling his way with his fingers, praying he doesn't back into something solid that will block his escape. He slides along the ground, his belly rustling against the long grass, and stops, his blood crystallising into ice as he feels a hand on his shoulder, the heat of somebody's skin pulsing through the fabric of his sweater. He opens his mouth to shout out and is stopped as a sweaty palm is clamped over his mouth.

'Shh! It's only me, you big, useless fucker.'

Alex rolls onto his back and lets out a low laugh that is frighteningly close to hysteria.

'Shut up, for Christ's sake.' Dane is looming over him, his eyes glistening like marbles set deep in his skull. 'We got him, Alex lad. We got the old fart out of his house and running like a scared fucking rabbit.'

Both boys back away from the house on their bellies, euphoria rushing through Alex's system, small pockets of it exploding in his veins. Only when they are out of the dense clump of shrubbery do they stand and run, their laughter ringing around the empty fields.

'Anyway,' Alex says breathlessly as they stumble out of the long grass and back onto the path, 'what was it you were going to tell me about him? You said there was a story that made the papers from years ago.'

Dane lets out another burst of laughter and shakes his head. 'Ah, God yeah, forgot about that. My old man told me all about it. It happened years ago, was all over the papers at the time. All I can say is that it's got something to do with a woman – an old girlfriend of his who went missing and was never found. Rumour has it she fell in a lake while on holiday in Scotland and drowned. It's a huge fucking mystery round these parts.' Dane widens his eyes in mock horror and lowers his voice to a whisper, staring at Alex, and rubbing his hands together, joy evident in his tone. 'All I'm going to say is this: did the poor bitch jump or was she pushed?'

17

She remains asleep, lying under the covers slumbering peacefully. Whatever Dominic has said or done to those youngsters to warrant being bothered like this is one thing, but for those boys to put his mother through such an ordeal is another matter. She doesn't deserve to be subjected to such levels of rowdiness. Regardless of whether or not she slept through it all, this is her house as well, and her safety is paramount. He needs to care for her, protect her. All they have is each other. The two of them together in this house. The rest of the world operates inversely to him, thinking differently, acting differently. They wouldn't understand his ways, would think him odd, stuck in a time warp. But so what? This is his life and he shall live it as he pleases.

His muscles slacken as he sits by her bedside, staring at her face, wondering again what it is he has done that is so terrible that these miscreants feel the need to taunt him: coming to his house, throwing sticks and rocks and making nuisances of themselves. This isn't the first time it's happened and he is under no illusions that it will be the last, but each time, it becomes more invasive, more hostile and he is becoming less able to tolerate it.

His pulse quickens at the memory, his knees throbbing where he fell. He trails his fingers over his legs, feeling for bruises and blood. Everything is intact; everything that is, apart from his dignity. News of his fall will be all around the school in no time at all. It's difficult enough keeping the students in line as it is, keeping a lid on the behaviour of the rowdier pupils whilst trying to deliver lessons, without something like this being thrown into the mix.

He scrutinises her features before closing his eyes and reaching out to touch her hand. He shivers. It's cold and dry. Snatching his fingers away, Dominic leans forward and pulls at the bed sheets, tucking them up under her chin, stroking the wisps of hair that frame her face. She doesn't move, continuing to sleep deeply.

Ice moves through his veins, the ambient temperature of the room doing nothing to warm him through. He reaches over, touches the radiator, recoiling at the heat pulsing out of it. Even in the sweltering heat of the summer months, this room remains cold. Darkened by trees, it is constantly in the shade, a chill ever present that he finds strangely comforting.

Pulling out another blanket from underneath the bed, he places it across her body, straightening it until every crease has been smoothed away. She needs to be kept warm, to feel safe, be kept apart from those boys, separated from the many ails of the world. She is all he has left. Without each other, they are nothing.

Stubble scratches at his fingertips as he rubs at his face, the sound of sharp whiskers against soft skin booming in his ears. He shuffles over to the window and stares out into the near darkness. Living here used to provide him a level of comfort, knowing there was some distance between him and other people; the other people out there who are disruptive and lacking in empathy and compassion, but as the suburbs have grown and expanded, their house is no longer so far from the nearby estate. It now encroaches their space, creeping closer and closer until only a field and a rutted track separate them.

He thinks of his early years, teaching at that school with his limited knowledge of dealing with people and the world in general, and shudders. So much has happened in the intervening years and yet here he is, still living in this house with his mother, still teaching at the same school, still battling the same problems. Still battling with the same people.

Robert Bowron.

Dear God, that name, that face. That voice. He remembers it all too well. Rob Bowron's distinct vocal reach, always eager to be heard above anybody else, his opinion clearly more important than theirs. Dominic winces. Like father, like son. Dane is quieter, surlier, his voice not quite as robust as his father's, but his nature is the same – that bristling anger, the sense of entitlement. Dominic recognised it immediately, cringing as he sat opposite the lad's father a few years ago, aware that Rob recognised him, aware that he still bore an unwarranted grudge for the years they spent holed up together in a classroom, Dominic trying to instil knowledge into an unwilling, closed mind, Rob resisting it every step of the way. And now here they are, many years later, older and purportedly wiser and yet nothing has changed. That resentment and inexplicable hatred is still present. There's no escape. Enduring it in the classroom is one thing; having to put up with it in his home – the one place where he should feel secure and content and relaxed – is unacceptable.

He tries to suppress his anger as he ruminates over what just happened: those boys surrounding his house, shattering his peace, making him feel frightened and unable to protect a vulnerable person who is completely incapacitated. Involving the police won't work. It will exacerbate an already delicate situation. Every day, he has to face those lads, to feel the wrath of their hatred and bitterness. Getting the police to issue a warning will simply stoke the flames of discontent. They will revisit, up their game and next time, they may even break into the house, do something unthinkable. Just the thought of it turns his guts to water.

All his life, he has tried to do the right thing, the honourable thing, yet time and time again, he is pushed down onto the ground, people holding him fast and grinding him into the dirt. At some point, this will all come to an end.

He has no idea of when that will be, but deep inside him, something has shifted, his ability to stomach any more of people's hatred towards him wearing thin, tapering to a point of invisibility. Perhaps it's his age. There was a time such behaviours would have washed over him, but these days, he can't laugh at it all as he once did. Maybe that's a good thing. Maybe his ability to ignore the indefensible has made him a target for all these years and he brought this on himself by being too lenient, too ready to forgive.

Behind him lies somebody who needs him to step up to the plate, to be her protector and keep her from harm. He can do that. He has it within him to be the tough guy, the one who will keep the status quo in their tight little bubble. All it takes is a bit of courage, the ability to switch from victim to victor when required. He can do that, can't he? He's a grown man, after all. He may even decide that he rather likes the sensation of superiority. Being downtrodden has never sat comfortably with him, leaving him as it has, susceptible to other people's moods and furies. The time has come for change.

* * *

He packs his briefcase, bites into a slice of toast, takes one last swig of coffee and leaves the house, closing the door behind him, a gentle, muffled click.

Sleep evaded him last night, ideas filling his brain, robbing him of any proper rest. He took a long walk at midnight, revisited the things that have led him to this juncture, tried to tell himself that this too will pass. At some point during the night, he crept into the cellar, his thoughts firmly focused on his father, on all the old man's mainly defunct farming equipment that still clutters up the place. He thought about how it should have been cleared out long ago. Something else he has neglected. Another job left undone. His dad was a stronger man than he could ever hope to be. He told himself that his father wouldn't have tolerated being victimised like this. He would have done something about it, taken firm action. Showed them who was boss.

After only a few hours' sleep, he rose both empowered and terrified, his senses and nerve endings firing and misfiring. Walking and thinking in the early hours helped him see through the fog, yet at the same time, left him light-headed and slightly nauseous.

The one thing he does know is that taking the higher moral ground hasn't worked thus far. All it has done is lengthen his agony, prolonging the attacks on his character and good nature, so why not test the waters, see what a bit of strict indoctrination can do? Whip these kids into shape. He saw it happen when he was a pupil, watching as tall gangly, young men cowered, terrified and wide-eyed at the hands of burly, cane-wielding house-masters.

Christ almighty, none of them dared breathe when he was a youngster sitting in class, watching as the teacher brandished that stick about, bringing it down across the back of anybody who dared look at them in the wrong way. Nowadays, pupils say or do what they like and nobody makes any attempts to stop them.

Times have changed, attitudes slackening and morals crumbling away. Soon, there will be nothing left but dust. No respect or deference or integrity, just a handful of nothingness where admiration and reverence used to be.

Nearby birdsong stills his thoughts. He has always loved these woods, recognising every sound, knowing every inch of the ground. This place balances him, keeps him grounded, keeping his thoughts in line and reminding him what is important in life and what needs to be forgotten and discarded.

He walks across the gravel track, stopping by his car, staring at it, feeling his pulse speed up at the sight of the gleaming length of metal and what is contained within it. The air is blessedly cool as he takes a deep breath, savouring every mouthful that slips down his throat, into his lungs. Everything begins to burn; fire flaring in his chest, pulsing under his skin. The ground tilts beneath his feet. He takes a couple of deep breaths, reaches out, leans against the bonnet for support. He's not sure he can go through with this. It's wrong. Deep down, he knows it. He has to stop these thoughts. It's not who he is. It's not who *they* are, the children he teaches. At heart, they are all good kids. Last night, two disaffected youngsters came to his home, not for the first time, and he has taken it personally, thinking all pupils are of the same mindset. They're not. He was, still is, angry and upset, but it's not something that should affect his thinking or alter his core values.

Dizziness grips him. He presses his palm down on the hard surface of the vehicle to stay upright. He needs to clear his head of these toxic thoughts. He's better than this, this *thing* that in the early hours of the morning, took hold of him, twisting his logic and knocking him off balance. Nudging him to do something violent and unforgiveable. Something final.

He taps at his briefcase, biting at his lip as he considers what to do next. He should go back in the house, perhaps even call in sick – something he hasn't done for many years – and stay at home, but then he will be conspicuous by his absence, his lack of presence duly noted by the pupils in question and any credibility he hoped to salvage from this sorry little mess will be lost.

No, he must go into school, face up to his fears, speak to those boys and be the better person. There's something he should do first though, something important, a decision that needs to be reversed. He made it when his thinking was impaired, when his emotions were running high, flowing through him untethered. He has to undo that decision, limit any further damage.

Dominic looks up to the sky, to the spread of cobalt above him, a thin blanket of the brightest blue. On impulse, he moves away from the car, twigs snapping underfoot as he moves backwards. Today, he will leave his vehicle at home and will walk into school, leave what it is he needs to do until tonight. It can wait. It's been years since he walked to work. The school is only a mile away. It will give him time to think, to prepare himself both mentally and physically. If he gets up a brisk pace, it will energise him, get some much-needed adrenaline pumping through his system.

God knows he could do with it after so little sleep last night. And who knows, he may even meet some of his pupils on the way there, get to mingle with them and remind himself of why he went into teaching in the first place. It will do him good to see them in a different setting, to not be viewed as the crusty, curmudgeonly, old bachelor who cares only about lessons and marking and standing at a board, barking out orders.

The sun makes a rapid appearance, its heat immediate and welcome as he strides over the gravel track and emerges out of the shadows and out into the light. He stops, stares up at the orb of watery, burnt ochre above and thinks that perhaps today won't be such a bad day after all.

18

Alex swings his legs out of bed, his vision blurred, eyes fogged up with sleep. His hair is tousled, a musty smell emanating from it. Last night was a laugh. No real harm done, apart from Mr Rose falling over. He got back up, though. He wasn't seriously injured or anything. More a case of his pride being dented than anything else.

They never did get to Miss Bennison's house. Too busy legging it home, stopping every couple of paces to catch their breath, their laughter at their antics ringing into the night sky. Dane's not so bad – a bit sullen and sometimes difficult to decipher but deep down, he's a good mate, not the type of lad Alex would ever have thought of pairing up with, but then, sometimes it's good to broaden your horizons, mix with people who aren't necessarily like you. He doesn't want to become like his mother – boxed into a small, predictable corner. It's a big wide world out there. He wants a bit of diversity, to have friends with differing opinions, not be the stereotypical, middle-class teenager everybody expects him to be. He's better than that. More accepting and open-minded.

Alex showers, dresses and turns to head downstairs. Joss stands on the landing, her hair piled high on her head, her pyjamas concertinaed up the back of her legs.

Their dad emerges from the bedroom, immaculately dressed, hair combed back and smelling of aftershave. 'Now then you two. Do you fancy scrambled eggs for breakfast?'

Alex nods. Joss gives a nonchalant shrug followed by a, 'Yeah, suppose,' before disappearing into her room and slamming the door.

Alex remains still, allowing his dad to pass him, then follows Joss into her bedroom. He stands at the door, checking over his shoulder, making sure his dad is out of sight before speaking. 'That thing you said about Mr Rose – well, you know, about him pressing himself up against you – is it true? Because if it is, we need to do something. File a complaint. It's serious, that sort of stuff, you know.'

Joss says nothing and turns away, her expression impassive. Alex waits, clenches his fists, unclenches them repeatedly. Why is his sister so difficult to read? Nothing is ever easy with her, the slightest of questions a drawn-out battle, as if any attempt at conversation is an attempt to pry into her sad, little world.

'Dunno,' she says finally. 'Probably. He certainly didn't try to move away when I was standing next to him. Why do you ask?' She pulls out the tight band from her hair and runs her fingers through the long strands, staring in the mirror at her reflection and frowning.

'No particular reason,' Alex says softly, thinking about last night at Mr Rose's house, thinking that his sister doesn't seem overly disturbed by the event. The purported event. He doesn't know a great deal about how most girls would react if this happened to them. He supposes that many would be horrified, too scared to go back to school, or maybe not, yet here she is, acting as if it was a minor episode, an everyday occurrence. It isn't. She should be horrified, anxious. She isn't, and it worries him. But then, Joss isn't most girls. She is confident, sassy. What if she's hiding her true feelings, covering it all up in order to keep face? That disturbs him.

'Right,' Joss says, her tone sharp, her gesture dismissive as she turns and stands, hands on hips, 'well, if you don't mind, I need to get ready.'

He backs out of the door, part of him wishing he hadn't brought the subject up at all. For all Mr Rose is quirky and eccentric and a bit of a sad old man, the guy doesn't strike him as some sort of pervert who would risk his job and reputation by doing such a thing. Joss is his sister. He knows her well. Too well. Perhaps she overreacted, saw something in the situation and misread the whole thing.

Or perhaps she is lying.

His breath is sour and warm as he leaves her and heads down the stairs, stopping briefly to stare at the door of his parents' bedroom. His mum is probably still in bed. Since moving here, she doesn't seem to care for early mornings, rising only as they are all about to leave for school and work. Gone are the days when she would get out of bed, fresh faced and sparkly eyed, excited at the prospect of what the next few hours might bring. These days, nothing they say or do has the power to snap her out of the low mood she is in.

He had no idea their other house meant that much to her. It was bigger for sure, but new when they bought it and as far as he could see, had no character. This place is smaller, quite a lot smaller, but it's cosy. Homely. He and Joss no longer have their own bathrooms although his parents still have an en suite here, and they don't have a huge living room and a music room and a games room but so what? It isn't the end of the world.

But of course, that isn't the only thing that is bothering his mum, he knows that. It's the status, or rather the lack of it, that is also dragging her down. No more cocktail parties, no more expensive holidays. No more paying a small fortune for both him and Joss to attend a private school where the fees cost more than many people earn in a year.

Rubbing at his eyes wearily, Alex heads into the kitchen, the smell of toast making his mouth water. He pours himself a glass of orange juice and sits at the table. His dad cracks eggs into a pan and stirs them vigorously.

'Won't be long. You can butter the toast, if you wouldn't mind?' It's as light as air, his father's voice, almost sing-song, as if he doesn't have a care in the world even though Alex knows the constant arguments and his mother's general demeanour must be wearing for him, dragging him right down. They drag Alex down. God knows how his dad feels about the tension that is now a permanent fixture in their once happy home.

Alex grabs at the butter tub and slathers each slice as they pop up out of the toaster, laying them on plates and placing them down on the table. He notices the empty wine glass in the sink, the bottom stained light pink, lipstick smeared on the rim. He wonders how many she had and whether she drank alone. He can't see any other glasses. Maybe his dad washed his tumbler before going to bed. Or maybe he didn't drink anything and left her to it, sitting here wallowing in her own misery, consoling herself with each consecutive swallow. That's the most likely scenario. It's been the pattern for the past few months. On occasion, he will have a tumbler of whiskey but given their recent rows, it's more likely that his dad sat in his study reading while his mum was in here, slumped at the table drinking alone, mired in wretchedness.

'There you go. Enjoy.' A plate of scrambled eggs is placed in front of him, the steam rising from the plate in tiny tendrils.

The chair is hard as he sits, his stomach tightening at the thought of his mum drunk. Again. Two minutes ago, he was hungry. His appetite is now waning by the second, visions of his failing family nipping at him, making him queasy. He wishes he could do something, say something to make it all better but has no idea where to even begin. The egg is hot and creamy. He shovels a forkful into his mouth and nibbles at the toast. It sticks in his throat, dry and rough edged.

'Dad, do you like living here?' The words are out before Alex knows it. Before he can stop them. It's time to start talking about this, not carrying on as if nothing is amiss, the four of them going about their daily lives while their world is slowly dissolving around them.

'Like it? It's a house. It's warm and dry. We have everything we need right here, son.' The chair creaks as his dad sits down next to him and takes a sip of juice. 'Why do you ask?'

Alex feels a pull deep in his chest, a fist grasping and twisting at his lungs, making it difficult for him to breathe properly, every exhalation an onerous and painful task. His dad must know why he is asking. Is he really going to make him spell it out? It's an inescapable fact that his mother is falling apart. They can either all carry on blindly or they can stop, assess the situation, and try to put a halt to her decline.

'I'm worried about Mum.' A flush creeps up Alex's neck, prickling his face, hot needles stabbing at his cheeks. His words were rushed, a wave of humiliation washing over him as he said them but they're out there now. There's no taking them back. He takes a deep breath, feeling the cold air stretching his lungs, a welcome breeze that steadies him.

'Ah,' his dad replies as he places his tumbler of juice on the table and lowers his eyes. 'Look, Alexander, all I can say is, give it time. Your mother isn't a fan of change. She had her friends, her routine, her big house and now all of that has been taken from her. She just needs some time to settle, that's all.'

Behind them, Joss enters the kitchen. She flops down on the chair, snatching up a glass of orange juice and draining it in seconds. 'Who needs time to settle?'

Alex shrugs and blinks, trying to clear his thoughts, wishing Joss had remained upstairs. She has killed the moment, stolen his precious time with their long-suffering father.

'Anyway, Dad,' Joss says, the conversation, the awkward moment in which she intervened, already forgotten, 'can I have some money for fabric for my lesson today? I asked Mum but she said to ask you. You're the money man, apparently.' Joss laughs, throws back her head and runs her fingers through her hair.

Alex shivers, feels himself shrink a little. She is unaware of the intended insult to their dad. Alex can hear his mum's voice as she said those words, her stinging and acerbic tone as she spat them out, and then Joss's features, bland and unresponsive, too locked into her own little world to notice or care about anybody else's, her thoughts geared only towards the cash that she needed.

'Sure.' Their dad dips into his pocket and pulls out a £10 note. 'This enough?'

Joss takes it from him and nods without a word of thanks, instead cramming a piece of toast into her mouth and chewing on it noisily. She stuffs the money into her pocket and carries on eating.

'Right,' Alex murmurs, standing up, unable to take any more of Joss's dismissive manner, her selfish, thoughtless ways, 'Thanks for breakfast, Dad. I'm going to go and get my things ready.'

He exits the kitchen, leaving a frosty silence behind him, wishing there was something he could say or do to make his sister and his mum realise that there are four people in this family and only one person working and bringing in the money and that if they don't start taking notice of that fact, something terrible and final may just happen, breaking them apart for always.

19

Nina picks her way through the detritus in his room, stepping over a tangle of wires, almost tripping as her feet become caught in the clothes that are strewn about the floor. She could leave it as it is, let Dane sort it, but then it would never get done and it has got to a point where she can no longer stand it. Even being downstairs, knowing it is in this state makes her teeth itch with anxiety.

Besides, this is a chance to search through his things, maybe stumble across those drawings she found a few weeks ago. She should have confronted him about them there and then but couldn't face the inevitable arguments: Rob backing him up, Dane claiming she is a terrible mother, prying into his business and that he should be left alone to do whatever he wants.

No, this way is better, easier on her nerves. She will never be a match for the pair of them, their voices filling the room, bouncing around her head, telling her she is imagining things, that she is reading too much into it and needs to get out more, not spend so much time hanging around the house and letting her mind go into overdrive. She has heard it all before, been subjected to the abuse and accusations, and isn't sure she can face any more rows and fights. Avoidance and apathy are now her default ways of dealing with the men in her life. She is always outnumbered and hasn't the energy for them when they close ranks and turn her words around, throwing them back at her like an unexploded hand grenade.

Ringing the school this morning proved fruitless. Even the idea that she would take matters into her own hands and sort out her son's education has backfired. Trying to get hold of the individual teachers was like trying to catch the wind. Three calls later, she decided to give up, each time having missed Miss Bennison and Mr Rose by a matter of minutes as they both returned to class to teach for the rest of the day.

It had seemed like such a great idea at the time. She had pictured herself sitting opposite them, working out a plan, helping Dane to get back on track but as the day progressed with no contact, it became increasingly difficult to keep up any momentum. Her energy waned and now here she is, snooping, intruding on her son's secrets in a bid to climb inside his head and decode his thought processes and emotions.

Perching on the edge of the mattress, Nina flicks through a notebook, looking for – she has no real idea of what it is she is looking for. Whatever she finds, she feels certain she will end up wishing she hadn't ever seen it. So why is she in here, searching? Biting at her lip, she closes her eyes and grips the edge of the bed. She needs clues. Something. Anything that will unlock the mystery as to what motivates her boy. If she can get an idea of how he thinks, it may be the key to forging a connection with Dane, a connection she is desperate to make before he becomes a stranger to her and she loses him altogether.

She spends the next half hour tidying up: nothing too drastic. Nothing obvious that will provoke a quarrel. She sorts through a few piles of clothes, changes the bed sheets and gathers up the trail of wires into a neat bundle, tucking them down the back of the cabinet that houses his many games. And that's when she finds it. A folder that looks out of place, incongruous and menacing, covered in black scribbles and words that make Nina's skin prickle with dread. This is worse than those drawings that she found a few months back – drawings of people in Dane's class with threats written next to them: ways in which he was going to harm them. That is bad enough of course, but it was childish nonsense – badly drawn images of classmates with words scrawled beside them. A stick man image of a boy called Josh that Nina remembers from primary school with the words *push off a cliff* written next to it. Another one was an immature drawing of a girl called Lori. Again, a stick image with curly hair and wearing a skirt, like something a six-year-old would draw, with the words, *kill the bitch* written next to it. Finding them had made Nina's stomach plummet, made her scalp tighten and her blood run like sand. But this wad of documents is something quite different. Something far more disturbing. Something horribly sinister.

On the front of the folder is written, *The Assassination Plan* and beside it is an array of pictures of countless types of weapons – a knife, some sort of homemade bomb, a rifle, a hand grenade, an axe – so many of them, it makes Nina's head spin. Her legs become liquid. She slumps down onto the bed, clutching at the sheets, the document laid on her lap. Her vision blurs. This can't be right. It must be for some sort of school project. It has to be. She tells herself this, knowing that such a notion is ridiculous and that this is the work of her son and isn't linked to any school assignments or essays. Her son did this. Her only child. Her boy. Ideas plucked from out of his head on how he wants to hurt people, to maim and terrify them. To kill them.

She swallows, the gulping sound a boom in her head. Her hands are trembling. She can't seem to stop them, her fingers fat and clumsy as she opens the folder and scans what is written there. Words: scrawled, horrific words that overlap and fill the paper; page after page after page, some decipherable, others making no sense at all. Then on the final sheet, something that stills her blood, turning it to ice. Photographs of teachers, at least ten of them. Beside each member of staff is a weapon. Nina tries to stop the tears from falling as she scans their faces, recognising the pictures from the school website: Mr Rawlings, the head teacher, his smiling face and next to it, a noose. Then Mrs White, the assistant head and next to her picture, a knife. Miss Bennison's photograph and next to her image is a pistol, then Mr Rose, his face split in half and a blood-covered axe jutting out of his head. On and on it goes. So many pictures, So many weapons. So much hatred and violence.

Tears fall freely now, running down Nina's face, dripping onto her hands. She throws the document aside, wiping away a rogue tear that lands on the edge of the page. She wants to take this folder and all the pages inside it and tear it into a thousand tiny pieces before throwing it in the fire. But she knows that she can't do that. What she has to do is put it back in its original place and then think long and hard about what she is going to do next. She can't broach the subject with Rob or Dane. One would back the other up, claiming she is overreacting and being neurotic. They would turn the whole thing around and act as if she is the one at fault, telling her she is unhinged even though it is their son who keeps a folder on what type of violent deaths he would like to inflict on his teachers and classmates. Somehow, the pair of them would find a way to defend this whole macabre incident even though it is an indefensible, atrocious thing to do.

All she is doing here is trying to understand why anybody would do such a thing. Why her only child thinks these thoughts and carries around so much malice and anger. She created him – this potential monster – and now wonders how and why and when it all went wrong. At what point did he turn from an innocent child into a potential murderer? Or has it always been there, lurking, waiting to emerge? She thinks of those earlier incidents, the killing of helpless animals, Dane's echoing laughter as he watched them die…

Nina stands up and puts the folder back in its original place, her head spinning. She is off-balance, barely able to walk in a straight line as she makes her way back over to the bed where she lies down, curling up into a tight foetal position, arms wrapped around her body, legs tucked up into her chest.

There is a chill in the room even though it's warm outside. Goosebumps prickle her flesh. She closes her eyes and shivers, wishing she could be transported away from this place, far, far away to a world where she is surrounded by like-minded people, to a place where violence and hatred are relegated to the annals of history and not present here in her home, the place where she should feel safe and protected – not wholly responsible for the actions of a troubled teenager who is enabled every step of the way by a father who sees it as his duty to ensure his boy is reared in his own mould.

Thoughts of what she should do next jostle for space in her head. She is tired. So very, very tired. She could try contacting the school again. But then what? They could reprimand him or possibly exclude him permanently and what good would that do? They would have to find another school or possibly even a behavioural unit. Is that what she really wants for her son? For him to be relegated to the periphery of the education system, set apart from others before his adult life has even begun? Such a disadvantaged and fractured start to life. Where would he go after such a move? To the bottom of society, that's where he would end up. Down in the gutter with the ne'er do wells. She can't allow that to happen. He's her boy, her baby. Every criminal, drug addict or lowlife is still somebody's child.

He could possibly be referred for counselling. It's better than moving schools but of course Rob would never agree to such a move and nor would Dane.

She can see it now, Rob's expression, his temper building as he attempts to defend Dane's actions, possibly even blaming Nina for not being a good enough mother. This would all be her fault anyway. Of course it would. Everything that goes awry in this house is always her fault. Rob is the worker, the provider. She is everything else. They have money – plenty of it. He would argue that he has done his bit, made them wealthy. Her side of the bargain has fallen far short of the mark. That is, if Rob would ever admit to there being a problem in the first place. He believes that men are strong and women are weak. Everything is black and white in his world, the lines clearly demarcated. There are no grey areas in Rob's life and counselling and therapy is for weaklings.

She curls up tighter, her world shrinking around her, her inability to do anything about this situation trapping her, the vines of this impossible scenario wrapping themselves around her limbs, around her torso, strengthening and tightening until she feels as if she can no longer breathe.

Nina sits up, tears still streaming, her chest bound with panic and frustration. Doing nothing feels wrong and yet what can she do, given her circumstances? She is hemmed in on all sides, living in a fortress that she should have broken out of many years ago but didn't, and now she is stuck here, in this house with these people; trapped in an impossible situation with no solution in sight. Everything suddenly feels so bleak, so terribly oppressive and impenetrable. All she can do is pretend. Pretend that her husband isn't having yet another affair. Pretend that her son isn't on the slippery slope to becoming a highly dysfunctional human being. Pretend that those notes, those horrific images and words don't actually exist.

Except they do. They are real, and she has no idea what to do about it. What to do about her son, the boy who, it would appear, is rapidly turning into a very unhinged and dangerous young man.

Standing up and smoothing down her clothes, Nina straightens the bedsheets where she has lain on them, puts everything back where she found it, making sure things look undisturbed, and leaves the room, wishing she had never set foot in there. Now all she needs to do is erase it from her mind, act as if everything is perfectly normal when she knows deep down that it is isn't and possibly never will be again.

20

1 JULY 1978

My Dearest Clara,

I am writing this letter knowing you will never receive it. This is a way of letting out my feelings, attempting to release the pent-up emotions that have been bubbling up inside of me. I am certain they will burst out of my chest if I don't do something constructive to alleviate the angst and worry and turmoil that sits deep within me.

I suppose that since you won't get to read this letter, I can say anything I like – anything at all – and yet you are still so much a part of me that I cannot bring myself to say or do anything insulting or to denigrate the memory I have of you in any way, shape or form. You are the love of my life and will remain as such as long as I have breath left in my body. I realise this may sound dramatic but at this moment in time, those are my overriding emotions and I cannot see any changes ahead. I feel what I feel and that, I am afraid, is that.

Again, Mother sends her best wishes. I realise you didn't always see eye to eye but I know for sure that she is still missing you, but not as much as I am, dear Clara. You are there all the time – in my dreams, throughout every waking moment. It is utter torture knowing I may never see you again. I am presuming you are staying up there, in Scotland? Your reluctance to reply seems indicative of your long-term plans. I *cannot imagine you coming back home to North Yorkshire, to the village of Ormston and you and I bumping into each other. I don't think I could stand it. Especially if you are with somebody else – another man, that is. It would end me both physically and mentally, seeing you on the arm of somebody else. I always felt so sure that you and I would spend the rest of our lives together – get married, have a family, grow old together – but here we are, apart, and here I am, alone and despondent. I am missing you so much, it hurts like a physical wound that continues to bleed profusely. I fear I may never heal without you in my life.*

I am going to end this letter now as seeing these words on the paper is a reminder of how far away you are. I would give anything to have you back, my darling, my love, my dearest Clara. I wish there were some magic formula I could use to win you over and return you to my side but it appears your mind is made up and that we are very much over.

I want you to know that I will never, ever replace you. There is only enough space in my heart for one woman and that woman, my darling girl, is you.

Take care, my love.

Dominic.

21

PRESENT DAY

The house is silent by the time she rises, everyone now absent, having left for work and school. A pain rushes through her skull, the room shifting and tilting as she sits up in bed. Kate pushes the pillows behind her head and sniffs the air like an animal searching for its prey. The smell of food wafts up from below – toast, eggs, maybe even a whiff of something greasy. Anthony probably had a full English, lining his stomach for his busy day ahead. She snorts, the smell making her retch.

Outside, the thrum of traffic pulses in her ears, every noise, every movement she makes, heightened and accentuated. She slips out of bed, heads towards the bathroom, her stomach clenched into a hard ball of anxiety as nausea sweeps over her, making her woozy.

She tries to remember how much she had to drink last night. One bottle, perhaps. Maybe even two. Since the argument with Anthony, she has found it hard to focus on anything anymore. Her heart simply isn't in it. She had hoped to talk him round, make him see that it is in all their interests to take Gavin up on his offer of that job, but he is holding firm, refusing to consider it. She had forgotten how stubborn her husband can be, a trait that served him well when he worked in a cut-throat environment, but not one that works well as a father and husband. This is his family. He needs to be more malleable, more open to her ideas. It's not just about what he wants. He has others to consider.

Her mobile phone sits by her side as she lowers herself onto the toilet and pees, the hot stream of liquid making her shiver. She finishes in the bathroom, phone clasped in her hands, and creeps back to bed, wrapping the quilt around her aching body. Drinking so much doesn't suit her. She should stop but can't seem to muster up the energy nor the will to do it. Not drinking casts an unpleasant light on her situation, highlighting the imperfections and flaws, reminding her of how low she has fallen. Drinking helps blot them out, those imperfections, her current status in life. Sobriety would be a step too far at this juncture. Once things pick up, she will consider it. For now, she is happy to forget, pretend none of this is happening. Until she wakes up, that is. Then it starts all over again, her lacklustre life. Her dull, impoverished existence.

In a moment of spontaneity, she sends a text message, asking if they can rearrange their date, telling him how sorry she is and that she will make it up to him. What else is she supposed to do with her time? Anthony is unreachable and Alexander and Jocelyn seem to be getting on with their lives, making the best of a bad turn of events. That's all she is doing here: turning this situation around to her advantage. Trying to dig herself out of a deep, dark hole.

She receives a message almost immediately.

> Sure doll. How about tonight at The Tavern? Nice and quiet in there. See you at 7.

A bolt of electricity darts through her, waking her up, shaking her brain into motion, forcing some life back into her tired, old bones. Sod Anthony and his low aspirations. She will make sure somebody puts this family first and if it means abandoning her morals and integrity to do just that then so be it. She may even have a little fun while she's at it. God knows she could do with injecting some humour and cheer back into her life. The kids can manage just fine without her while she does it, and Anthony – well, she feels sure Anthony will barely notice her absence. Most evenings, he has his head stuck in a book or some pamphlet or other while she watches TV alone. They are living separate lives, passing one another silently, the ghost of their marriage rapidly fading until it disappears altogether.

Buoyed up by the sudden response, she showers and tidies the bedroom. It's so hard to find places to store things in this shoebox of a house. Her clothes are crammed into a tiny wardrobe and her make-up and jewellery are stuffed into boxes that fill every surface of the bedroom. Doing her best to remain upbeat, she cleans the bathroom, tidies upstairs and curls her hair ready for later on tonight.

* * *

The rest of the day is a blur of housework and cooking. She cleans the kitchen, the living room, the children's bedrooms, making sure it's presentable for when everyone returns from school and work. It may even help put her in a better light, let them see she isn't just some miserable old soak who sits about the house all day painting her nails.

She knows how she is viewed by her husband and children and knows also that she drinks too much and that they want her to stop. Misery has pushed her into a rut. She is trying to climb back out of it but it isn't easy. In fact, it's very bloody hard. Some days, a blackness descends and it feels as if she is suffocating, every last pocket of air being pushed out of her lungs. Perhaps tonight will help lift that blackness. She hopes so. She deserves this time, this slither of happiness. She needs it.

The Tavern is perfect, she thinks – tucked away at the bottom of a lane, frequented mainly by locals, none of whom will know her – she will be able to relax, be herself and not be the uptight individual she has become of late. The thought of it makes her blood fizz with excitement. Her skin tingles as she visualises his face, the way his eyes shine whenever he glances her way. She can't remember the last time Anthony looked at her the way he does. She shouldn't get too attached to him, she knows that and will do her utmost to keep a healthy distance from him but she cannot be held responsible for what happens when her marriage is falling apart and her husband is a cold individual who hardly notices whether she is dead or alive. It's a bit of fun, that's all. A way of reminding herself that she's still breathing, that she is still here and in need of some love and affection. She is more than just somebody's wife, somebody's mother. She is a person in her own right and is worthy of being treated as such.

By the time Jocelyn and Alexander arrive home, she is floating on air, happier than she has been for many weeks. Trying to keep her newfound enthusiasm under wraps, Kate keeps her make-up to a bare minimum and dresses conservatively, telling Anthony she is meeting another of her friends from her yoga classes, telling him that Sylvia will also be there and that it's an informal get-together and she won't be late back. He seems relieved to see her happy, even giving her a peck on the cheek as she leaves. *Maybe he prefers it when we're apart,* she thinks as she slips out of the door and into the night.

She drives there, keen to take the car, to stop herself from drinking too much. It's midweek. She needs to stay alert, keep her wits about her, not get carried away by the moment. Besides, last night's alcohol is possibly still swilling around in her bloodstream. Two bottles. Or was it three? She has a memory of searching for a fourth. Or maybe not. Perhaps that was the previous evening. Or the one before that. Her face burns, shame creeping under her skin. Driving is better. She needs to dry out.

'You look stunning.' In the corner of the pub, he sits, half hidden in the shadows. He stands to greet her, his green eyes twinkling, sending a dart of desire through her. God, that smile. And those eyes.

A vision of Anthony pushes into her mind, his expression as she left, the fact he attempted to say something which she brushed off as she grabbed at her jacket and closed the door behind her, the dull click of it making her head thump. She ignores it. He has had his chance to make good the bad things in their life. Now it's her turn to grasp at this small goblet of happiness, to take it and drink it down greedily like a woman dying of thirst.

A glass of wine is placed in front of her. 'I'm driving,' she manages to say, her voice husky.

'It's a white wine spritzer. Just the one and you'll be fine.'

She nods, takes a sip, savouring its slightly acidic taste, and smiles at him. 'I can't stay out late. Anthony thinks I'm with the girls from my yoga class.'

He gives her a knowing smile and takes a slug of his beer. 'Always running away from me.'

'No. Not running,' she replies softly. 'Just cautious.'

The pub is almost empty save for a few stragglers at the bar, locals who pay no attention to the couple in the corner. Relief finally settles in her bones, softening her sharp demeanour. She can do this. It's just possible that a small amount of happiness is within her grasp.

He is evaluating her every move. She feels excitement mingled with fear as he reaches over and places his hand over hers. His skin is warm and reassuring against her cold, clammy flesh. 'This place has rooms. I took the liberty...'

It's wrong, she knows that, but she can't remember the last time she felt so alive. She can't remember the last time anybody paid her this much attention, caressing her bare skin, kissing her body, murmuring her name over and over until she feels like she might explode.

His lovemaking is a slow and sensuous affair. Not what she expected from him. This is another side of the man she thought she knew. This is his gentler side, his tender self that is reserved solely for her.

'I have to go. It's getting late.' She attempts to sit up. He begins to knead her breasts, his fingers moving over her naked body with the softest of touches.

'Like I said, always running away from me.'

'No, like *I* said earlier. Just cautious. We both have a lot to lose if anybody ever found out about us.'

'They won't. Come on, just ten more minutes and then we'll leave.' His voice is so seductive, it takes her all of her strength to drag herself out of the bed and slip into her underwear.

'You're a tease, Kate. I need to see you again.'

She mentally rakes through the week ahead. Could she really manage another night like this without Anthony getting suspicious? She wants to, dear God, every inch of her wants to. Her skin is burning with desire, her nerve endings tingling and tight with lust, but she also knows that she has to be careful here. Getting caught is unthinkable.

'How about tomorrow during the day? Everyone will be out. We could meet here again. Or somewhere else.'

He watches her as she gets dressed. 'I hope you're not messing me about, Kate.' There is a sliver of ice in his voice. 'I hope you're not about to cut me off. I don't like being cut off before this has even started.'

She hears the coldness in his tone. She hears it, dismisses it. He's a man, driven by sex and power. They all have it within them to suddenly turn, their moods dipping and changing as they intimidate people to get what they want out of life. She knows that. It excites her, fires up her deadened senses. Anthony is a shadow of the man he used to be: a dispassionate being who no longer makes her feel alive. And she wants to feel alive. Dear God, she wants it so much it's a constant, gnawing sensation that sits deep in her guts.

She shivers and throws on her jacket, buttoning it up against the sudden blast of cold air that is running through her. 'No, not at all. I'm just being careful, trying to avoid being seen.'

He nods and she surreptitiously lets out a breath that has been compacted deep in her chest. She can't lose this before it's begun. Besides the amazing sex, this man has exactly what she needs – money. Getting him to allow Anthony to manage some of his finances could be their lucky break.

'You'll have to tell me about your property portfolio.' She hopes she hasn't overstepped the mark, making him think she's only interested in his wealth. She is, but not in the way he might imagine.

'Course I will. Got some amazing developments on the go at the minute. A new set of office blocks right in the centre of town that should be going up next year. Just need to get the planning department to not be so fucking anal and get them on our side and we're good to go.'

She smiles, knowing she's on safe and steady ground here. He likes nothing better than talking about himself and his achievements and future developments. Rob is motivated by money which is why introducing him to Anthony could work well in their favour. Even Rob isn't so dense as to mention their affair. He doesn't want to lose half of everything he owns any more than she does. It's all about the money with him. She knows how he thinks – cash is king.

'Well, if ever you need any assistance with the financial side of things, Anthony could always help you out. He's an experienced hedge fund manager, really knows his stuff.' Her words appear to fall on deaf ears as Rob reaches across and grabs at his phone, scrolling through it with the interest she wishes he would show towards her suggestion. 'And he also has contacts in the planning department that could benefit you.' She has no idea why she is saying such a thing. Anthony has a friend who used to work in the planning department and whether or not he holds a position of authority is debatable but she had to find a way in, to get Rob to listen to her.

He sits up straight and throws his phone to one side. He's listening now, his eyes gleaming with longing. 'Who? Have you got a name?' His voice is suddenly loud, rich with interest, his words coming out in an unstoppable stream. Gone is the gentle, demure tone he used with her only moments ago in bed. The Rob Bowron of old is back – loud, brash, demanding.

'No. Sorry, but I can get Anthony to contact you if you like? Maybe he can also give you advice on your investments. He's one of the best.'

Rob is shaking his head, his interest now honed back in on his phone, which he snatches up and reads, his eyes narrowed in concentration. 'Got an adviser, thanks. Don't need another one.'

Disappointment and resentment bristle within her. Rob needs Anthony. He needs his expertise and knowledge to increase his wealth. He just doesn't know it yet. One more meeting to try and persuade him, that's all she needs. Then she can back off, cool her ardour and they can all get down to business. The business of improving her life, her wealth, her status. The business of getting her old life back.

'Tomorrow?' she says with a wink, leaning over and kissing him softly on the lips. 'Same place?'

The sun is a distant memory, the moon silvering the ground as she crosses the car park and slips into her vehicle, failure nestling and unfurling in her abdomen. He just needs more time to come round to her way of thinking, that's all it is. The way he made love to her, so gently, so tenderly, that's how she knows that she will eventually win him over, get him to consider taking her up on her offer. Her body, her female charm, she will use it to her advantage and get exactly what she wants.

It's just a matter of time.

22

Dominic's day passes quickly but not without incident. The memory of that girl, her fixed gaze, the way she turned her head – it causes him to stop and take stock of everything. It's that look that she has, the curve of her mouth, the colour of her skin. The skittish way she acts when her name is called out in class, as if she has been caught out doing something untoward – it reminds him so much of her – his Clara. Except she isn't Clara and he needs to remember that, to stay focused in her presence, not get bogged down in thoughts and recollections that tug at his heartstrings, knocking him off-kilter.

Clara is gone, even the scent of her no more than a distant memory. He knows that. Clara chose a life without him.

This Jocelyn child is just that – a child. A child in a woman's body with the wily ways of somebody much older and wiser.

Clara definitely wasn't the same sort of person that this Jocelyn is – troublesome, brash, over-confident – and yet there is something about her that evokes images from his past, stirring acid and bile in his gut and forcing him to mislay his sensibilities when he is around her. Last week, he had to speak to Jocelyn about her behaviour in class, how she was losing focus and not contributing to the lesson in a positive manner.

His eyes mist over, a pebble-sized lump lodging in his throat as he thinks back to that day, the way she moved closer to him, as if she could read his thoughts, his innermost needs and desires. It unnerved him, made him uncomfortable, wanting to jump out of his own skin. He told her to leave the room, his tone sharp and unaccommodating. She and her friend left, both full of sniggers and sarcasm. A sense of impending doom sat in his gut for hours afterwards.

Dominic snaps back to the present, shaking off all thoughts of Jocelyn, of Clara, of a time when he felt sure life would go his way and didn't.

Alexander is sitting at the back of the room. Dominic evades his gaze, can feel the boy's eyes on him as he addresses the class, telling them their learning objective for the next hour. In the corner is the other miscreant, Dane Bowron: the boy who is destined to follow the same route as his father, his path in life already mapped out, its trajectory deeply embedded in the boy's DNA. There is no escaping his father's genes: his loutish ways, his fixed opinions, his dismissal of education.

'Why spend weeks and months stuck in college when he can be out there earning money?' was Rob Bowron's cry when Dominic had made a rare appearance at a parental consultation evening one time. Dominic had spoken honestly, telling Dane's parents that he feared for the boy's future if he didn't start applying himself and putting more effort into his schoolwork. 'Learning how to make things that people want to buy, that's the key to success, not sitting here reciting bloody poetry or spouting off a load of Shakespeare. It's all bollocks anyway.' Rob had laughed at his own statement before telling his wife to get up, that he had heard enough and it was time for them to move on. 'Problem with you education types is, you've never been out there in the big, wide world. You've got no idea what makes people tick. I can tell this much – it ain't Shakespeare and Dickens that will earn the boy good money; it's a solid day's graft.'

'He's a capable young man and could go far but not if he doesn't produce the work and study hard,' Dominic had said, hoping for some sort of recognition at his words. The mother had sat quietly: a submissive creature with features that reminded Dominic of a frightened rabbit startled by an oncoming vehicle, too scared to move or react before shifting in her seat and standing up. She had given Dominic a meek smile and moved away, her feet clicking on the tiled floor as she hurried to catch up with her brute of a husband.

You never can tell, thinks Dominic as he stands in front of the board and asks the class to open their books at page 115, *how these youngsters will turn out later in life.* Some of them do surprising things, breaking out of their mould and taking flight away from their often impoverished upbringing. But Dane Bowron's future is as predictable as the passing of time. There is no doubt whatsoever in Dominic's mind that that boy will go the way of his dad. You can love your children, educate them, teach them right from wrong, but in the end, the genes will out. That boy is destined for a life of delinquency.

The next hour passes quickly with only the odd sarcastic remark when Dominic mispronounces a word and has to quickly correct himself.

He asks everyone to finish the sentence they're writing and prepare to leave. Should he ask the two lads to stay back? He considers it but wonders what will be achieved by such a decision. There will be no other witnesses to what he is about to say, only two resentful teenagers who would vouch for one another should things turn sour. After the last time, when Alex's worldly-wise sister, a girl who thinks herself advanced for her years, did her damnedest to get close to him, making his muscles twitch and his head ache, he decides to let them go, dismissing the class and reminding them to complete their homework in time for the next lesson.

Packing up his bag and tidying his desk, Dominic ruminates over the thoughts that passed through his head in the early hours of the morning, how close he came to doing untold damage to his reputation. Perhaps it was a rare flash of madness, events of late becoming too much for him: recurring memories, moments of doubt and terror coupled with an invasion of his personal space. They all crowded his mind, nearly sending him toppling over the edge into the dark, gaping mouth of insanity.

Despite the warmth of the room, he feels cold, a chill brushing over his flesh. He shuffles on his jacket, pushes his chair under his desk. His battered, old briefcase dangles from his fingertips, its weight digging into his skin.

It's time for him to go home. It may have been a positive day today and the learning that took place has given him a buzz. It's a long time since he felt that sensation. But he now needs to get out of this place, to feel the sun on his face, see the azure sky. But more than anything, he wants to shut off his mind, close his eyes and simply forget.

* * *

She is sitting in the bedroom chair when he arrives home. Today, he didn't make it back at lunchtime to check up on her. It worried him, the thought of her being stuck here on her own. Her head is dipped to one side, her eyes closed against the thin slant of watery sunlight that filters through the blinds. He wonders what goes through her head. Does she still think about him? Is she even aware of where she is? Who he is?

The dim light smooths out the fine lines on her face, painting her complexion a fresher, clearer shade of grey. Because she is grey; so little life running through her, everything she used to be, slowly ebbing away. A ghost of a woman, that's what she is. A ghost of her former self. Her hands sit on her lap, dry, loose and veined, her thin flesh the texture of old paper.

He allows his mind to roam back to a time when she was able-bodied, when she had a brain, ambitions, was able to formulate thoughts, speak coherently, be a fully rounded person. He places his arms beneath her tiny, frail body and lifts her back onto the bed, her soft exhalations caressing his face as he straightens the covers and reaches down to softly kiss her head. The mattress sighs under her weight, the floorboards groaning and creaking as he moves away and closes the door behind him. He's glad she's still here. Her body and mind may be weak and he is aware she is suffering, but just having somebody else around is enough to keep the loneliness at bay, to stop that black dog from howling at him and dragging him off into the depths of the darkest night.

He isn't sure he could have carried on living in this house alone. The nights are long, hour after hour of silence and emptiness. Her presence has helped him get through those evenings, given him a reason to rise each day and face the world. Some days are easy, others not so much. It's not been the same since Clara disappeared. Nothing has been the same.

A freezing fog billows through his mind. He thinks back, remembering how he had planned to drive up to Scotland to see her all those years ago.

After repeated requests for her to get in touch, she maintained her radio silence, making no attempt to reply to his many letters. He should have just let her go, allowed her to sever their relationship at that point. He knows that now, but he just couldn't shift her from his mind. She was in his head all the time; every waking moment, ever present in his dreams, a ubiquitous presence he couldn't shake no matter how hard he tried. He knew then that he couldn't carry on without her.

It was the not knowing. Did she have somebody else? What had he done that was so wrong? It ate at him. It was the not knowing that he couldn't handle.

And then the day he was due to leave, his mother took ill. Her sickness altered his plans. He was forced to stay home, had sat by her bedside, watching, monitoring her condition, making sure she didn't deteriorate. She stabilised and slept for most of the day but leaving her was unthinkable. He was all she had. With Clara out of the picture, they only had one another.

It was later that week that he heard about Clara's disappearance. Her parents paid him a visit, detailing the events of that day. They were closely followed by the police, who questioned him relentlessly. Clara had gone for a walk to the nearby lake and failed to return. Her grandparents had alerted the police later that afternoon. The area was scoured, every available officer out searching for her, but Clara was never found. She had vanished into thin air.

Dominic slumps into the chair, the living room a swathe of undulating shadows. He sits in silence, contemplating the past, the present, the future. Sometimes, when the sun is shining, when the sky is clear, summer close by, nudging its way into view, he feels sure he can cope with losing her, then there are other days when the pain of her absence is as acute as it was the day she went missing. Winters are the worst. Those endless, grey days. The long, dark nights.

He still has the letters he wrote to her, piles of them stuffed into his wooden box, carefully straightened out, neat and tidy, just how he likes them. Many a time, he has considered disposing of them but can't seem to bring himself to do it. Seeing her name written there is a sharp reminder that she existed, that she was once his. That he was once hers. He hasn't read them for such a long time now, he's not sure he could bring himself to open them, to sweep his eyes over those words or think about how much she meant to him. Still means to him.

There hasn't been anybody since Clara. It's crazy, he knows that. He should have moved on, found somebody else, but knows that nobody would have matched up. What they had was unique. That's why he has hung onto the letters. Just knowing they're around is enough. By storing them, he has been able to cling onto the very essence of who she is. Or who she was.

No.

Who she is. Clara is still locked in his heart, in his head. She is everywhere and nowhere. He sighs, stares up at the ceiling. It all happened such a long, long time ago and yet it was only yesterday.

His hand is trembling as he pours himself a large whiskey. He's earned this. Despite knowing it will make him groggy the following day, he swallows it down in one long gulp, his gullet a trail of fire as the amber liquid trickles into his belly. He pours himself another, just to blot out the memories, drinks it down and then pours one more for good measure.

With each consecutive drink, the desperation lifts, clearing a space in his head, his heart not so cumbersome and heavy. Not so full of Clara. Empty. That's how he is now, he thinks as he drains the last of the alcohol. An empty husk of a man, hollowed out and cavernous. Still, he has his work and this house and his mother for company. And whiskey. When all else fails, whiskey will always be here for him. It's a solid, reliable entity in his life, alleviating his stress. Helping him to forget. Forcing him to remember. He shivers, closes his eyes, tries to draw a line under it all.

It happens as the edges of his musings have begun to blur – the noise, the commotion outside. Stumbling to his feet, the alcohol softening his reflexes, Dominic heads to the door, aware he can't defend himself or his mother in his current state. He turns the door handle and all but falls outside, his feet twisting under him as he lurches forward into the shadows. Righting his posture, he looks around, craning his neck and peering through the growing darkness to the spots of light beyond the trees.

'Hello?' It sounds ridiculous to his own ears, his tinny, whiny voice echoing through the woods. Pitiful and pointless. 'Come on, old boy,' he murmurs, shaking his head at his own ineptitude. 'There's nobody here.'

And then he feels it – a rush of air, somebody brushing past him, a shadow on the edge of his line of sight that shoves him sideways, his body being pushed into the doorframe, his spine crunching against the wooden jamb.

The shadow darts inside the house and Dominic feels his legs fold under him. He flexes his fingers, straightens up and runs after them, his heart a steady thump in his chest.

Dear God, his mother. She is upstairs in her bed. Alone and helpless with an intruder in the house while he is down here trying to drum up enough courage to stop them. Always a coward. His father was right. He has always lacked enough courage to be considered a true man.

The shadow flits ahead of him. His skin ripples with dread. He turns to follow it, his head a mass of terrified thoughts. It's dark outside and in, this house full of dim shadows, sharp corners, surrounded by foliage. He is alone here. *They* are alone here. He and his mother. Nobody around to help them.

'Stop!' No response. His voice echoes through the house, a tinny, cowardly squeak.

And then up above him, he hears the creak of a floorboard, the thud of feet as the trespasser moves from room to room. He bristles. Fear and anger flood through him.

'I'm calling the police!' If somebody were to ask him afterwards how he reacted, he would find it hard to give a clear answer. Everything is indistinct, his logic clouded, panic taking over and muddying his thinking. His head pounds, blood thrums in his ears. He eventually breaks out of his torpor, races upstairs and can see the intruder standing outside his mother's room, their fingers curled around the handle. In slow motion, they push open the door a crack and peer into the darkness of the bedroom.

With a sudden rush of strength, he lunges forwards and grabs at them, trying to lock his arms around their midriff, knocking them sideways onto the floor. The shadow is lithe, stronger than he is, more agile. Younger. It scrambles up on its feet and slips around him, pushing him with strong hands, an inordinate amount of strength behind them, slamming him into the wall. He gasps, hears the voice as they call out to him and knows then. He knows who it is that is here in his house with him, trying to scare him, prowling around. Trespassing.

'Fucking creep, Rosey. You're a fucking creepy old bastard.' Dane Bowron hurls himself down the stairs and out of the door, slamming it shut, rattling the frame, shaking the windows.

Dominic chases after him, his feet thundering down the stairs before he follows the boy out into the night, stumbling and hurtling through the trees, squinting ahead, knowing that this is a futile chase. The boy is younger, fitter, leaner. He will easily outrun Dominic's ageing body.

Slowing down to catch his breath, he catches sight of the lad as his silhouette pelts into the woods. He's alone. No sidekick tonight. A small amount of relief blooms within Dominic's chest as Dane weaves through the trees before disappearing out of sight. Alexander needs to distance himself from this boy. He's trouble. His father was trouble and he is following the same route, too like his father to ever think for himself and carve out a more positive life trajectory.

His mind already geared to tightening the security around the house, Dominic makes his way home. He locks the door after himself and drops into the chair with a heavy sigh.

23

Alex turned Dane down and now it's not sitting well with him. What if his friend suddenly takes offence? What if he throws a hissy fit at Alex's reluctance to go along with his plan and refuses to speak to him? Dane is a moody one, his face set in a permanent scowl, always on the cusp of tipping over into a fit of pique.

It's just that Alex thinks they've done enough to old Dominic Rose. They have hung around his house making nuisances of themselves and scared the old guy senseless and Alex doesn't fancy doing it again. Dane was insistent he go along and, in the end, Alex used his dad as an excuse, telling Dane he had promised to go fishing with him. Neither he nor his dad have fished for years and years but it was the first thing that came into his mind and now he'll have to think of something to say when Dane asks him about it this morning.

Alex finishes his juice, throws his satchel over his shoulder and heads for the door. 'I'm off. See you later.'

His dad has already left for work. Joss is upstairs doing her hair or her nails or something to preen herself, and his mother is still in bed, dead to the world, bitter and hungover. *What she needs,* he thinks idly as he winds his way down the path and out onto the pavement, *is a job.* Something that will give her a purpose, a reason to get up and face the world every morning. He thinks of speaking to his dad about it, how he could phrase it to cause the least amount of upset and offence. Somebody has to do something. His father and Joss are trapped in a web of apathy and denial. It's easier to do nothing that be proactive, he knows that, but doing nothing can lead to disaster.

Dane is waiting for him at the school gates, a cheesy grin plastered on his face. His eyes are black and full of something that Alex can never quite put his finger on, something questionable and suspicious, but his smile is a mile wide, a rarity for the lad, who is normally full of solemnity and malevolence. Alex just thanks his lucky stars that the resentment that constantly swills deep in the pit of Dane's abdomen isn't directed at him.

'You missed it all last night, mate,' Dane says, his voice a hoarse whisper as they fall into line and head down the path towards the large school yard where a gathering of teenage boys stand, kicking at stones and elbowing one other, their guffaws rumbling around the sprawl of asphalt. 'I did it. I actually fucking did it!'

Alex stares at his friend. He can see that Dane is bristling with excitement. Alex wants to ask. He doesn't want to ask. It doesn't matter. Dane will tell him anyway. Alex's absence made no difference and any fears he had over being castigated for not going along were completely unnecessary.

'I got into his house! I sneaked past him and got inside his ramshackle old place. Christ, what a bloody dump.'

Alex's guts tighten. At least he wasn't part of it this time. At least he was at home. What the hell was Dane thinking, going inside Mr Rose's house? Hanging around outside is one thing. This is trespassing. A whole new level of stupid. 'His house?' The incredulity he tries to keep out of his voice creeps in. He clears his throat, attempts to dampen his dismay, keep his tone sober and even. Easier that way. Safer. Alex stares down at the ground, kicks at a stone and shoves his hands deep in his pockets, his stance conveying borderline boredom while his insides shift and squirm.

'Yeah. Man, it was awesome. I even managed to sneak upstairs. Got a peek in one of the bedrooms. The place stank of piss. I reeked of it all night when I got back home.' Dane glances at Alex for a second before dipping his head and looking away into the distance. 'You missed a cracking night. How'd the fishing trip go?'

'Yeah, not bad.' Alex's blood rushes up to his neck, settling in his face. He's a rotten liar. Always has been. That's the problem with spinning a yarn; it inevitably comes back to bite you when you least expect it. More lies are then needed, more and more heaped on top of those already told until in the end, it becomes impossible to continue, the complications of said yarn too difficult to remember. 'What you up to tonight?' He is saying anything at all now to cover his embarrassment, to move the topic of conversation along, steering it away from his non-existent fishing expedition.

'Nothing much. Why – you fancy doing something?'

Alex wants to bite off his own tongue. He was just making conversation and now he thinks that he's going to be forced into going back to Mr Rose's house when it's the last thing he wants to do. Last time was a bit of fun, a way of blowing off a bit of steam. He doesn't want to do it again. 'Not sure, really. Was just asking.'

They walk in silence towards the main doors that lead into the large assembly hall.

'I think my old man's having another of his flings.'

Alex's skin burns at Dane's words, at the casual way he hangs out his dirty laundry as if what his dad gets up to is normal family behaviour. Alex can't imagine his dad ever having an affair. He can't imagine his parents ever being young and enamoured with each other, come to that. Stiff and formal would be how he would describe his mother and father and yet here Dane is, talking about it with breath-taking ease and simplicity, as if they are chatting about lessons or the weather or the price of fucking bread.

'Right,' Alex mumbles, unsure how to respond to this latest piece of news. Unsure why Dane even told him. He has enough to deal with at home with his own family issues. The last thing he is about to do is start oversharing personal problems, telling Dane that his mother is a miserable alcoholic because they don't have the money they once had.

'It'll come to an end,' Dane replies nonchalantly as they pass a group of giggling girls in the corridor. 'They always do. It's what he does. One woman once tried to get him to leave Mum and move in with her. He told her to piss off and broke it off with her.'

Alex feels his heart speed up as Dane talks openly and readily about things that, in Alex's family, would remain deeply private. 'Doesn't your mum mind about, you know – all of this?' He clears his throat, discomfited by this unexpected revelation. It's an alien experience, listening to this sort of talk. He thinks of Dane's mum, her nervous smile and disposition, and feels a small amount of pity for her swell in his chest. Dane's dad is a loud, formidable man. He and Dane's mother are polar opposites. He hopes she is okay.

But then, Alex doesn't know the full story. Maybe Dane's mum is a different person behind closed doors. As his dad is so keen on telling him, there is always two sides to every story. He wonders about the story behind his own parents' troubles and who is right and who is wrong and whether the lines are so blurred and tangled that it's impossible to tease them apart. He wants to remain loyal to his mum but she doesn't make it easy. It's as if she wants her own family to turn against her.

Dane shrugs listlessly, as if moving his shoulders is too much effort. He juts out his bottom lip and gazes ahead. 'Dunno. Doesn't seem to. Hard to tell. S'pose it's between the two of them to work it out, isn't it? Nothing to do with me, really.'

Alex thinks that perhaps Dane is glossing over things, ignoring what could possibly be an impending family disaster but doesn't push it any further. It's none of his business. He's not going to poke his nose into anybody else's crumbling home life. 'Yeah,' Alex says quietly. 'Suppose so.'

They go off to their different classes, Dane's solitary figure soon swallowed up by a moving throng of youngsters who fill the narrow corridors within seconds of the bell sounding.

They meet later in the morning as they are making their way towards the English classroom, Dane's face set in a scowl. Alex doesn't ask him what the problem is. There's no need. He already knows what his friend's thoughts are regarding Mr Rose.

'Fucking hate this lesson. Longest hour of my life every time I come in this shithole of a class.' Dane's voice is a bark, his eyes once again dark pools of hatred as he finds his chair and slumps down into it, his body languid, apathy and animosity oozing out of him.

Alex doesn't reply, slipping instead into his own seat in the row opposite Dane, his desk set slightly behind his friend. He pulls out his text book from his bag and stares ahead, waiting for the initial furore to simmer down. He likes it in here. Despite Dane's inescapable hostility that is directed towards Mr Rose, Alex enjoys English. His mind is geared up for each lesson, ready to absorb each word, to ruminate over the workings of language and how it can be used to demonstrate a range of emotions from festering malice and malevolence to passion and love, and everything in between.

The hour passes quickly, Alex too engrossed in the nuances of J B Priestley's characters to notice Dane's body language and whether or not he engaged with the lesson.

It's as they're leaving that Mr Rose nods to Dane to indicate that he needs a word. Stepping to one side, Dane waits behind while everyone else files out, the rest of the class too busy to notice that he has been singled out.

Alex waits behind, hoping to team up with his friend and offer some moral support but feels himself guided out by the surprisingly strong hand of Dominic Rose. He is propelled forwards and the door pushed closed behind him. Through the glass pane, he watches as Dane is asked to sit, Mr Rose also lowering himself into a chair opposite and staring at him with a steely look of determination in his eyes. Alex swallows and waits.

24

Dominic thanks God for glass inserts in classroom doors. Dane Bowron is the kind of kid who would think nothing of making a false allegation, claiming Dominic abused him in some way. He has given this boy so many chances but last night's intrusion was a step too far. This type of behaviour has to be stopped one way or another. He simply cannot allow this boy to get the better of him. Bowron is the son of a man who would gladly see Dominic rot amidst the ruins of a fabricated accusation that would tear his life apart. Now is the time to step up to the plate and show them he isn't about to be bullied by a youngster who can barely string a sentence together. He's better than this. He's better than the Bowrons. No more the victim. Those times are behind him, starting from today.

'Do you have anything to say to me, Dane?' He has thought long and hard on how to approach this, running through various scenarios in his head late into the night and again on his way to work this morning. He concluded that there is no easy way to have this conversation aside from letting the boy take the lead and allowing him to become trapped in his own web of lies. Dominic will let him speak, will allow him the sensation of being in control rather than cornering him, and then he will make his move and strike. Boys like Dane don't take well to figures of authority barking commands at them. He needs to tread carefully.

Dominic observes the lad slumped before him, assessing his body language: the slight twitch of his jaw, the dipped eyes, the heavy breathing. They are all indicators that he is stressed, desperately trying to think of a way out of this situation. He could lie, deny that it was him in Dominic's house last night – but they both know that his friend Alex will immediately capitulate if questioned, admitting that they have been hanging around Dominic's property and trespassing on his land, thinking of different ways to annoy and scare him. This boy has a history of loutish behaviour and isn't eloquent enough to defend himself when placed under pressure.

Dane shrugs and twists his body away, his chin tucked neatly on his chest.

'I think you would be better speaking now when there is just the two of us, rather than waiting, don't you? Ask yourself this: do you really want your head of year, your form tutor and the head teacher present to hear what it is you've got to say? Or would you rather we sorted this now, just you and me? I know which I would prefer if I were in your position.'

Dominic tries to stem his erratic breathing, to slow down the bursts of air that are firing out of his lungs in rapid succession. He can do this. He just needs to *appear* controlled even if he doesn't necessarily feel it. Why does this boy have such a hold over him? The Bowron family have been the bane of his life for so many years now and it's time to put a stop to it. All he wants to do is educate this boy and yet it seems that he and his father are doing everything they can to put barriers in the way.

He has no idea how these people think and has no desire to find out, to climb inside their heads and discover what drives them. They are worlds away from his own ethics and beliefs but even knowing the chasm between them, he is willing to give this lad the chance to own up. Even now, after what the boy has done, he is going easy on him, giving him the breathing space that many others wouldn't especially after he entered Dominic's home uninvited, rampaging through the house, even having the audacity to peer into his mother's bedroom. It's appalling behaviour. Completely unacceptable.

'Sorry.' The word is a low mumble, a scratch in the emptiness around them but it's definitely there. Dominic isn't mistaken. Dane Bowron has just admitted his guilt and apologised.

A streak of air passes over Dominic's skin, cool and comforting. He pulls at his collar and tries to appear nonplussed at this unexpected response. He was prepared for surliness or silence, even the odd swear word. He wasn't prepared for this.

'Okay,' he replies softly, his heart hammering out a dull, thudding sensation beneath his layers of clothing. 'That's a good start. I accept your apology on the condition it will never happen again. Do you understand?'

Dane shrugs, his usual indifference still apparent as he slumps farther down into the chair. Even now the boy still can't quite bring himself to yield completely. Still the defence mechanism is present, a solid wall between them, keeping them apart.

'I'm sorry? I didn't quite catch that.' Dominic waits, the atmosphere charged with expectancy, fear and anticipation heating his blood.

'Yeah, okay. Whatever you say.' Another shrug. More shifting and twisting in his seat. That dark-eyed look from under a furrowed brow.

'My mother is a frail old lady. You could have hurt her.' Dominic wants to bite off his own tongue. That last bit of information wasn't necessary. He was winning. There was no need to say anything, no need at all. The less this boy knows about his private life, the better. He's a pupil and a healthy distance should be maintained at all times.

Dane doesn't reply. His body remains in the same position, his legs jutting out in front of him. Dominic isn't even sure the kid is listening anyway.

'So, I won't be seeing you or your friend anywhere near my house ever again?' He waits for a reply, angling his head down to try and catch a glimpse of the lad's reaction to his question.

'S'pose not.'

The steady tick of the wall clock and the occasional grunt from the teenager sitting opposite boom in his head. At what point does he accept that the boy is going to stick to his promise and allow him to leave? He has to do something to cement this moment in this youngster's head, to make him ever so slightly fearful of further repercussions should he decide to go back on his word.

Dominic's chair scrapes over the floor tiles. His skin puckers at the sound of metal against plastic. He shuffles forward some more and lowers his voice a fraction, an inflection in his tone that's just enough to convey his simmering anger at having Dane enter his home. 'Do it again, and I'll hurt you. I'm not talking a slap here. I'm thinking a big bullet straight between your eyes. Do you get it now, Dane Bowron? Do you?'

The teenager looks up, startled, shock creasing his face, those dark, unforgiving eyes stripped of their perpetual, simmering fury, replaced now by panic and a creeping look of distress.

'And of course, what I've just said never happened. You and I have spoken in a civil manner about your behaviour and what is expected of you when you are in my classroom. Just so we both understand one another, yes?'

No reply. Nothing.

Dominic tries again. 'Yes?' Firmer this time, harsher. Not loud. Authoritative. Imposing.

It works. Dane nods, his face colouring up, a flash of crimson spreading over his sallow skin. The web creeps across his throat, resting there. A glowing spread of humiliation that warms Dominic's heart. He is willing to bet that this lad has spent his whole life being pandered to, getting exactly what he wants and never knowing the pain and indignity of being spoken to in such a manner or being denied anything he desires. This will be a new experience for him, being put in his place and told that for once, life isn't going to go his way. He had better get used to it because Dominic isn't willing to relent. His home is his sanctuary and nobody, especially this young offender that is slumped in front of him, is going to get close to it ever again.

A warm sensation shifts across Dominic's belly, an unfurling spread of heat that inches and edges its way around his body, settling deep in his bones. It's a pleasant feeling, exerting his authority, being a dominant force and showing this young slip of a lad that he is the one who is in charge around here.

'Get up. And remember what I said: if I see you again near my house, you'll know about it.'

Dane jumps up as if burnt. He spins around, unable to orient himself to his surroundings.

'Right, young man,' Dominic says lightly, striding towards the door and opening it wide, 'as I was saying, your work is definitely improving. You just need to give that extra 10 per cent and you're on course for some half decent exam results at the end of the year. Well done. Good to see you putting in that extra bit of effort. I'll be sure to pass this great bit of news on to your form tutor. And your parents, of course. I'm sure your mum will be delighted to hear from me.'

Dane staggers out of the door and into the corridor where his friend Alex is still waiting. Alexander Winston-D'Allandrio. A pupil Dominic thought he knew. He was so sure he had that one all worked out. How wrong he was. Alex is just another jumped-up little shit who cares only about himself. They're all the same, these kids. Selfish, thoughtless, arrogant bastards, every last one of them.

'And well done to you, Alexander. You gave some sterling answers today. Keep it up.' He nods at the awkward-looking youngster and gives him a half smile. Alex returns the gesture, his eyes twinkling with delight at the unexpected bit of praise that is being thrown his way.

'Thanks, sir. It was a really good lesson. I like *An Inspector Calls*. One of my favourite texts.'

Dominic leans against the doorframe as the two lads saunter away, their voices echoing in the stairwell. He hears the pound of their feet as they make their way to their next lesson and heads back into his classroom, thankful that he has a free period to mark books, tidy the classroom and steady his breathing. That was easier than expected and yet adrenaline is still whistling around his system, making his head swim. He hopes that Dane takes this seriously, remembering his threat.

The odd thing is, Dominic isn't so bothered about the boy running off and telling somebody about what he has just said – he would simply deny it and with an impeccable record compared to Dane Bowron's abysmal history of surliness and rude behaviour, he knows who everyone would choose to believe – no, Dominic is more bothered by the fact that the boy will ignore his threats and continue visiting his house and terrorising him and his mother. After a day spent at the chalkface, he needs time away from this place, not be faced with that boy's presence in and around his home.

He spends the next hour marking books, planning lessons and tidying the classroom, although his efforts at smartening up the place seem to have little effect. With blinds that are hanging by a thread and windows that haven't been washed for as long as he can remember, the room has all the appeal of a prison cell. He makes a mental note to approach Pat, the deputy head, to ask for some new blinds and to enquire after the services of a half-decent cleaner who can get rid of the grime that covers the glass. The pupils in this school deserve better. *He* deserves better. He has given over forty years of his working life to this school and it's about time they recognised that fact. Making this a pleasant environment in which to learn is the least they can do. He's not asking for anything palatial: just surroundings that are clean and comfortable.

By the time lunchtime comes around, he feels fired up, brimming with energy and ambition. It's been a good morning – eventful and successful. He pushes his papers into his briefcase and makes his way downstairs.

* * *

'It's a school, Dominic, not a hotel. Kids are here to learn. They don't come for a spa day at a luxury resort.' Pat Miller, the deputy head, is sitting behind her desk, a small pot of yoghurt set in front of her. To her right sits a framed photograph of her family. Behind her is a large picture window affording her a grime-free view of the hills in the distance.

Dominic makes a point of staring at it then averting his eyes back to hers.

She sits ramrod straight, her long, manicured nails spread out on the wooden surface but has the good grace to lower her gaze, a small look of embarrassment obvious in her features. 'Look, I'll see what I can do. My office, as you know, also doubles up as a meeting room for governors and visitors. When I'm not in here, I also teach in a room like yours. Money is tight. Our budget has been slashed. As I said, I'll speak to the bursar and see what she has to say about any spare cash we might have.'

'I would be very grateful for that, if it's not too much trouble. I'm sure you'll agree that a decent learning environment makes all the difference.' He wants to say more, to remind her that she teaches for just five hours a week, the rest of which she spends in here, in this spacious, impeccably clean and beautifully furnished room that gets dusted and polished every single day, whether it needs it or not. Her flushed face and inability to look him directly in the eye say more than words ever could.

Dominic turns to leave, resentment bubbling through his veins, suppressed anger leaving a sour taste in his mouth.

Making sure he closes the door with just enough force to let Pat know what he thinks of her office and her privilege and her lack of commitment to the pupils of this school, not to mention the staff, he shuffles along the corridor, his stomach slowly sinking to his boots, his feelings of earlier buoyancy abandoning him, then does something he never ever thought he would consider and heads out to the car park, his latent anger building, burning and scorching him, an unstoppable furnace flickering and combusting deep within him. He opens the boot of his vehicle and stares inside at the bag that has been lying there since last week. The one he forgot to remove. He picks it up, slings it over his shoulder and heads back into his classroom.

25

Things have turned sour. And Nina is the one who has soured them. She has done this. Nobody else. Just her. She could have just let things be, waited for this affair to burn itself out. Just like the others. But she hasn't. She has taken decisive action and is now questioning her decision. Maybe she should have let things be. Or maybe this course of action is long overdue.

She sits with her hands tucked between her knees to stop them from trembling. This is the first time she has ever done anything like this and hopes it will be the last. Temptation got the better of her and now she is sitting in her car, watching for signs of her husband through the small windows of the pub. He's here. She knows he is here because she followed him, keeping two cars behind, making sure she kept herself tucked in and out of sight. Rob isn't one for watching others anyway. He's too wrapped up in himself to notice anybody else. For once, his selfishness has served her well.

She turns off the radio, savouring the silence. Before he left, Rob's voice had bellowed through the house, complaining that there wasn't enough food in the cupboards. 'What the fuck do you do with yourself all day, Nina?' he had bawled, his voice like the cry of a spoilt child who has been denied sweeties.

She didn't reply and instead salted herself away in the bedroom, myriad thoughts whirling around in her brain. A million ways of killing him kept her entertained until she decided that following him would be easier and far less painful for both of them. Spending the rest of her life in prison terrified her, although it flashed into her mind that such an existence would not be too dissimilar to the life she is currently living.

He had showered and got ready, the odour of his pungent, cheap-smelling aftershave filling the house. At over £100 a bottle, Nina thought it should at least smell a little less noxious, perhaps containing traces of an appealing, musky aroma but instead, Rob left the house smelling like a crusty old sock and now here she is, sitting in her car, wondering what he is up to in there, visualising who he is with. Is she younger? Blonde or brunette? How big are her tits? Because Rob is shallow enough to be attracted to the obvious bimbo, somebody who will satisfy his immediate needs and massage his ego, making him feel like the big man that he isn't. He will have dropped hints about how rich he is, how big his house is, how successful his business is. That's what drives him. Money makes him amorous – it's his aphrodisiac. Without it, he is nothing.

She is here out of curiosity more than anything else. Although the thought of leaving Rob and starting out again on her own terrifies her, she knows now for sure that she feels no love for the man. She will stay for Dane, not for Rob. They are very different people. He has his life and she – well, she would like to say that she too has her own life, but that would be a complete lie. She exists. No more, no less. Apart from Sally, she has nobody. No life worth speaking of. Her parents have both passed away which in itself is a blessing. They didn't live long enough to see their predictions about her doomed marriage come to fruition. She also has the house. *The house.* The big, glossy, ostentatious building that is her home, but even that, with all its modern gadgets and top-of-the-range comforts, is something that is designed to trap her and keep her in place to serve Rob and Dane. It's not a home – certainly not *her* home. Homes are places full of love and warmth.

Last week, when she was in town, her eyes had been drawn to the high-rise maisonettes towering over the main shopping precinct, homes that fill many local people with horror at the thought of living there. She had stopped, her breath trapped in her chest as she realised that moving into one of those poky, damp flats was more appealing than going back to her soulless house and loveless family.

A flicker of movement draws her eye back to the pub. Next to the entrance, she sees a woman, dark haired and slim. She slides out of a car, this woman, this confident-looking woman, decked out in high heels and a red, tight-fitting dress with a matching bolero jacket. Nina's heart leaps. She knows instinctively that she is the one. It's her. She can sense it – Rob's latest squeeze. The most recent notch on his bedpost.

Nina leans forward, squinting to get a better view, willing this vixen-like creature to turn her way. As if prompted, the woman spins around, her chin raised, eyes narrowed. She glances around the car park, scanning the immediate area, clearly looking for somebody and at that very same moment, Nina's heart misses a beat.

She claps a hand over her mouth. Her teeth chatter, her tongue feels too big for her mouth. This is a mistake. She's got it wrong. This isn't her husband's latest fling. It can't be. It's all a horrible coincidence. Nina is tempted to get out of her own vehicle and move alongside to say hello. Were it not for the fact that right now, Rob could be sitting inside watching, she would do just that, just to settle her mind, to tell herself that Kate Winston-D'Allandrio isn't the woman who is having an affair with her husband.

Sliding further down into her seat, Nina tries and fails to stem the sickly feeling building in her gut. She watches as Kate checks herself in her compact mirror, adjusts her hair and reapplies her lipstick before heading towards the entrance.

And then Nina's world tilts on its axis as he appears, framed in the doorway like a huge spectre. Rob. Her husband. His movements are swift and steady. He steps outside, slips his arm around Kate's waist and guides her inside.

The sound of Nina's blood pounding through her ears is deafening, an ocean of it bashing against her bones, tearing through her veins. Throwing open the car door, she vomits onto the tarmac. This can't be happening. It just can't. *This* she didn't expect. This she wasn't prepared for. Tears blind her as she wipes at her mouth and slams the door closed, leaning back into the headrest, gulping in air.

A couple of seconds pass, minutes perhaps. It's too difficult to tell, her thoughts tangled, her logic and lucidity in freefall.

She pushes the keys into the ignition and starts the engine with thick, clumsy fingers. The pedals beneath her feet feel light and airy, her feet too heavy and lacking the dexterity to drive properly.

She expected a young blonde, somebody attractive and predictable and completely forgettable. She didn't expect this. Kate Winston-D'Allandrio, the woman who has been to their house to drop off and collect Alexander, the smart and polite young man Dane has teamed up with. Nina secretly hoped that the pairing would have a positive effect on her son and drag him out of his permanent state of angst and misery. But that hasn't happened. Instead, their families have become entwined in the worst possible way. An intimate and unforgiveable way.

Fury pulses through her. It didn't take Rob and Kate long to hook up together. There must have been an attraction from the very beginning. Rob has had affairs in the past but never this close to home. It's always been some impressionable young airhead, somebody he met in the pub, someone he could use and dispose of without too much trouble, but this – this is in a whole new league. He has outdone himself this time, tearing up all the usual rules, scattering them far and wide and trampling over her feelings in the process.

She swings the car out onto the main road, tears blurring her vision. Her mind is empty, her soul crushed. She has no idea what to do next, how to react to this latest discovery. Her husband is sleeping with their son's best friend's mother. Nina slams her hands against the steering wheel and lets out a deep, throaty growl. 'For fuck's sake, Rob! What the actual fuck do you think you're doing?'

The journey home is a blur, her reflexes taking over as she steers the car through busy traffic, her thoughts a miasma of hurt, anger and confusion.

What if she were to just pack her bags and leave? Would the two men in her life beg her to rethink her decision, to come back home, or would they cheer, hoping she never returns? She wishes she knew them better. They are strangers, their thinking on a different wavelength to hers. Rob and

Dane are two peas in a pod. She is the outsider here. The outlier. Would they even miss her if she left? They would miss the meals she provides for them and the level of cleanliness in which they live, but they wouldn't actually miss *her*. Two family members and a marginalised woman all living together under the same roof, that's what they are. She co-exists with her husband and son. Does she love them? A mother will always love her child no matter what. Even when Dane is being downright rude to her, she still loves him. There are days when she doesn't like him, but she is hardwired to always be there for him, to give of her best to her child despite his constant rebuffs and sarcastic comments and insults. She has had to grow a second skin, to be impervious to his moods and temper.

Does she still love Rob? That particular question gives her pause for thought. She loves the *idea* of him. She loves the thought of not being alone and having to struggle through life on her own but as for the actual man – no, she definitely no longer loves him and finds herself wondering if she ever did. She is here for Dane, that's all. Once he is up and doing his own thing, she will leave. Rob's latest affair has sealed his fate and put an end to their marriage. Two more years. She will give it two more years, and in the meantime, she will start to prepare, to squirrel away money and look around at available affordable properties. She doesn't care where she lives, as long as it's not with him, the man who has emotionally abused her for as long as she can remember. The thought of facing him after tonight's discovery, having to sleep next to him every night, makes her skin ripple with dread and revulsion. It's going to be a long couple of years.

The thought crosses her mind that she should confront him about this latest dalliance as she pulls up on the driveway, locks up her car and enters the house. Why should he get away with it? After Kate, there will be another and then another and then another – a long stream of women that will fill the void in her husband's life while she sits at home alone.

Rage ignites inside her. What sort of woman is she that she has allowed her husband to get away with such despicable behaviour? Theirs isn't an open, swinging marriage where anything goes. That isn't why she got wed. She married Rob because she truly believed in love and a lasting partnership and family. She didn't bargain for this. It's about time she confronted him and what better time to do it than now, when he is fucking the mother of his son's best friend?

'Hiya. Where've you been?' Dane is standing in front of her, a small amount of concern etched into his features as she kicks off her shoes and pushes her feet into her slippers.

She stares down at them – pink, fluffy, childlike things. So silly. Inappropriate and unnecessary. She kicks them off and they slide under a nearby cabinet out of view. 'I just fancied a drive to clear my head.' Her keys rattle as she throws them onto the console table and moves away from him. She isn't in the mood for dealing with any of his nonsense either. Not tonight. She has had a gutful of being trodden upon and taken for granted.

Behind her, she can hear the shuffle of her son's feet as he follows her into the kitchen. Apprehension builds in her chest. Not now. She hasn't the energy for his moods or his barbed remarks. If it's an argument he's after, he can go elsewhere to pick a fight. She is bone tired. Too exhausted for quarrels and disagreements. Too exhausted for anything.

'D'you want a cup of tea?'

Her flesh prickles. Something is wrong. Dane doesn't make tea. Dane doesn't initiate conversation other than to fire a volley of insults her way.

She nods and gives him a half smile, unable to commit fully to engaging with her own child. Such a shameful thing to think. Something needs to change.

He fills the kettle and prepares the cups as she sits down at the table, her legs suddenly weak, her bones dead weights. It's exhausting being permanently anxious and on edge, worried where the next insult is coming from. She feels sure she could sleep for a hundred years and still wake up weary.

The clatter of crockery and the low hiss of the kettle allow her to drift off into her own thoughts, a world of her own making where none of this is happening. She visualises a life where she and Rob are happily married and very much in love, a life where Dane is settled and chirpy, is doing well at school and has so much to look forward to. Such families exist, it's just that hers isn't one of them. They are a fractured household, their cracks glossed over with money and status and everything many other less well-off families could only ever dream of having. Money isn't everything. In their case, it is nothing at all. She would sacrifice this big house and their many cars for just one ounce of love and tenderness.

'Mr Rose said I was working well at school today. Said if I keep it up, I might get some half-decent exam results after all.' Her tea is handed to her, Dane attempting a smile as he passes it over.

She is lost for words. She wants to laugh, to ask if aliens have kidnapped her son and replaced him with this person, but instead smiles, tells him that this is great news. Nina daren't hope that Dane is at long last emerging out of his decade-long bout of petulance and fury. She won't pin her hopes on such a thing, but clings onto this moment, treasuring her son's softer side, the side she sees rarely. That letter from school getting home has obviously worked. Dane is starting to take his education seriously. And not before time.

They sit together in companionable silence, each locked in their own thoughts, until he speaks again, this time his disclosure cutting her to the quick. 'I also got into a bit of trouble.'

Her flesh flashes hot and cold. She should have known this was coming – the tea, the easy conversation. It was all a ruse. A breath is suspended in her diaphragm, trapped in place as she waits for him to speak again. This is bad. She can sense it. That's what it's all about – his softness, his gentler approach – he was breaking her in. Preparing her.

A bit of trouble.

It could mean anything. She bites at the inside of her mouth, braces herself.

'I was messing about near Mr Rose's house last night and slipped inside. I didn't do no damage or nothing. It was just a bit of a laugh. I saw his mother asleep in bed upstairs then ran out.' His eyes are lowered, his voice bordering on remorseful. Or could it be a fear of having crossed a line that could result in untold trouble landing right at his feet?

Nina swallows and tries to still her thrashing heart, taking small, regular breaths and gripping onto the edge of the chair for stability. 'So, I'm guessing Mr Rose spoke to you about it today? Did he mention calling the police for trespassing?' She has to be careful here. Her son has opened up to her: a rare occurrence. She doesn't want to tip the balance and push him away by being too domineering, or scare him into silence. This is a defining moment.

'Yeah, he gave me a warning. Said his mother is really ill and stuff.' He fiddles with his sleeve, pulling at a piece of loose thread with semi-dextrous fingers.

Nina sees his hands and notices how grimy his nails are, an arc of dirt embedded under each one. The hands of a child. She lets out a sigh and tries to remove herself from the emotional tug of this situation. He is still so young, so deeply juvenile, yet to develop into a fully grown man. Will he ever mature and think of others? How did she ever produce somebody who goes his own sweet way with no thought of how his actions affect other people? She sighs. Perhaps she is being too hard on him. Just look at the things other young lads get up to – shoplifting, fighting, bullying – Dane's misdemeanours pale into insignificance compared to some of the other local teenagers. It could be a whole lot worse.

They sit once more in silence. She reaches across and briefly touches his hand. This is a step forward. She has to see that. He opened up to her. They had a civil discussion without any shouting or name calling. Whether she likes it or not, this moment they are sharing, despite it being tinged with apprehension and a small amount of concern, is a positive thing.

Nina stands up and breaks the quiet with no desire to further their discussion. She doesn't want to spoil the moment, wanting to leave on a positive note. 'I think I'm going to go and have a bath.'

Dane nods, gathers up the cups and puts them in the dishwasher, something else he has never done before. Hope unfurls in her abdomen, tiny tendrils of optimism reaching out and spreading through her, small, green shoots springing to life.

She takes the stairs two at a time, a warmth she hasn't felt for as long as she can remember spreading over her skin. Has he finally returned to her? After all this time, has her little boy finally emerged back into the light? Despite his awful confession about what he has done, she hopes that her boy is trying to forge some sort of connection. He did something wrong and came to her to speak about it, unburdening himself and admitting his guilt. That has to count for something, doesn't it?

She closes and locks the bathroom door behind her, allowing herself a small, expectant smile at what may lie ahead. If she can get Dane on her side, then perhaps she can take the next step and confront Rob. It's a possibility. She has no idea what else to do. Her life is currently collapsing around her. She can either sit and watch it happen or take pre-emptive action and limit the damage.

The bath is hot, scalding her skin as she steps into it and lies back, the burning sensation a welcome reminder that she is still alive, is still able to feel something apart from sadness and hopelessness that for so long now has dominated her life.

She closes her eyes and imagines Rob far away, living another life. She imagines that soon she will be free.

26

He should distance himself. That's what his brain is telling him, but his heart is saying that Dane is his main friend and to shake him off now would be like losing a limb. Dane actually trespassed inside Mr Rose's house. He could get permanently excluded for it. It's really serious stuff.

Alex slumps onto his bed and stares up at the ceiling. He doesn't believe all that shit about Dane being kept back in class so Mr Rose could congratulate him on working hard in lessons. It was a bit of subterfuge. They obviously spoke about him entering Mr Rose's house last night. Dane does nothing in lessons except stare down at the floor and flick pieces of saliva-soaked paper at the back of girls' heads. The last thing Mr Rose would do is congratulate him and tell him he's heading for a clear pass in his exams.

It's stupid really, as his friend is a bright lad but he's prepared to give up the chance of getting any decent exam results so he can go and work on a building site with his dad. As much as Alex loves and admires his own dad, he wouldn't want to work alongside him day after day. And as for being on a building site in the middle of winter – Alex couldn't think of anything worse. It might appeal to some, but it's not how he would want to spend his life.

He doesn't tell anybody at school what he wants to do once he leaves school, what his ambitions are. It would leave him open to ridicule. What he really dreams of doing is working as a scientist, possibly an epidemiologist. He isn't dead set on that particular branch as yet but he does know that that science is the thing he wants to study. Saying this sort of stuff in the school he currently attends would make him a laughing stock, especially where Dane is concerned, so he keeps his mouth shut and his head down and just gets on with his work. That's his route to survival and success. It's how he makes it through each and every day.

Beside him, the glare of the clock catches his eye, glinting in his peripheral vision. 11.30 p.m. His parents have finally stopped arguing. His mum came in shortly after 10.30 p.m. and it started almost immediately: the hissed accusations, the relentless questions about where she had been, her barked replies telling his dad to shut up and leave her alone.

They thought that both him and Joss were asleep, even peeking around the door at one point to check before shutting it behind them and continuing with their tirade.

Alex wonders if his mum is capable of having an affair. Maybe that's where she's been. He can't imagine it. She's so aloof and frosty, it seems impossible that she could ever succumb to anybody at all. As much as he hates this atmosphere, he doesn't want his parents to split. He wants them to grow up, get their heads together and work things out. They're adults. It's what adults are supposed to do – they evaluate and assess situations and try to make them better for everyone concerned.

His mother isn't a bad person, just upset and lonely. He wonders if she is planning on leaving them all for somebody with more wealth and glamour. It means a lot to her, the status that money brings, but does it mean more to her than her own family? Alex hopes not. He hopes she comes to her senses and realises that cash isn't the be-all and end-all, that they have a comfortable life here – better than most. He hopes that she realises that her family would miss her if she left.

He is surprised to find that tears are stinging the back of his eyes. Crying has never been his thing. He usually has a good handle on his emotions but just lately, events seem to be spinning out of control and there is little he can do to stop it.

Did Joss hear the rowing? He thinks not but also thinks that even if she did, it would wash over her, leaving no mark. She is oblivious to their parents' disintegrating marriage, oblivious to what direction their lives could take if either of them were to leave. It's about time his sister woke up to the world around her instead of being so wrapped up in her own life, cocooned in her own little bubble of happiness.

Alex closes his eyes and tries to switch off but his mind refuses to shut down. He thinks of Dane and how he got inside Mr Rose's house. He thinks of his mother and what would happen if she left them. He thinks of Joss and her selfish behaviour and then thinks of his dad and how they would all cope if anything really bad happened to their family.

He finally succumbs to exhaustion, slipping into a fitful sleep where nightmares fill his head: visions of Dane being arrested; images of his dad trying to strangle his mother; the sensation of falling into a deep, dark void, his body plummeting and gathering speed as he travels through the inky blackness, waiting to hit the bottom – until he wakes, perspiration coating his skin, his heart a rapid thump under his ribcage.

His eyes are gritty, his back a solid ache. He checks the clock, climbs out of bed and steps into the shower where the hot water rushes over him soothing his sore limbs. At least it's Saturday. He can spend it doing whatever he likes. No Dane, no trying to avoid the obvious troublemakers in class. Just him and his thoughts. He isn't sure if that's a good thing or not. Sometimes his mind goes into overdrive, assuming the worst is going to happen. It might be a better idea to do something productive today rather than just sit about, letting his imagination run riot.

Joss is waiting outside the bathroom as he comes out, her eyes rimmed with mascara.

'You look like a panda. Mum'll love the mess you've made on the pillowcase.'

She slaps his arm and pushes her way past. 'Shut it, swot boy and get out of my way.'

He laughs, steam still billowing off his glistening skin.

Downstairs, the phone rings. His dad's voice is a low murmur, suddenly developing into a loud, staccato din. It makes Alex's head swim. Anxiety punches at his chest. Something is wrong. His dad is unerringly polite when talking to others. He and his mum may argue but when speaking with other people, his manner is reserved and gracious. Always. But not this time. Something is happening. Something really bad. Something that is causing him to be gruff, demanding. The crescendo fills Alex's head, setting his senses alight.

Closing his bedroom door, he gets dressed, tripping over his own feet as he rushes to get down there, see what's happening. He has no idea what can do, if he will be of any use, but not knowing what is unfolding on the other end of the line is, he feels sure, worse than knowing. If he is close by, he can help, maybe calm things down. He can be there for his dad.

The phone conversation is coming to a close as Alex enters the living room. His father sits slumped, the receiver in his hand. His eyes are vacant, his skin bleached grey, as if all of his blood has suddenly emptied out of his face.

The protracted silence is interminable. An impending sense of doom threads its way through Alex's veins, filtering into his organs, anchoring him to the ground. He is heavy, cumbersome as he staggers over to where his father is sitting.

'Dad? What is it? Who was that on the phone?' His voice cracks; he coughs to clear his throat. Tries to act natural even though his innards are suddenly loose and watery.

'Hmm?' His father snaps out of his trance-like state and gives Alex a tight smile. 'It's fine, son. Nothing for you to be concerned about.'

He *is* concerned and whatever it is that has just taken place feels anything but fine. 'So who was it you were talking to on the phone, then?' Alex stands over his dad, focusing on his breathing, every rattling breath that leaves his body low and controlled. The room appears smaller somehow, nearby objects farther away. Everything is skewed, out of perspective. He grips the back of the sofa and tenses his muscles, his senses heightened to every movement, every whisper of air that passes by him.

'Oh, that? It was work. Like I said, nothing for you to worry about.'

He's lying. His dad is a terrible liar. Always has been. His voice has a slight warble to it. His skin is suddenly pale and waxy. His eyes have clouded over and he can't bring himself to look directly at Alex, staring off instead into the distance, his gaze fixed on a point somewhere over Alex's shoulder.

'Work?' He should leave it, let his dad be, but something is driving him on, making him dig for the truth. Lies multiply. They fester and grow, leading onto bigger untruths and if there is one thing Alex cannot tolerate, it is deceit. Not here in his home. They have enough to contend with as it is. Lies will only make things worse. 'It didn't sound like work. It sounded more like an argument. As if something awful has happened.'

'Look, Alex, my boy. I'm a completely worn out today so if you wouldn't mind, let's just leave this conversation until another time, eh?'

With eyes that mask nothing, his dad looks up at him and Alex's flesh creeps and rucks, squeezing tightly against his bones. 'Okay. Whatever you say, Dad. Have you had breakfast?' He wants to protect his father from whatever is going on, to let him know that he is here for him even if nobody else in this family is.

'That sounds perfect, son. Right now, a cup of coffee sounds damn near perfect.'

Alex spots it as he shuffles past – the unshed tears that his dad blinks back, the sudden mottling of his skin, the darkening of his eyes – he sees it, registers it and wishes there was more he could do to alleviate the pressure his dad is under. Being there for him, he thinks, as he fills the kettle and spoons coffee into the cups, is about as much as he can do for the man who has always been there for him. For the time being, that is. Until he knows what the issue is. Then he can step in and help.

* * *

It's bad. Really bad. The shouting downstairs is so loud, he is forced to cover his ears to drown it out.

Joss left the house a few hours ago, heading off into town with a gaggle of her girlfriends and a fistful of money given to her by their dad. She has pestered him for cash as he had sat in the living room, head dipped, skin ashen. And now Alex is left here, alone in his bedroom, sitting it out, wishing he had gone off somewhere far away from here.

It started shortly after Joss left, the almighty rowing, the hollering and screaming. The terrible accusations.

They seem to have forgotten that he is still in the house. He can hear them now, their voices filtering up through the floor, the carpet and thick rugs doing little to muffle their anger. There is no let-up. He has caught snippets, enough to know what's going on and is wishing he hadn't been present when those words were said. He can't unhear them. They are out there, those hissed accusations, that dirty revelation, the grisly details of his mum's sordid little affair. He was right all along. He had wondered if she was having a fling and he was right. With every fibre of his being, he wishes he was wrong, but knows that he isn't. Alex has heard enough to know that his mother is sleeping with another man. And not just any man – Rob Bowron.

Christ almighty. Rob frigging Bowron.

He lowers his head onto his knees and closes his eyes, squeezing them shut against the screaming and hollering that is taking place in the living room below him. It shouldn't bother him. Most teenage lads would shrug it off, consider it none of their business, get on with their lives, but he's not like most teenagers. Stuff like this affects him, eats away at him, making him think there is worse yet to come. Which there is. Separation, divorce. Everything is set in motion now. No turning back the clock.

He never thought he would ever think such a thing, but he finds himself wishing they had never moved here. If his dad had continued working at his old job, none of this would be happening. Alex opens his eyes and raises his head. Or maybe it would. Maybe his mum would have got bored of that lifestyle as well and gone out searching for something different. For some*one* different. At least it wouldn't be Dane's dad. That's the worst part of it. Another man, *any* other man would have been bad enough, but this – this is beyond the pale. Talk about shitting on your own doorstep.

He feels like marching down there and shaking some sense into his mother, shouting at her that not everything is about her and what she wants and needs, that there are four of them in this family and it's about time she sat up and took some notice, but he doesn't. Of course he doesn't. He will be his usual docile, incompetent self. Soft in the middle. Lacking the courage to do the right thing. So he sits, anger and anxiety building up in his gut, his heart thumping, his head woozy with the thousand thoughts that collide and crash in his brain.

And then there's Dane to consider. The thought of facing him on Monday fills Alex with utter dread. Does Dane even know about this latest revelation, and what type of reaction will it provoke in him if he does? Anger, resentment, embarrassment. That's just for starters. Life will become unbearable for the both of them, their friendship on the cusp of fragmenting. All because their parents couldn't be bothered thinking outside of their own selfish needs.

Alex lies back on his bed, consumed with so many emotions that it is impossible to pick them apart. A great, big mash-up of hurt, anger, hatred and humiliation. Why is his mum so fucking selfish? They could all be having a nice, easy life here but now she's ruined everything. The one friend he had has been inadvertently dragged into Alex's family crisis and now he has no idea what the future holds for any of them. Everything is one big, fucking, awful mess.

At this moment, he hates his mother – really hates her, the sensation gripping him. It's an overwhelming feeling that he can't shake. It twists its way under his skin, digging deep into his chest, nestling in the warmth of his beating heart where it waits, biding its time. A killer waiting to strike. There's no easy way out of this situation now, no way to undo the damage that she has done. Everything is in tatters, their lives in ruins and he has no idea how to get any of it back.

27

Nina replaces the handset. She didn't know what else to do. She can't even remember dialling the number and was shocked into action when she heard the voice at the other end, asking who she was and demanding to know what she wanted. Another part of her took over. A part she didn't know existed. It feels good to know she still has some fight left in her, that somewhere hidden deep within herself, she still possesses enough courage and resolve to confront her problems.

Her nails break and split as she nibbles at them. Perhaps she did the wrong thing making that call, but it doesn't matter anymore because she has done it now. Too late for regrets. Her kickback is long overdue.

Last night, she confronted Rob about what she had witnessed and he turned it around, telling her she was going mad and that she needed to get out more, that she was turning into a lonely, bored housewife who had no friends and was borderline frigid and even if he was having another affair, was it any wonder living with her and her constant refusals of his sexual advances.

She had gone cold at his words, and after he left the house early this morning to visit some building site or other – or maybe even the woman herself, Kate Winston D'Allandrio – Nina picked up the phone and made the call. She did it without any preamble, not wanting her nerves to get the better of her, unwilling to take the cowards way out by backing out and continuing to live a huge, fucking lie with a man she no longer loves or, indeed, ever loved.

Her body feels weightless, as light as air. A heavy burden has been lifted. She is free; filled with both terror and excitement in equal measure. Upstairs, Dane is sleeping peacefully, blissfully unaware that his life is about to change into something unrecognisable now that she has done this thing, revealed her husband's heinous deed and set free the beast of his sins. The truth is out there and she cannot recapture it. There is no way to take back those words. Everything is in a transitionary phase. Rob is still unaware of what she has done, but soon he will know and although she feels fear and unease at the thought of him finding out, she isn't utterly terrified. It had to be done.

She can see a chink of light at the end of what seems to have been an endless tunnel. For so long now, she has stumbled about in the dark, crashing into things, falling and injuring herself before getting back up and dusting herself off only to fall once more, always harder than the last time. But not anymore. Everything is at an end. An end that offers a fresh start. It will be tough, she knows that, but ahead of her lies a whole new beginning.

She spends the next hour showering, styling her hair and painting her nails, something she hasn't done for as long as she can remember. There seemed little point when her life consisted of cleaning and cooking but since making that call, she feels imbued with an energy that she can't quite define, a spurt of adrenaline that is pulsing around her body, spurring her on.

She hears the turn of Rob's key in the door downstairs and stops. Her heart speeds up; her palms are damp and clammy. Now it's real. Her act of defiance is about to lose its shine. She will tell him what she has done and watch as his temper takes hold.

Her slim fingers grip the edge of the mattress, her stomach shrinks. She will have to speak with him. Sooner rather than later. There's no escaping that fact because she is under no illusions about what will happen next. Anthony Winston-D'Allandrio will get in touch. She doesn't know when, but it will happen. What she needs to do now is to still her thumping heart, go downstairs, tell Rob that she has made the call and ride the oncoming storm.

Beneath her, she can hear him as he raids the fridge, slamming doors, his footsteps clattering across the stone flooring, crockery spinning on worktops where he has placed plates and cups down with such clumsiness, she wonders how he ever manages to build houses that remain upright. The noise is an indication of his mood. Their argument from the previous evening is still in the forefront of his mind and now she has taken it one step further, calling Kate's husband and telling him what she knows about the affair between their respective spouses.

If she thought things were bad before, they are about to get a whole lot worse.

She stands up, hoping Dane remains asleep, hoping Rob doesn't react too badly to her news, yet knowing deep down that he will. Her skin tingles and burns at the thought of his face, the roar of his voice as he tells her she is an interfering old bitch. Worry swills like acid in her stomach.

He moves across the hallway, stopping at the foot of the stairs before going into the living room and turning on the television so loud, it causes her to jump.

This is it. This is the moment that will stay in her brain long after it happens: the moment her life takes a different route, leading her down a path she has never before walked. She has no map, no compass to help her. She is going to have to trust her instincts, go with her gut and hope that for once, her judgement is steering her in the right direction. Not like last time when she went against her instincts, following her heart instead of her head, and married Rob. She is older now. Wiser. She has paid a hefty price for refusing to take heed of her father's advice.

The stairs sway under her feet as she heads down to the living room, the blare of the football commentary an assault on her ears, the roar of the crowd making her flinch. She enters the living room to a wall of noise, Rob's voice accompanying the almighty din as the ball hits the back of the net with a resounding thump.

'Fucking God almighty! My nan could have stopped that fucker going in!'

She closes her eyes, prays that for once, luck will play its part, that she will be saved the terror of one of Rob's adult tantrums and that this confrontation will end peacefully and amicably, yet also knowing deep down that it won't.

He turns and scowls at her.

The words spew out of her mouth, a stream of syllables that echo around her head, telling him what she has done, how his latest lover's husband has been informed and that she is not going to put up with his liaisons and boorish behaviour for any longer, that she has had enough and deserves better than to be ignored, her feelings shoved aside, treated as if she is some feral creature that should be cast out into the wilderness.

For a moment, she thinks that he has softened, taken on board what she has said. His eyes glaze over, a rheumy film obscuring his thoughts, but it doesn't last long. Within seconds, everything changes.

He catapults out of his seat and grabs her shoulders, shaking her until she is dizzy, her head bouncing and flopping, her vision distorted and clouded with fear. Even when he is wrong, he is right. Such ignorance and conceitedness. He is beyond redemption. She knows that now. Should have known it earlier, saved herself years of misery and heartache.

'You stupid, fucking bitch! You stupid, useless waste of fucking space!' Flecks of spittle land on her face. His eyes bulge with rage, spidery veins spreading over the sclera.

Nina stares at him, wants to laugh at how ugly he looks, how all the years of bile have built up inside of him, turning him into the monster he is today, but she knows better than to do such a thing. Rob is a ticking time-bomb and the best thing to do is stand clear, say nothing, do nothing, just watch, mesmerised as he detonates and hope she is able to dodge the shrapnel.

Wrenching herself free of his grasp, she steps back into the soft body of Dane who is standing directly behind her, a small moan escaping his lips.

'What's going on?' His eyes dart from one parent to the other, panic in his tone.

'Ask your mother! Ask her what she's gone and done now.' Without giving the boy a chance to reply, Rob cuts in, his voice a near shriek. 'She has told your mate's dad that me and his mother are having an affair. Can you fucking believe it, eh? Your mother has lost her bloody marbles, son. She's completely sodding deranged.'

Her son gulps nervously, his Adam's apple bobbing up and down. A tic takes hold in his jaw. He blinks and brushes his hand over his face as if trying to swat away an unwanted insect. 'What have you done, Mum?'

Her stomach ties itself into a tight knot as she listens to the sour tones of spite in Dane's timbre, the softened version of him from earlier, now a distant memory. *This is how it is,* she thinks dejectedly, *and how it will always be. Dane is his father's son and will always choose his dad over me.*

No matter how terrible the misdemeanour, how upsetting and hurtful Rob's transgressions are, her son will always take his side. She is alone in the world now. Alone and lonely. A terrible place to be. And yet still she tries to defend herself, to get her only child to see through the fog of bias that swirls around his head, masking the truth.

'Ask your dad what he has done first, Dane. Ask him who he is having an affair with.' She shudders at her own words, not quite believing she is saying these things to her own child, using him as a human shield to deflect from her own wrongdoing after making the call to Kate's husband. Things are slipping out of her grasp. She is losing this battle. She is losing everything.

'An affair?' Dane's voice breaks and she thinks that maybe this is the point where her son sees his father for who he really is. 'Well, maybe if you were nicer to him and paid him a bit more attention, then he wouldn't have to go looking elsewhere, would he?'

Freezing water flushes through her, crystallising in her veins. She hears Rob's snort of laughter, sees Dane take a step closer to his dad. The floor spins; the walls lean in drunkenly.

'He's sleeping with Alex's mum.' Her voice is disembodied, a remote noise that bounces and reverberates inside her head, banging off her skull. She wants to sit down before she falls. She wants to vanish into the ether, to be anywhere but here.

The next few minutes are a blur, the noise and commotion too much for her addled brain to decipher.

She can hear Dane as he shouts at his father but cannot make out the words. She stands close by as a scuffle takes place. She watches as Dane storms off upstairs shouting that he hates this place and wishes they were both dead.

* * *

The rest of the weekend she spends in a dreamlike state, staggering around the house, soundless and close to tears. She hears Rob shouting about this thing that she has done and wonders when he will realise that he is the one who started this charade, that he is the one who has done something unforgiveable.

Nina sucks in a lungful of cold air. It's like a scene from a soap opera and she is caught up in the middle of it – her life, a seedy, low-budget daytime soap. This is what she is reduced to, what her life has become.

Dane stays holed up in his room, eating on his own and refusing to engage with either of his parents.

At least he hates both of us equally, Nina thinks with a small amount of triumph, *and no longer sees his father as a hero, an untouchable icon who is beyond reproach.* They are both worthy of his hatred and contempt. That affords her a modicum of comfort, knowing she isn't alone in this mess. Knowing that the seemingly unbreakable bond he once shared with his father has finally been severed.

Her son's anger and loathing are a palpable force, leaking through the walls and filling the entire house. Nina can hardly breathe for it, every room stuffy with rage and bitterness. There is no escape, no corner of the house free of his fury. Nina can almost taste it: the sour flavour of hostility directed their way.

And then there is Rob, the man she is no longer sharing a bed with. The man who stooped so low, he is practically slithering across the ground, snake-like, his moral compass smashed into unrecognisable, tiny pieces. She does her best to avoid him, leaving rooms as he enters, eating alone and trying to build up enough courage to speak to her son without risking another argument.

She is all out of energy, her levels depleted, her ability to reason her way out of this non-existent. She did what she thought was best for her family and now everything is broken, her marriage in tatters, her life cracked and splintered beyond repair.

Losing her husband is one thing but the thought of losing her son cuts her in half. She thinks about his moods, his permanent state of angst, and wishes there was something she could do to drag him out of it, to help him realise that better things lie ahead, that one day, he will have a job and a family of his own and that this time in his life will pass. Better things are coming; it's just that he can't yet see it. He hasn't the vision, the experience or the advantage of her wisdom to see beyond the here and now. He thinks his life is at an end. It isn't. It's just beginning.

She sits in one of the spare bedrooms, staring out of the window, reflecting on it all: regretting the past, despising the present, welcoming the future. Soon, this will be over. Soon, her life will refresh itself. She can start again, be a different person. A better person: braver, happier. If only there were a fast-forward button to bypass the hurt and pain that the stark truth brings. Right now, it feels like the beginning of the end, but it isn't. In the not-too-distant future lies another life for her and her son. A life without Rob. And it can't happen soon enough.

28

20 JULY 1978

Dear Clara,

    I have held back from writing any further correspondence but woke this morning with these words burning deep inside me, so here I am, pouring out my feelings to a woman I know will never reply. This letter isn't meant for you though, dear Clara. It will never reach you. This one is for me, to attempt to assuage the heavy ache that sits in my heart day after day with no signs of it lessening. This letter is my therapy, a way of getting through this period of my life. I have nobody else to turn to. Nothing will ever be the same without you, Clara, and I think you know that. You've always known it. I had no idea how callous you could be, how easy you found it to trample over my feelings, casting me aside for a life elsewhere, then ignoring my pleas for us to be reunited. But I know it now. Now I am all too aware of it and believe me, it is a heavy burden to bear.

    We never really knew one another at all, did we? I was mistaken, carried away by my feelings, swamped by the flush of love I felt for you. But it meant nothing to you, our relationship, did it? Nothing at all. I was standing in your way, blocking your route to freedom and was simply too enamoured by you; too enamoured and too blind to see it. I see it now, though. It is painfully plain to me.

As I stated in an earlier correspondence, your dismissal of my interests and hobbies is another bone of contention between us but now I can see that it was fear of being recognised for who you really are that drove you to say such things. My studies into the features of the human face have taught me many things and one of those is the mask you wore when you were in my presence, dear Clara. I have seen through it now. I couldn't recognise that at the time such was my heartbreak and desperation at your departure and subsequent refusal to communicate with me, but it's all so clear to me now.

Physiognomy is dismissed by many – you included – because it makes people feel uncomfortable in their own skin. It forces them to delve deep into their own thoughts to discover who they really are.

And delve I did. I discovered who you really are, didn't I, Clara? And I didn't like what I found. You knew that though, didn't you, which is why you left, never to return. Your high cheekbones and full mouth that I once thought of as strikingly attractive and a thing of beauty are in fact an indication of your arrogance and conceit, making you predisposed to a level of callousness that is breath-taking in its ugliness. Your dark eyes and small, upturned nose that made other men stop and stare are a sign of your savage nature, your ability to switch off your own feeling and sentimentality when dealing with others. The shape of your face is a strong indication of how cruel you really are, its oval shape displaying your lack of empathy with no idea of the suffering of others, neither caring nor making any attempt to soften and yield to them when faced with their sorrow and anguish in its purest form.

This is you, dear Clara, the woman I loved, the woman I thought I knew. This is the real you, the ugly, detestable you that nobody else saw. You hid it well, dear Clara, but I saw it. I see it and I see you for who and what you really are and I can tell you, it isn't pleasant.

I am better off without you. I know that now. My path in life is free of the clutter that my relationship with you brought. No more heartache. No more pining after you. No more you.

I am going to end this letter now, my mind clearer than it has been for some time. I have eased the load that I have been carrying around and can now continue with my existence, putting my efforts into things that are worthwhile instead of chasing after a pointless dream that only ever existed in my head. We never had a shared vision, Clara. You were always looking for a way out, using me to fill up your days then casting me aside after you had grown tired of our time together. After you had grown tired of me.

You are gone and it is better that way. No more hurt, no more rejection. No more torturous nights wondering where I went wrong. I have my work, my house and my solitude and that is the way it is going to stay.

Goodbye, dearest Clara.

I loved you once. But not anymore.

Dominic.

29

PRESENT DAY

They meet in the kitchen, her eyes downcast, his gaze furtive, darting about as he tries to evade her scrutiny. Rob left for work over an hour ago, exiting the house in a blaze of glory – slamming doors and revving the engine as he sped off the drive like a Grand Prix driver. And now here she is, locked in a battle of wills with her son, both of them too stubborn, too anxious to speak openly and honestly about what is going on in their lives. How everything is unravelling. It's temporary; she wants to tell him that. She wants to hug him; tell him there is a life beyond this, but doesn't know how or where to begin.

'Would you like some toast?' Her voice is a whisper, lower, weaker than she intended it to be. Nina clears her throat, asks again. 'Dane, would you like me to make you some toast?'

He shakes his head, instead grabbing a bowl and filling it with cereal, pouring on milk in a clumsy rush. The creamy splashes land on the surface as he overfills it. Nina watches, has to stop herself from wiping them away. Tidying up is who she has become, an integral part of her personality. She has little else to define her.

'Anything good happening at school today?' This is a weak attempt at breaking the silence, trying to patch things up between them. Like they were ever fully healed to begin with.

'They're all cunts.' He slurps at his breakfast, a trail of white dribbling down his chin.

She winces at his words, wanting to rub away the trickle of milk, is almost able to feel his coarse skin beneath her fingers, the slight stubble of his chin, the transformation of his bone structure from boy into man. She won't ask him to curb his language. It will achieve nothing except to set them even further apart.

'I'll cook you your favourite meal tonight. Lasagne and chips with garlic bread.'

He doesn't reply. He spoons the last of his cereal into his mouth before standing up and throwing his utensils into the sink with such force that the bowl breaks in half. Flinching, she wants to grab him, to shake some sense into him and tell him that this isn't her fault, that the blame lies squarely at the feet of his father. Instead, she stands up, retrieves the broken crockery and drops it into the bin. Dane marches out of the kitchen, slamming the door behind him.

The chair is hard beneath her as she drops into it, unable to drag herself out of this moment. She is all out of ideas as to how she can make it up to her son. Maybe she can't. Maybe they will always be disparate souls, forever set apart. He hates her. He hates everyone. Perhaps she should just accept that fact, realise that this is how it is and stop trying to mould him into something he isn't.

The thought of spending the day on her own in this place makes her bones ache, her muscles shrivel. She should have a hundred places to visit, dozens of people to see, but in reality, has nobody. Nobody at all. No one to talk to, nowhere to go.

'Fucking hell! What an awful fucking mess.' She doesn't care whether Dane hears her or not. She doesn't care about any of it anymore. Why should she?

Above her, she hears her son as he thumps about, dragging things around his room and stomping down the stairs. She prepares herself for inevitable door slam, the house shaking as he leaves.

Now she is alone. Now she can let it all out. Tipping her head back, Nina lets out an ear-splitting scream, thumping at the table and banging her feet on the floor until her voice cracks and her entire body throbs and burns.

Then she rests her face on the cool wooden surface and weeps.

30

Alex can barely bring himself to walk through the gates, every step he takes resulting in a painful jarring sensation that travels up his body. The closer he gets, the greater his uneasiness. It grows exponentially, swelling in his chest, making it hard for him to stay focused. He grits his teeth, wondering if Dane knows about any of this, wondering his parents kept it secret from him and yet knowing all the while that that won't be the case at all. He's met Dane's dad, seen his brash manner, how he commandeers a room, refusing to allow those around him to have their say, projecting his own thoughts onto them, his voice carrying more weight than anybody else's. There is no way their house will have functioned normally over the weekend. And if it did, then life is completely fucking unfair. There is no real justice in this world if Dane has had an easy weekend while his has been shit.

Every noise is amplified in his head – the din of distant laughter, the shriek of the bell, even the sound of his own blood as it pulses around his body – they all clang against his skull, forcing him to slow down and steady his breathing.

He needs to do this, to face his friend and hope that the sins of their parents don't drive a wedge between them.

Heart pumping, he heads inside, his senses attuned to everything around him. Huddled in the corridor is a gang of Year Elevens. He inhales deeply, steeling himself for a torrent of abuse, and is relieved when he passes without so much as a titter from any of them. They are all grouped around somebody's phone – even though phones are banned – and stand guffawing at something on the screen.

On the other side of the corridor is a group of girls. They eye him as he passes, giggling and murmuring, one of them giving him a wolf whistle while the others shriek with laughter.

All of a sudden, he hates this school. His life, his family and all their tawdry little secrets crowd his mind. They are written all over his face, evident for all to see. He feels sure of it. His skin glows hot. Perspiration coats his neck, his back. He should have stayed in bed, avoided everything and everyone but then that would have meant being around his mother and he doesn't think he could have faced that either. There is nowhere to hide. No shelter from this particular storm.

Behind him, footsteps move closer, running toward him. He turns, his head thumping with anxiety, half expecting to see Dane approaching, his face lined with annoyance but instead sees Bobby, his gangly form swaying, his arms and legs uncoordinated as he rushes over to where Alex is standing.

'Yo, bro. What's up?'

Alex grits his teeth. He hates that kind of stupid talk, as if they're living on the streets of Los Angeles, hanging out with members of The Crips or The Bloods. They live in North Yorkshire for Christ's sake, the county of market towns, of farms and moorland where sheep wander aimlessly and hikers ramble through the heather.

'Nothing's up, Bobby. What's up with you?' His tone is sharp. He can't seem to help it. He wants to be elsewhere, anywhere away from this shitty mess. He thinks of his grandparents living down south and marvels at how lucky they are, being away from all of this heartache and drama and then he thinks of his uncle Ralph going off to Tibet and wishes he was there with him. Maybe that's what he will do when he leaves school – go travelling, get away from people. They only cause trouble anyway, making everyone around them miserable. Why bother staying here when there's nothing worth hanging around for?

'Nothing up with me, man but sounds like you're having a bad day.'

Guilt spears Alex. This isn't Bobby's fault. Bobby is one of the good guys, a friend. Alex smiles and cocks his head. 'Sorry. Got out the wrong side of the bed this morning, is all. Ignore me. I'm being a dickhead.'

'Anyhow,' Bobby says, the moment already forgotten. 'I was wondering if you and the big man fancy another get-together at mine sometime soon? The last one was awesome!'

Alex can't help but grin. Bobby's laughter is infectious, his permanently upbeat mood impossible to ignore. 'Maybe. I'll have to see what Dane is up to. You seen him around anywhere?' A fist clutches at his guts. Dane usually meets him on the way into school. He's conspicuous by his absence. *He knows.* Alex can sense it. Dane knows and is avoiding him. Just as he expected and feared. As well as his parents' marriage disintegrating, so is his friendship with Dane, the one person who has been there for him since he walked in this building all those months ago. A broken friendship and all because of a stupid fucking affair.

'Funny you should mention that. Saw him earlier. Called out to him but he ignored me. Maybe it's me?' Bobby gives Alex's shoulder a light push, smiling broadly as he leans closer. 'You two had a falling out, yeah?'

'No. Definitely not.' Alex stops and hoists his bag higher up over his shoulder, the strap digging into his bones, causing him to grimace. 'I'll keep an eye out for him later. Got PE first thing, straight after registration. Gotta get moving or old man Harding will have my arse on a plate.'

They part, Alex's feet feeling as if they've been glued to the ground. His entire body feels ten times heavier than it did a few minutes ago. He traipses over to his tutor room, his mood low, his thoughts tinged with images of his parents and Dane and how this will all end. A bit of circuit training might be just what he needs to rid himself of this heavy feeling. The feeling that things are about to spiral downwards at a rapid rate of knots.

Registration is over in minutes and Alex heads to the sports hall, buoyed up by the thought of an hour of mind-numbing exercise. He speaks to nobody and nobody approaches or tries to engage with him. It suits him. Alone is better. Alone is therapeutic, giving him space to think. To breathe.

Slipping into his kit, he runs his fingers through his hair then shakes his limbs about to loosen up before heading into the hall, a chill biting at his bones.

* * *

He'd be lying if he said it didn't help elevate his mood because it did, running around a large hall, clearing hurdles, doing press ups, pushing his body as hard as he could, but it didn't eliminate all the dark thoughts and worries that loiter at the back of his mind. They're still there, waiting.

Beads of sweat run down his face, the salt burning his eyelids as he heads for the shower. It feels good to punish himself, to sweat it out and yet knowing that the worst is still to come. He may be able to cleanse his body but clearing his mind seems like an unsurmountable task, especially when it's other people who are creating the problem. And what a fucking awful problem it is.

Ignoring the childish jibes of other lads in his class as they flick towels at one another and bare their arses to raise a laugh, he cleans himself up and gets dressed, glad to be out of the changing room and into the cool and relative quiet of the small yard.

Next lesson is English, where he will see Dane, where he will be sitting close enough to reach him. Maybe things will be okay between them. Maybe they won't. It's not unusual for them to go separate ways for hours at a time, their timetables differing. But now he is going to have to face him, to see what his mood is like and to try and determine whether or not he knows. Rubbing at his face wearily, Alex heads over to the English block, grit lodged behind his eyelids, perspiration still beading his hairline.

He knows. Dane knows. It's obvious by his stance, by the way he refuses to meet Alex's gaze. The way he blatantly ignored Alex as he greeted him and slapped a friendly hand on his shoulder when they entered the classroom. He knows.

So now they sit, only feet away from one another yet worlds apart, Dane's head lowered, his body rigid and angular. Alex watches him, sussing out his body language, trying to work out whether he is likely to soften or whether this thing will continue indefinitely. He hopes not. He wants to find a way of approaching him, a way that will let Dane know that the actions of their parents shouldn't affect their friendship. Easier said than done, he knows that, given Dane's sullen behaviour and mood swings, but it's worth a try. It's better than doing nothing. Their friendship, although still in its infancy is, he thinks, worth fighting for.

At the front of the classroom, Mr Rose stands, his long arms reaching up to the board, the squeak of the whiteboard pen setting Alex's teeth on edge.

'*An Inspector Calls*,' he says, his voice louder, more authoritative than it has been in the past. 'I want you to think about how Priestley explores the theme of class divide in post-war Britain.'

There is a slight groan from the back of the class. Probably from Ed Preston, the only person who hates this lesson more than Dane.

'What do you think the Birlings' opinion was of Eva and the fact she was working class?'

Alex raises his hand, clears his throat before speaking. 'That she was only interested in money and wasn't as good as them because she didn't have it?'

It's an indiscernible movement, a slight twitch of Dane's head as Alex gives his answer, but Alex sees it all the same. He wants to move closer, to tell him that just because their parents have fallen out doesn't mean they should, but knows it's impossible. Not here. Not now. But maybe later. Maybe once this lesson is finished, he can sidle up to him, tell him that stuff between them hasn't altered in any way, that their parents can go to hell. What they do or don't do shouldn't affect their kids and their friendships. He tries to visualise Dane smiling and nodding, agreeing with him, giving him one of those infamous dark, brooding looks, the ones that make others fearful of Dane Bowron. But not Alex. He's not fearful. He knows Dane, has bonded with him in a weird, asymmetrical fashion, two ill-fitting parts of a jigsaw that somehow sit alongside one another and complete the picture.

'Yes. Good answer, Alexander. And what else? What message is Priestley trying to get across to his audience?'

Alex swallows, wishing he wasn't being singled out, wishing he hadn't drawn attention to himself by answering in the first place. 'He tried to highlight how inequality was rampant in Britain and felt that upper class people saw those with less money as being beneath them.'

'Like you, Winston-D'Allandrio. Stupid fucker.'

It's a whisper, a low muttering, but he hears it all the same. A pulse thumps in his temple, a small gavel repeatedly bashing against his skull.

'Sorry?' Mr Rose says brightly, his gaze resting on Dane, who has slumped even farther down into his chair. 'Have you got anything to add to Alexander's answer, Dane?'

There is a collective inhalation of breath as Dane rearranges his body, sitting up carefully in his chair and pulling at his collar, his voice stilted, each syllable clipped.

'Fuck right off. Dirty, perverted bastard.'

Alex squeezes his eyes shut, unable to believe what he has just heard. Or thinks he heard. It was quiet, barely a sound at all. And yet it was there. Other people heard it. He is sure of it. He wants to twist around in his seat, to stare at the sea of waiting faces behind him, to gauge their mood and try to work out whether it's just him and his imagination running wild or whether it actually happened and isn't some weird illusion borne out of stress and exhaustion.

'Sorry, Dane? I didn't quite catch that. Can you speak a little louder so everyone can hear your answer?'

Everybody waits, the tension in the room a physical force. All eyes are focused on Dane, watching, waiting to see and hear what comes next. Alex wills him to do the right thing. To say the right thing. To let their differences remain just between them and not spill over into a public domain.

'I said, fuck off you dirty, perverted bastard. You can fuck off and Alexander Winston frigging D'Allandrio and his desperate slut of a mother can all fuck right off!'

There isn't time to do anything, for the shock to set in. Dane turns and brings his fist into Alex's face.

And that's when it all begins to fall apart.

PART III
THE END AS IT HAPPENS

31

Dane is upon him before he has a chance to think or breathe or do anything at all. Alex feels himself being propelled backwards, his head hitting the hard floor with a crack. A pain whooshes up behind his eyes and everything spins. He tries to sit up but the pressure on him is too great, Dane's weight pinning him to the ground, his face leering down at him – that furrowed brow, the dead-eyed stare, a drool of glistening saliva bouncing like the string of a yo-yo close to his flesh.

Another hit to the face, a stinging sensation at first then a burst of pain exploding behind his nose, travelling up behind his eyes. He tries to turn away, his cheek resting on the cool surface of the floor, his vision gauzy and indistinct.

'That was from my mum, and this one is from me.'

Alex hears the crack, feels the crushing pain travel up and down his face, layer upon layer of agony and knows then that something is broken. Dizzy and sick, he tries to sit up but is pushed back down, strong hands pressing on his sternum. He is weakened by the blow, by the waves of pain that crash into him.

He brings his hands up, sees the blood and hears the screams, the shouts for Dane to get off him, to leave him be. Relief blooms somewhere in his chest. Somebody will help. One of the bigger lads will prise Dane off, pulling them to opposite ends of the room. Alex lets out a shaky breath and tries to speak, to reason with him, but before he can utter two words, he feels another explosion in his face as Dane's fist connects with his cheekbone.

More room spinning, more bile rushing up his throat. The weight on his chest loosens but he is too tired to roll away, the agony in his head too great. He can't seem to move, is rocked by the intensity of it all.

He hears the scuffle of Dane being dragged off him, his shouts of protest as he is restrained. Through bloodied eyes, Alex sees a scrum above him, arms, legs, fists lashing out, foul language circling in the air above where he lay, girls crying and huddling together in a tight, terrified mass.

A thump as the scrum falls to the floor. The din of a dozen young men fighting and trying to pin Dane to the ground.

And then the roar of Mr Rose. The sight of him towering above everybody as he stands on his chair and waves his arms about, his fingers clasped around something long. Something solid and metallic. Alex squints, tries to clear his marred vision, wiping away a viscous, gooey mess of blood, snot and tears.

And then he swallows hard and groans.

A rifle.

Jesus Christ. Mr Rose is holding a rifle.

Alex hears himself shout, screaming for everybody to stop, to get down onto the floor and take cover. His throat aches, his voice is hoarse. He has no idea if he is doing the right thing but it seems that his reflexes have taken over, a survival instinct kicking in. The words sound muffled as he says them, blood and saliva hindering his enunciation.

A sudden silence.

Then sobbing. And more screaming. Followed by a sinister stretch of nothingness where time seems to stand still, everyone suspended in the moment. An interlude from the fear.

'Try it, son, and see what happens.'

Alex turns to see one of the lads attempting to leave the room, his fingers curled around the door handle, his face stricken.

Mr Rose lowers the rifle and waves it at him, indicating for him to step away and back into the class. 'Move. Get over there in the corner. All of you! I said get over there in the corner!'

The mass of bodies shifts backwards. Alex watches through swollen eyes as they stumble, terror ravaging their faces, dread that this is the end etched into their expressions, fear of their imminent demise all too obvious in the way they tremble and cower, their voices weak, subdued.

It's strange, he thinks, how in times of distress, people often focus on the inane. He hears the trickle of water and sees a damp patch appear on the floor, pooling at the feet of a petrified girl. He can't seem to look away as she weeps, a soft, unassuming cry that makes his blood run cold. Transfixed by the puddle of urine, he waits for the dizziness to ease, thanking God that his major organs received no blows and he can at least breathe properly. Small mercies, he thinks as he attempts to sit up, to take stock of this bizarre and chilling situation, only to be pushed back down again by the butt of a rifle.

'Stay right there, lad. Nobody moves unless I say so, okay?'

It's Mr Rose and yet it isn't. How can it be? How can this insane-looking creature before him be the quietly spoken man who week after week struggles to control the behaviour of a class when teaching? It doesn't make any sense.

Alex turns his head. The man he once taunted paces around the room, wild eyed, a frightening level of volatility perceptible in his stance: the way his eyes narrow as he surveys everyone; the way he twists and turns his body in a rapid, threatening motion to monitor and control the people in the room. His hair sticks out at divergent angles, wiry and uncontrollable, his lined skin is colourless, almost translucent, his voice loaded with menace. Perched on the end of his nose, his glasses sit awkwardly, skewed at an angle.

Alex's breathing becomes erratic again, shallow gasps sticking in his throat, fighting to be out. This isn't his teacher, the mild-mannered man they all know. He has snapped. Something inside him has broken and now anything is possible.

Alex knows that he has to do something – anything to stop this. He cannot just lie here and let something terrible happen. Something final.

Over in the corner, Dane struggles, straining and thrashing against the sets of arms that hold him fast. He doesn't speak but Alex can hear his grunts and shouts of protest as he bucks and bends his body, hatred driving him on, oozing out of him. An unstoppable torrent of anger.

To stop the struggle, to halt Dane's muted attempts to free himself, Mr Rose brings his hand down on the desk, the thump bringing forth a series of screams and shrieks.

Head still spinning, Alex forces himself upright, ignoring Mr Rose's orders to remain as he is. 'Stop it, sir. You need to calm down.' Alex closes his eyes and tries to breathe through his nose, choking on blood and phlegm while wishing this scenario away. He is barely able to believe his own words; having to reason with a teacher who has snapped and is currently hurtling into the deepest pit of madness.

He waits, unsure what it is he is actually waiting for. For a beating perhaps, for the cold metal of the barrel to be poised at his temple. For something deadly to happen.

Nothing.

Just the arrhythmic battering of his heart, the surging of his blood, the thudding of the pain that is beating its way around his head, pummelling at his face. He swallows down vomit. Fire traces its way down his gullet. He swallows some more, rubs at his eyes.

'Please, Mr Rose. Just put the gun down.' He has no idea where this bravery is coming from. Something is driving him on, willing him to do the right thing, the decent thing. After his past behaviour, mocking and provoking this man, he has to speak up, to move things along and make sure nobody gets hurt. It's the least he can do. It may be a futile attempt. It may be dangerous. He has no idea what is going through this guy's head, no idea of his capabilities, but doing nothing isn't an option.

'Mr Rose, please.'

A grunt, then a step closer as he gets down off the chair and shuffles towards Alex, the squeak of his shoes echoing around the room.

His face looms over Alex's, his eyes wide and glassy, his skin drained of all colour, mouth twisted into a grimace that abates the boy's movements and thoughts. Jagged stones dig into his bones as he stares up.

Then Mr Rose's voice – a deadened drone, a string of sounds that lack inflection or emotion. Saliva gathering at the corners of his lips, his yellowing teeth as he grins and speaks.

'Stop it, boy. Just shut the fuck up.'

Alex shakes his head, tears streaming, blood bubbling out of his nose, coursing down his face, dripping on the floor. He tries to respond, but the words won't come.

Instead, he tries to move, to get closer, but is stopped in his tracks as the door bursts open, slamming into the wall with force. A figure comes hurtling in. Face stained with tears, Joss stops next to him, eyes bulging, mouth gaping. Then a shriek as she calls out her brother's name, her body bent double with shock.

As if in slow motion, Mr Rose reaches out, his long, gnarled hands pushing her into the corner with the others before dragging his old wooden desk over to the door with one hand, the other still holding the rifle, his finger curled around the trigger. Chair after chair is stacked next to the desk, behind it, on top of it, making entry into the room almost impossible.

Alex's sister. Here. With him. His younger sibling. He has to do something – anything – to stop this escalating, to protect her.

That's when he lunges forward.

32

Pat Miller, the deputy head of Ingleton Secondary School, sits at her desk, stomach churning. Her professional demeanour is crumbling away. She keeps her fingers splayed out on the desk to disguise the tremble there, remaining seated for fear of falling to the floor in a heap if she stands up. No teacher, no member of management, however skilled, should ever have to deal with anything of this nature.

She has run through a scenario like this one before, simulated versions where members of staff roll down shutters and gather pupils in the classroom, annoyed at the disturbance to their lesson while the management team stand with clipboards, ticking off procedures, making certain staff have followed them correctly.

But this is different. This is real, and it frightens her, decimating her thoughts, stripping away her illusion of proficiency and control.

Ron Pierce, the head teacher stands near the door, speaking to the police officers, their sombre expressions, barked orders and pointed fingers telling her everything she needs to know. Another team of officers arrive. She hears the click of their boots on the laminate flooring, the buzz of their radios, the concerned murmurs of terrified office staff as they open the doors to allow them in.

She wants to be elsewhere. Anywhere but here. Ron is being proactive, the consummate professional, while she can barely think straight. She needs to do something, to start overcoming this panic, to free herself from its iron grip and so suddenly, she stands, her head woozy, her stomach threatening to eject its contents. She clears her throat. She can do this. She has to. Doing nothing is not part of her plan. Lives are at stake here. Children could die while she sits mute, immobile, trapped by her own anxiety. This is what she is paid for: to take on this level of responsibility, to make sure this school is a safe environment for all.

'We need to get in touch with parents,' she finds herself saying. 'I'll ask the office staff to print out a list of contact names and numbers.'

The police officer standing next to Ron nods. 'Pass them onto us. We'll speak to all the relevant parents and carers.'

'Yes, of course.' She clears her throat, feeling useless and cumbersome, a bystander on the periphery of this calamitous event. That's why the police are here. They will take over. She will do the small things, the administrative tasks that, whilst still important, require no high level of accountability.

'Onto it now,' she says quietly as she picks up the phone and makes the request.

33

Nina knew this was going to happen. Her gut instinct was correct. She knew when she received the phone call, when they gave her the barest of details, insisting they visit the house so they could speak with her face to face. The two police officers stride into the room and lower themselves onto one of the large, white, leather couches. Nina sits opposite, a vice clamped around the base of her skull. She wants to cry, to scream, to tell them that whatever it is they are about to say, she doesn't want to hear it, but remains silent instead, her voice absent as dread takes over, its hold on her so great, she can barely keep herself upright.

Her life is about to turn to dust. If she thought things were bad before, they are a million times worse now. They don't need to enlighten her, to speak of the events at the school. She already knows. She can sense it – the way her son was this morning as he left the house, his deteriorating mood, his mounting anger. And those pieces of paper up in his room. She was right all along.

Nina freezes, her tongue suddenly too large for her mouth, her throat shrinking as she gasps for breath. A thought occurs to her. What if they ask to search his room? She should have disposed of the incriminating evidence while she had the chance, saved her son from further trouble. It's too late now. Everything is just too damn late.

'There's an ongoing incident at the school, Mrs Bowron. Do you have a number so we can contact Dane's father?'

Nina's head vibrates. Her skin burns hot then cold, perspiration coating her top lip. 'Is he dead? Has he killed somebody? Oh God, what's going on?'

No change in their faces, their eyes remaining impassive, giving nothing away. *Consummate professionals,* she thinks. She should trust them. They know what they're doing. She speaks candidly, hoping to offload her worries, to let them know of Dane's state of mind, how desperately angry he is. How his father caused it. How she caused it, her impulsive actions leading to this moment.

'We've had a few troubles at home. Me and Dane's father. They both left the house this morning really upset and angry, especially Dane. Whatever he's done is my fault. You can blame me. He's young – distressed and hurting. I'm the one at fault here. Me and his dad.' She can't stop the tears. They cascade now, a river of them tumbling down her face, dripping off her jaw onto her lap.

'Dane hasn't done anything wrong, Mrs Bowron. There is an incident at the school and your son's class is caught up in it, but as far as we are aware, Dane didn't instigate it.'

Relief and confusion meet and merge in her head, her ability to think clearly attenuating with every passing second. She has no idea what to do. What to say. 'How do you know? What's going on? How do you know that Dane didn't start this thing?' Shame washes over her. *Listen to yourself,* she thinks, *throwing your own child to the wolves, trying to implicate him when they have already established that he is an innocent bystander.*

Her fingers are cold. She clasps them in her lap, wringing her hands in desperation.

'We can't divulge too much information at this point but what we do know is that a firearm is present in the classroom and we're doing all we can to defuse the situation and bring out all of the pupils unharmed.'

Nina stares at the officer. He has kind eyes, his demeanour softening as he speaks. She should offer them a hot drink, perhaps some biscuits, but can't summon up any energy, afraid she will drop to the floor if she attempts to stand. She almost laughs out loud at the absurdity of it all. She is indoctrinated to a certain way of thinking. Even in times of dire need, in the worst possible circumstances, she feels the need to offer beverages to try and make everything better, to ease the shock, like her nana making tea for everyone in the street after their houses had been bombed, their lives shattered and ruined. *It's what we do,* she thinks numbly, *a way of bringing people together. Tea and coffee – the universal glue of humanity.*

'There's coffee,' she says weakly, 'in the kitchen. In the percolator if you want any...' She isn't able to say anything else. Her throat is constricted, her mind skewed, the process of talking suddenly a gargantuan effort.

One of the officers leaves the snug and heads over to the kitchen worktop, pouring out three cups before striding back and placing one of them in Nina's hand, carefully wrapping her fingers around the base. 'There you go. I didn't add any sugar.' Her voice is gentle, considerate, this female officer who sits down next to her. This person doing their best to inform and prop up a woman whose son is in danger.

Nina takes a sip, allowing the heat to soothe her, to clear her thoughts. She takes a breath, formulating the words in her head before saying them out loud. 'He got into trouble recently, at school.' She looks up, observes their faces, searching for something – anything to show that they are interested in what she has to say.

The other officer nods and waits for her to continue.

'He went to one of his teacher's houses and somehow got inside. I told him he was trespassing and could even be arrested for it. He seemed sorry afterwards.' *As sorry as Dane can ever be,* she thinks sadly. As sorry as she has ever seen him be for any of his transgressions. It was a start at least. And now look what has happened. One step forward, a hundred steps back.

She swallows down her tears and rubs at her face with her free hand, a small amount of coffee splashing onto her lap. 'Sorry. I'm a bit...' She isn't sure what she is, or how she feels or even what it was she was going to say.

'Do you know which teacher it was?' the male officer says, his authoritative tone present once more.

'I, er.' Nina takes a sip of the coffee, its strong tobacco flavour coating the back of her throat. 'It was Mr Rose. He got inside Mr Rose's house and even sneaked upstairs where his mother was sleeping.' She looks up, renewed fear creeping up her spine. 'I told him it was wrong and that he should never do anything like that again, especially when there is a frail old lady in the house.' She dips her head and squeezes shut her eyes to stop any more tears from escaping. 'He's just immature, that's all. Easily led and impressionable. He'll change. I know he will. It's just a matter of time.'

The officers exchange a knowing glance and her stomach plummets. 'Is everything okay? Did I say something wrong?'

'We really need you to get in touch with your husband, Mrs Bowron. We would rather he didn't hear of this from another source.'

34

'We're trying to establish a motive. Our team need to negotiate with Mr Rose, to work out a way to get everybody out safely.'

Pat watches through bleary eyes as officers buzz about, taking over her office. A full lockdown situation. A teacher brandishing a firearm. A nightmare scenario.

Her head thuds, her mind slows down, all previous training preparing her for this situation abandoning her as shock sets in, a concrete slab that sits at the base of her stomach, rigid, heavy, unyielding.

'We need to know everything about this man.' The officer leans down, his large hands spread over the table. 'Everything. Past history. Family. Work. Pupil disagreements. Everything.'

She swallows, nodding and riffling through papers on her desk, thinking of Dominic, the way he has plodded through life, his deep, intellectual mind, his quiet ways. Her abrupt manner when she spoke with him recently. Flames sneak beneath her skin, white hot, fiery. She dabs at her face, rubbing at her eyes, trying to think of something to tell this man, anything that will help them understand what is going on inside her colleague's head.

Nobody could have predicted this. Nobody. It's always the quiet ones, isn't it? They sneak up on you, take you by surprise. She isn't prepared for this, probably never will be. Regardless of training, regardless of how many practise runs she has experienced, nothing could ever prepare somebody for an event of this magnitude. It's terrifying, mortifying.

The officer turns away, speaks into his radio in hushed tones, his words mumbled and indecipherable. The crackle rumbles through Pat's head, making her squirm, pinpricks of terror and dread darting through her pores. He listens intently then utters a few more words and turns back to face her, searching for something she feels sure she cannot give. Dominic has ambled through life, through his career, upsetting nobody, keeping his head down, doing what needs to be done then going home at the end of the day. His presence is a whisper, his manner quiet and unobtrusive. His visit to her office was out of character. Was that a sign? If so, it was a subtle one. Too nuanced to be of any note. This current situation isn't something she could have ever predicted. A slight change of character isn't necessarily indicative of a tormented, broken mind. People have bad days, they get tired, jaded. And then they go home, rest, regroup and come back the following day rejuvenated, ready to tackle whatever life throws their way. They don't bring a rifle into school and point it into the faces of terrified children.

She thinks back to when they were younger, to the time they spent together in college, she and Dominic, both of them applying for and accepting job offers in the same school. All that time, all those years that have passed and yet his life has remained static, nothing changing while she left this place to further her career elsewhere, only returning here decades later to take up a managerial post: older, wiser, married and with three children.

Dominic was still the same, she thinks sadly, his life still stuck in a familiar, old groove, his life as a bachelor after Clara going missing, a route from which he never deviated. A clever man, he could have gone so much further up the ladder of success but chose to stay as a classroom teacher, working at the chalkface, his skills directed towards the pupils as he filled their heads full of knowledge. That is still a decent thing to do, but has it left him too rigid in his beliefs, his vision blinkered to the views of others? Is that what has happened here? Has a lack of experience and diversity in his life led to a lack of compassion and empathy towards others?

'We have a report of a pupil breaking into Mr Rose's house a few nights ago. Do you know anything about this?'

She shakes her head, shockwaves running through her. 'No, nothing at all. This is the first I've heard of it.'

'A parent has informed us that their child recently admitted to breaking into the house while Mr Rose and his mother were both inside. The pupil got upstairs into his mother's bedroom while the old lady was asleep in bed.' Other officers crowd around the desk, hemming her in as they hear this latest piece of information. She can feel the heat from their bodies, knows that this could be serious and yet is unable to conceal her confusion.

She clears her throat and has to project her voice to be heard. 'I think this must be a mistake. Whoever said this is possibly playing some sort of twisted prank.'

The commanding officer locks his gaze with hers, his pupils dark pinpricks. 'Well, if you could let us know your views on this matter, we'd be most grateful. We need to take every lead seriously and breaking and entering is a serious offence. This gives us a possible motivation.'

'I realise that, officer. It's just that the statement doesn't quite add up. I'm not saying the pupil, whoever they are, didn't break in; it's just that they must be mistaken about Dominic's mother being in bed. She can't be.' Pat inhales, her chest and throat tight, the room suddenly at an angle, her head fuzzy as she clears her throat and speaks again. 'You see, Dominic Rose lives alone and has done for quite some time now because his mum has been dead for over forty years.'

35

Dominic doesn't have to time to react. A vice-like grip attaches itself to his ankles and he is down on the floor before he is able to do anything at all. He feels the rifle leave his grasp, hears the heavy, metallic clatter as it skitters across the floor, Alexander's fingers still tightly curled around his leg.

He gasps, winded, having landed awkwardly, his old bones incapable of taking the force. His glasses bounce off his nose and slide out of reach. Fingers outstretched, he rummages around to try and find them, his vision limited, seeing only a blur of outlines, his nails raking along the hard surface as he claws and snatches at thin air.

Behind him, he can hear the high-pitched crying and shrieking of pupils and knows that he has to get up, to take charge again before one of them decides to steal his weapon from him. It's the only thing stopping him from being ambushed by a gang of terrified, angry teenagers. He didn't plan on this happening but it's underway now and he has to finish what he has started.

It's all gone horribly wrong, he can see that now, everything falling away from him, spiralling downwards. It's out of control. He is out of control. Not that it matters anymore. His life is over. Like it ever really began. A life without Clara was no life at all.

He refuses to fall into his own trap – to be reeled in by those dark, dark memories that he has suppressed, keeping them hidden for so many years – he will not allow them to rise to the surface and consume him. He will fight against them, giving them no space in his head. Instead, he will focus on the present, shake off this boy, this inconsequential slip of a lad, and get back up. That rifle, his father's old farming rifle, is his property. It belongs to him and nobody can take it from him. This is his chance to show them all who's boss. Years and years of being ignored and browbeaten, kicked aside and forgotten. Year after year of loneliness and heartache and desperation; they all have taken their toll both at home and here at work. He has at long last grown teeth, found the courage to stand up to those who have wronged him. And not before time. Maybe his father was right. Maybe he is a weakling, a lesser man. But not anymore. The time has come for a drastic change, for him to prove to himself that his dad wrong, and to start fighting back.

With a sudden roar, he rises, pressing himself up off the floor with his hands, his bones creaking and protesting as he throws himself forwards and grabs at young Alexander, the boy he thought would help steer Dane in a different direction. The boy he had such high hopes for. It didn't happen. Instead, he was dragged along in the slipstream of Bowron's bad behaviour and now look at him, at what he is doing, trying to stop Dominic from keeping order in his own classroom. He's the teacher here, not this Alex lad, this inexperienced child who knows nothing about life or how to manage people. Dominic is the teacher, the adult, the one who holds the position of authority in this room.

He slips and lands short of grabbing back the firearm, Alex pulling it away and holding it aloft.

'Stop it, sir. Just fucking well stop it!' The lad's voice is thick with tears. There was a time a plea like that would have worked, stopping Dominic, pulling him up short, tugging at his emotions, but not now. He has reached his breaking point. Besides, what good would it do at this late stage? He's stepped over a line, an invisible boundary that for years he has tip-toed around but never crossed, and now he has advanced over it, there is no turning back. He must do what has to be done. Finish this thing once and for all.

In his peripheral vision, he sees a flicker of a movement and turns.

Through the glass pane, the slither of light that isn't obscured by the barricades he has constructed, he is aware of a sea of faces peering in and knows that time is against him. Soon they will come with their rules and regulations, a team of highly trained officers who will restrain him and hold him fast, cuffing him before throwing him in the back of police van, the sort you see on the evening news, the sort that houses the most dangerous of criminals, and he can't let that happen. Not yet. Not when he still has work to do here.

With one last burst of energy, he throws himself forward, feeling the welcoming shape of his father's gun as he snatches it out of Alex's hand, the warmth of the wood, the reassuring heft of it sending a dart of desire through him. This rifle can save him. It could also end everything. Maybe that isn't such a bad thing. Life is looking rather bleak at the moment, as dark as he can ever remember, his carefully crafted little world unspooling. Everything unravelling at a rapid pace.

His mood oscillates wildly, ranging from childish giddiness to the darkest anger he has ever known as he tips his chin forward, his voice projecting across the room. He smiles, liking the way it sounds – authoritative, commanding. Powerful.

'Over there!' He waves the firearm at the young lad who responds by crossing his arms and shaking his head, eyes glassy with tears yet sat the same time, so full of fire. *Such bravery and courage and valour,* thinks Dominic with sadness. *And yet such foolishness.* 'I said, over there.' He is hissing now, his voice dropping to a whisper. It resonates around the room, clipping bare walls, hitting the cold, tiled floor, a weapon in its own right.

'No. I'm not moving. You'll have to shoot me.' The boy's response takes him by surprise. Gasps from behind him cause his to skin prickle; anger and shock and even a little bit of glee pulsing through him at the temerity of this boy, this once obedient and hardworking student who has suddenly developed a steely side, a rod of iron running through him as he defies his teacher.

'Very well.' Dominic says, rising to the challenge. 'Whatever you say.' He brings the rifle up to his line of sight, aims it at Alex, takes a shaky breath and pulls the trigger as a shadow propels itself towards him from the back of the classroom, hurtling straight into his line of vision, her screams cutting through the moment.

Joss stops moving, stares down at her abdomen, at the spread of crimson that is pulsing through her white blouse. She places her hands over her chest, continues gazing down at her bloodied hands and drops to the floor.

36

Kate wonders how it ever came to this. Alexander, her boy, her gentle, sensitive son locked in a classroom, brandishing a rifle. Where the hell did he get a rifle from?

Christ. She shivers, pulls at her skirt, straightening out creases. Her fingers are numb, thin slivers of ice. Beside her, Anthony sits, his spine stiff, eyes unmoving as he stares straight ahead. The police contacted him, insisting he come home immediately, said it was for the best and now he is wearing the same mask he wore at his previous job when his life was at its lowest ebb, his emotions hidden, unreadable. Both of them sitting next to one another, together side by side. Both of them alone.

It all happened so quickly. Pupils outside the classroom alerted management, who alerted the police, who are now positioned outside the door, watching it all unfold.

She can't bear to think about it – her boy doing such a thing. Her boy, his hand curled around the butt of a firearm, his fingers tugging at the trigger. There has to be a mistake. Alexander is a nice boy, a sensible boy. The sort of boy who always sees reason when others have lost their heads and succumbed to irrationality. This isn't him. Besides, where in God's name did he get a rifle from? They don't possess such a thing. Maybe this is some kind of sick prank that has gone horribly wrong and now he doesn't know how to pull back from it. There will be others involved. He wouldn't do this alone. Not Alex. Not her baby, her thoughtful, beautiful boy. It's absurd.

And then she contemplates the atmosphere in the house recently – that phone call from Nina Bowron and the resulting arguments. Kate's face burns. Shame slithers through her. Her blood boils and cools in her veins. She shivers, wraps her arms around herself. This is on her. She did this. For once, she needs to stand up and take responsibility for her actions. Alexander has listened to the rows and the acrimony and been pushed too far. She has read about incidents like this – children who snap under the strain. It's always the quiet ones, the receptive, impressionable ones. Still waters run deep. But not this time, not her Alexander. Please God, not her boy.

She feels a strong, warm hand on her back as she lowers her head into her lap and weeps. Anthony leans down, whispering unexpected yet comforting platitudes into her ear, his breath soft and sweet against her skin and so wonderfully reassuring. The barriers between them slowly drop and she thanks God that he's here. She wouldn't be able to do this without him. He is the strong one. He is the one who almost ended his own life while she was too blind to see it, too selfish to help him climb out of the deep, dark hole that almost swallowed him.

They shuffle closer together, their bodies touching, their minds focused on one thing and one thing alone – their son and making sure he gets out of this unharmed.

And then they mentioned Jocelyn. What is her involvement? Since arriving at the school premises, information has been scant, the chaos of the lockdown situation resulting in a heavy police presence around them with little communication being passed their way. Plenty of probing questions about their private life, about Alexander and Jocelyn and their reactions to moving here and whether or not they are coping. As if they would go on a shooting spree because they moved to a new school and felt marginalised and lonely. It's ludicrous, insulting and degrading, and Kate will have none of it.

A police officer nods into his radio, clears his throat and speaks. 'We're now have news that the teacher brought the firearm into the school and threatened pupils. Somehow, Alex retrieved it from him and is now in possession of it. We're processing any new information that we receive as quickly as we can. There has been an attack by Alexander but the details are still unclear.'

Kate stems rising vomit, brings her hand to her mouth to stop it. She swallows, runs her fingers through her hair and rubs at her eyes. 'I want to know what's going on. Where are my children?' She tries to stand up, to assert her authority both as a law-abiding citizen and as a mother but feels Anthony's hand firm on hers, pressing down, stopping her from doing anything.

All life drains out of her, a tide of fear and doubt washing away her zealousness, the protectiveness she feels as a mother. Her bones are made of lead. Even breathing feels onerous.

And then she sees movement outside the school office, a sudden burst of energy, people rushing, clambering past one another, like the contents of a shaken bottle of fizz, all spewing out in one direction. She knows then that the worst has happened. She knows it and is utterly powerless, stuck here in this room with her husband and a team of officers who remain mute despite her many questions and protestations. She is rooted to the spot, her limbs refusing to respond to the signals that her brain is firing off. She watches it all happen from another plane, her body, her mind detached from reality. Her son, her daughter. Their children, trapped in a classroom while both she and Anthony sit here doing nothing. They should be with them, helping to get them out of that room safely.

Through the window, she sees an ambulance screech to a halt and a team of medics spill out onto the pavement.

'No!' Wrenching herself free of Anthony's arm, she hurtles towards the door, a scream stuck in her throat, releasing itself as she presses her hands against the glass, an ear-splitting stretch of noise that reaches every corner of the room. It echoes in her head, sapping away every bit of her strength until, for the second time in less than an hour, she falls to the floor, her body folding in on itself like a crumpled piece of linen.

People all around her, pulling her up, smoothing down her hair, giving her sips of water. She chokes on it, spits it out, drinks some more, feels the cool liquid trail its way down her chin and heaves, her stomach convulsing violently as it rejects the icy spike of water.

This is it, she thinks miserably. *This is as bad as it gets. There is no way back from this point, no way to undo all the damage or take back all the hurt.* She is falling into an abyss that has no end; a deep, dark, endless void that will strip her of everything she holds dear.

And it is all of her own doing.

37

Dominic didn't mean to do it. Except he did. Denying it is pointless. If he cannot be true to himself, to admit his many failings inside his own head, then what is the point of it all? He was angry. His authority had been questioned and he felt duty bound to assert himself. But then of course, the girl stumbled into view. He hadn't been expecting her. It all happened before he could stop it. And now he is stuck here in this moment, trying to contain the terror and chaos that rages inside him and coming up with no easy way out of this awful, chilling mess. The bullet was meant for the boy. Not for her. Not for his Clara. He would never do such a thing. Not after last time.

He wants to scramble over to her, to lie beside her, stroke her soft skin and whisper in her ear that everything is going to be all right, that he didn't mean to hurt her. Not now and not back then when everything broke and fell apart.

It takes just seconds for his thoughts to cause him to lose focus, for the gun to be snatched away from his hands, and for him to find himself staring down the barrel of his father's rifle. He is transported back to that time, all those years ago, when his father did the exact same thing to him, calling him names, telling him to get a grip and be a man, not a mummy's boy, that his quiet, cowardly ways would get him nowhere in life and that he had better start helping out around the place instead of having his head stuck in a book.

What the hell good is reading Dickens novels going to be in life, eh? Need to get yourself a decent job instead of moping about in your room. Get yourself moving, boy. Start helping out around this place. Start earning your keep. Now move it, lad. Do you hear me? Move it!

He lets out a low moan, shoves the memory of his father's face back into that dark place in his head, that shadowy corner that remains untouched for the most part. Except for now, when it has chosen to creep its way back into the light. Seeing the rifle at that angle, the barrel so close to his face, feeling that fear again has brought all those memories hurtling back.

Dominic closes his eyes, waiting, counting, senses attuned for that moment, for that sudden click of the trigger that will bring everything to an end.

He waits, his breathing laboured, his limbs aching, every nerve in his body tensed and ready.

Then a sudden pain as something connects with side of his face again and again and again. Something hard, cold, heavy, the crushing agony rocking his world, making him curl into a ball. Not a bullet, but a rifle instead, used against him over and over and over, pummelling his face, knocking everything out of shape, breaking bones and tearing flesh. And suddenly, a final thrust as the gun is shoved once more into his broken and bleeding face, pushing him into the loneliest of places where everything is the darkest shade of grey.

38

Alex stares at Mr Rose, then over to his sister who is lying on the floor, bleeding. He can't recall what happened. Instincts kicked in after she was caught in the middle of this fucking awful nightmare scenario and he did what he had to do, but now Mr Rose is dead and panic is clawing at him.

Teenagers spill out of their huddle, gathering around Joss and dragging the table and chairs away from the door. Alex sits, his heart thumping, logic wrestling with anxiety inside his head. Christ almighty, he's killed a man. Was it self-defence? He isn't so sure. He kept on hitting and hitting, the butt of the rifle smashing into Mr Rose's skull long after he was knocked unconscious, something taking over Alex's senses, driving him on. Anger, fury, retribution, making him do things he didn't know he was capable of. What he does know is that he can't go to prison for this. It would be the undoing of him. His life would be over. Coming back from this is going to be hard enough, but trying to start again as an ex-convict? No chance.

He turns and stares at his sister, at her twisted body. And the blood. *Oh God, so much blood oozing out of her.* A sob catches in his throat. He did it for her. Mr Rose shot her and he had to do something. He was trying to end this, to rescue them all from the clutches of Mr Rose's deranged mind, and now he's a murderer himself. He is as bad as the man who shot his sister.

Terror rages inside him as all around, movement kicks in, people moving, scrambling over each other, screaming for help, sobbing uncontrollably. Girls calling out Joss's name, boys shouting at him to hand over the rifle, to lay it down on the floor. But he can't. His fingers are locked around it. There's something he needs to do to bring this all to an end.

He sits, legs outstretched, head tipped back against the wall, and places the barrel of the gun under his chin, his fingers carefully curled around the trigger. He's not scared. Going to prison terrifies him more than dying. Dying is a brief moment. Prison, no matter how short the sentence, will stay with him forever, crushing his dreams. Ruining his life.

Whilst turmoil rages all around him, he is overcome with a sudden calm. He thinks of his dad, feels his comforting hand on his shoulder, a reassuring heaviness that helps to steady his breathing, lowering his blood pressure, enabling him to do this. Alex hopes that his father knows that he did it for him, to save their family from the shame of having a son who ended somebody else's life. Nobody should have to live with that. They're all better off without him.

He closes his eyes and counts, waiting for the darkness to take him, for that brief second of eternal bliss where nothing and nobody matters.

His voice is a whisper amidst the melee.

'3… 2… 1…'

He takes a juddering breath.

He pulls the trigger.

39

Nina cannot bring herself to look at him, the way he is just sitting there, looking contrite and unassuming, nodding as the officer speaks, giving the poor woman the occasional sideways smile. Even at times like this, her husband is a flirtatious, conniving little shit, unable to control his urges, seeing an opportunity, a friendly, attractive face and trying to find a way in to her affections. Nina is willing to bet that PC Gibbon has dealt with dozens of men like Rob. She has plenty of weapons in her armoury for keeping them at bay, tried and tested strategies that will cut Rob off before he can say *piece of skirt*.

They are sitting with other parents in the caretakers' old house set directly outside the school gates, some of them crying loudly, some stunned into silence, some murmuring inaudibly while others simply weep.

Her eyes sweep around the place, scanning, looking for *her*: Kate Winston-D'Allandrio. The woman who helped end her marriage. The woman who inadvertently did Nina a favour, saving her from further humiliation and many years of torment. She wonders where they are – Alex's parents. Why are they not here, holed up in this stuffy room with all the other anxious parents who are being forced to sit this thing out with no idea of what is happening at the other end of the school? Dane is in most of

Alex's classes. They are bound to be together inside that school. So where are his parents?

The officer finishes her bland spiel that says plenty but tells them nothing, and moves onto the next set of people – an elderly pair whom Nina assumes are grandparents. They stare at PC Gibbon with rheumy eyes and pallid complexions, their skin appearing to melt from their faces like hot candle wax as she speaks, telling them that a situation has occurred in one of the classrooms and that the police and emergency services are doing all they can to gain access and get everybody out safely.

How long? Nina wonders idly. How long are they supposed to wait here, crammed together in this room that stinks of cigarettes and fried food, before they know what is going on? Every minute is an hour, time stretching on and on with no end in sight. She thinks of Dane and how he might be responding to this. He's still her boy, her baby. Is he frightened? Trying to put a brave face on it?

She chews at the inside of her lip. What the hell is happening inside that school?

Outside, sirens blare. All heads turn; a silence followed by shouts of panic as ambulances trundle past the window, pulling up outside the reception area. She feels herself being pushed aside as everyone in the room clamours to get a better view, pulling aside yellowed net curtains, pressing their faces to the glass, a collective cloud of breath misting up the window.

PC Gibbon speaks into her radio, asks for backup, calling for everybody to remain calm and to get back to their seats. Another officer steps into the room, a man of towering proportions, at least six foot six, Nina thinks as she stares up at him, assessing his face, looking for his reactions to the sudden spurt of bodies that bang into each other, jockeying for position at the window as another ambulance passes, stopping outside where they are seated.

He shouts for them to move away from the window, to sit back down, his voice a wave of noise that penetrates every corner of the room. Some respond, sliding back into the chairs; others stare outside, demanding access to the school, to find out what has happened to their offspring.

'We're doing all we can,' he replies, his voice carrying an element of exasperation as he looks around the room at the sea of expectant faces, anger and fear evident in each one.

'Well, do a bit fucking more, will you?' A man stands up, fists clenched, a pulse ticking away in his jaw. 'It's our children that are stuck in there. We have a right to know what the fuck is going on!'

Beside her, Nina hears the soft weeping of the elderly woman. Moving away from Rob, she shuffles closer, places her hand over the woman's fingers, cold to the touch. The elderly lady lifts her head, sniffs and attempts a smile.

'It'll be fine, I'm sure. They know what they're doing,' Nina tries to whisper, to shrink away from the wall of noise and confusion.

The woman nods and thanks her, dabbing at her face with her sleeves. Nina has no idea whether or not the police know what they're doing. She has to have faith in them. That's all they have going for them at the minute. Blind faith in the law enforcement team and the fervent hope that every pupil will leave that school unharmed.

She thinks of Dane, where he is now and how he is handling this, and then turns to look at Rob, who is staring ahead, emotionless, unblinking. A part of her softens but only momentarily; a brief second of relenting before she reverts back to her unbending stance. Too much water under the bridge. Too much hurt to ever alter her current thinking. To others around them, they look like every other married couple, sitting here, waiting for news of their child. As if he is able to read her thoughts, Rob moves closer, their bodies almost touching, the musky scent of his aftershave lingering in the air between them. He places his hand over her shoulders, his fingers curling around the back of her neck, resting on her shoulder, gently caressing her collar bone with his thumb. She turns to look at him, noticing how handsome he still is, how the years have been kind to him, strengthening his features, making him even more striking. She twists her body, sagging slightly under the pressure, feels herself give ever so slightly, then straightens her spine, removes his arm and slides away.

40

Plaster rains down on him, scattering over the floor, sticking in his hair, gritting up his eyes. Beside him, Dane lies, his breath coming out in ragged gasps. He is crying. Tears are rolling down his face, long, wet streaks clogged up with grime and dust, turning his skin pale and ghost-like. Alex is unmoving, his body stiff while his brain tries to catch up with events. The shotgun. His hand sweeps around but already somebody has snatched it out of reach. He spots it on top of a bookshelf, the muzzle turned to the wall.

'Fuck sake!' Dane screams, sitting up and facing Alex. 'What the hell were you thinking, man?' He places his arms around Alex's neck, leans into his friend's chest and cries, great gulping sobs that leave him breathless.

Alex feels his throat constrict at the memory of his friend leaping across his legs and knocking the gun out of his hand, the bullet hitting the roof, splitting it apart. He remembers the sound, the power, the howls of terror and thinks about what he almost did to himself. What he almost did to his family. How he nearly lost it all. It felt so right at the time, so fitting for what he has done. But now, just seconds later, he is swamped with relief.

He can't stop the tears. They run down his face, dripping onto his lap, small, dark orbs of misery and regret. He's here. He has no idea what the future holds but he is here and breathing. Then he thinks of Joss. It hits him full speed. The gun, her blood. Her still, lifeless body...

Everything seems to happen at once, police officers and medics pouring in, pupils being led out, his hands being held behind his back, the feel of cold metal against his skin as he is cuffed.

'Joss!' He screams her name, tries to twist his head to see her but feels himself being pushed down to the floor, his vision obscured by a large hand that presses down on his face. 'Jocelyn!'

Footsteps close to his face, the smell of mud and dust and sweat. He makes another attempt to get up but is held firm, his shoulders screaming with pain at being pinned down while he attempts to twist and writhe his way out of it. Then Dane's voice, his protestations as he tries to explain what happened, that it wasn't Alex's fault. Nobody listens. His words fade into the ether as he is led away by an army of adults who refuse to listen, their minds already made up.

He needs to see Joss, to make sure his sister is still alive. He thinks of her dead. He thinks of his parents, how they will cope once this is all over, and lets out a howl of protest, raw and animalistic.

He is hauled upright, his voice dulled by the ferocity of the movement, by the strength of the arms that pull at him, dragging him across the room. Everything swirls. His head pounds. Vomit courses up his throat, his stomach contracting. Still, the strong hands hold him, lugging him forwards, his feet gaining no purchase on the floor until fear and shock and dread win over, stars bursting behind his eyes as he falls forward and everything diminishes before vanishing completely.

41

It's dark, all the curtains drawn, the musty aroma of unwashed clothes and dirty dishes hitting them full in the face as they push open the door and step inside. The place reeks of neglect.

Noise filters in from outside where a team of officers scale the perimeter of the property, torches lighting their way even though it's still daylight. DI Rahman can hear them trampling through the tall reeds and tangle of shrubbery, pushing aside bramble bushes and thistles with their bare hands whilst scanning the area, their voices a distant murmur.

Rahman brushes his hand against the wall, fumbling for the light switch, slapping at it with his palm. A bare bulb illuminates everything, its white glow making him blink. He shields his eyes, glancing around the room, a breath trapped in his chest. He tries to ignore the mess, the feeling of being transported back in time as he takes in the dated furniture and décor and scans the immediate area for signs of anything suspicious.

'Christ almighty. It's like something from a bloody museum – you know, one of those rooms you go in to see what it was like living in the 1950s.' Beside him, his colleague, Sarah Gallagher stands, shaking her head and smiling as she surveys the living room. 'Could do with a lick of paint, don't you think?'

Rahman lets out a soft chuckle and sighs. 'I'll bet a local property developer would give their right arm for a place like this; get it done up and sell it for a fortune. Come on,' he says quietly as he picks his way through the piles of newspapers and dirty cups that litter the floor. 'Let's have a proper look around. See what we can find.'

'Do you want to have a look down here and I'll go upstairs?' The young female officer stares up at her boss, waiting for his reply. Standing at just over five feet tall, she has become accustomed to craning her neck upwards when conversing with colleagues, many of whom, like Rahman at six foot four, tower over her.

'Tell you what,' he says, his voice suddenly quiet, his expression sombre, 'let's go upstairs together. See what we can find.'

'Not exactly sure what it is we're looking for, sir.' Gallagher raises her eyebrows, searching his face for any signs or clues.

'No,' he murmurs softly. 'Me neither, but I'm pretty sure we'll know what's relevant and what isn't if we find it.'

* * *

Rahman is busy pacing around the front bedroom when he hears the shout. He gave Gallagher the task of checking the bathroom and then the back bedroom while he scours Dominic Rose's room. He feels sure that that's where they will find something. Or at least, he did. Judging by the shouts from the next room, he thinks that perhaps he has got that wrong.

He finds Gallagher standing in the doorway, hand clasped over her mouth, eyes watery with shock. She's new to this game. Rahman has been on the force for nearly twenty years and seen plenty but his stomach roils as he steps forward, gently pushing Gallagher to one side so he can get into the bedroom and get a better view.

'Good God.' Her voice comes from behind him. 'What the hell is it?'

Rahman says nothing, edging forwards towards the bed, his footfall hushed against the decades-old rug and a pile of dirty blankets spread across the floor.

'How long has it been here for?'

He doesn't answer, speaking instead into his radio, calling for assistance, his voice muffled. Urgent.

He looks down at the desiccated corpse on the bed, at its skeletal features, the wisps of hair swept across its bare, bony scalp and the clothes that cover its frame – a pair of old jeans and a crocheted sweater – and tries to work out how long it has been here for. Twenty years, perhaps. Maybe thirty. Maybe even longer. Probably longer. He's no expert, forensics and pathology aren't his field, but he does know that this corpse is probably a damn sight older than his colleague, young Gallagher here, who at only twenty-five years of age is a novice to this sort of discovery.

'Keep the blinds drawn in this room. We'll let the crime scene manager take over from here.' Rahman backs out, his legs suddenly weak. He has seen a fair few dead bodies in his time but nothing quite as macabre as this one. They're usually recent deaths. Battered, bloodied faces, bloated corpses after being fished out from the river, their flesh tinged blue, but nothing like this – a fully dressed dead person, their few remaining strands of hair combed into place, shoes on their feet, propped up in bed like a mannequin. An undrunk cup of tea sits on the bedside cabinet alongside a plate of biscuits. This is like nothing he has ever experienced. This discovery is in another league.

At least he hasn't become desensitised to it, he thinks as he closes the door and heads back downstairs. At least it still gets to him, catching him in his solar plexus, knocking all the air out of him, which is as it should be. Many of his colleagues can down a bacon sandwich and a gallon of coffee after discovering a dead body or after reading the pathology report of a murder victim who has been battered to death and left unrecognisable. Not him. He hopes it will always get to him, leaving him slightly discombobulated, wondering what goes through people's heads when they carry out these atrocious acts. He is glad he is who he is, and not someone who has the capacity to take the life of another person. Or in this case, dress them up, feed them biscuits, prop them up in bed and pretend they're not actually dead.

***

It's coming to an end. Dominic knows it, is conscious of what is going on around him, his nerve endings absorbing every sensation, every nuanced word and look. He may be ill, his body broken and damaged, but his brain is as active as it has ever been, and he knows that the game is up, that the future looks grim and he has nowhere left to go. No more hiding places. Nowhere left to call home.

He has no idea what day it is, how long he has been here, confined to this hospital bed, but he does know that police officers are lined up outside the door, waiting to question him about Jocelyn, about Alexander and what took place in that room. To question him about Clara.

There is little to say. Everything that he knows is stored in his head and that is where it will stay. Releasing it would tarnish her memory and sully her good name. As for the events that took place in the school – there are plenty of witnesses who can give accurate accounts of what happened in that classroom. Their stories will all marry up. They don't need to hear his version. He has his own story resting somewhere inside his mind, the one that he prefers. The truth is a strange thing: flexible to a point but brittle if bent too far. But then, they will discover that soon enough; that is, if they haven't already. He made his life, shaped and moulded it as best he could to alleviate the heartache, the unending loss he felt for his dearest Clara.

He wonders if they have already forced their way into his home, their size ten boots trampling through his little house, desecrating and defiling the place, violating his memories, his property, his life.

They can do whatever they want now. It's not as if he has the power to stop them. The only thing that concerns him is his lack of access to the letters. They will find them easily enough, the police and their team of investigators. He never hid them away. He simply stored them in a locked box for posterity.

He recalls the last time the police visited him after Clara disappeared. They descended on his home, questioning him about his movements the day she went missing. They didn't stay long. There was nothing for them to see. No startling revelations. No visible signs that anything was amiss.

That's because they didn't look hard enough.

Dominic closes his eyes and rests his head back against the hospital pillow, the crisp, slightly yellowing linen soft against his bruised flesh. He tries to visualise his future: what sort of life lies ahead for him. This isn't how he planned it but then, isn't that how things often pan out? Life is full of twists and turns and unexpected deviations. His time with his dearest darling Clara has come to an end, that's all it is. He once had her and now he doesn't. His secret is about to be exposed. The general public will gorge on his story like hungry locusts, stripping bare the carcass of his life, leaving him with nothing but the bare bones.

Sleep comes quickly, a welcoming, warm place free of misery and hurt, where nobody can judge him or tell him what to do. He savours it, knowing it may possibly be the final time he will ever be truly free.

42

6 A.M., 15 JULY 1978

'You're better off without her. She was never any good. Beneath you, she is. You can do far better if just put some effort in and got out more.' His mother's voice fills every room in the house. It's her way. It's always been her way, making sure she gets heard. Making sure she has the final word.

Dominic zips up his jacket, pulling the collar straight before checking himself in the mirror, slicking back his flyaway hair and stepping outside, closing the door behind him with just enough force to let his mother know exactly what he thinks of her comment. She just doesn't know when to stop, her pointed, snide words always finding the chink in his armour and wounding him in ways only she can. Sometimes, it's as if she saves up all her bile ready to spew out in his direction, each insult finding a special place to lodge in his heart, skewering him and cutting him to the quick. It's a gift she possesses, being able to wound deeply without leaving any visible scars.

He slides into his car, the sudden solitude sitting well with him. He's looking forward to the drive. She is right about one thing, his fiery old mother: getting out of the house is good for him. Getting away from her relentless jibes and tirades lessens his load, easing the tension that sits across his chest whenever he hears her voice, his shoulders hitching up to his ears to block out the hurt she inflicts.

The engine is a low purr as he turns the key and crunches his way off the small, gravel drive and heads out onto the main road.

* * *

The early start worked well. He checks his watch. Just under five hours to get here. Still a long journey but setting off at 6 a.m. has ensured he has made it in time to catch her. They will have time to talk, to sort things out. He feels confident that they can make it work. He'll buy her lunch, talk her round, get her to see that they are meant to be together. Once she sees him, she'll know. It will all come flooding back to her. Distance has placed a wall between them, cutting off the familiarity and love that they once shared. Now he's here, they can start to rebuild that familiarity, restoring the bond they once had, strengthening and securing it. And then everything will be perfect.

He has pulled into a layby rather than park up outside her grandparents' cottage. Here is better, more isolated, the nearest shop over five miles away, no pubs or restaurants. Not much of anything except the shimmering lake and the squat, white edifice of the small bothy in the distance. Were it not for the current circumstances, he would think this place perfect, with its rugged countryside and complete silence.

Above him, clouds gather then part, scudding across the sky, the breeze forcing them towards the horizon. The weather is different here too: cooler, sharper, the light less translucent, a wash of grey covering the landscape, the air thinner and cleaner. He looks around at the scenery – a perfectly acceptable outlook in the summer months but bleak and barren come the winter, he imagines. He can see why she is struck by the place, why her head has been turned.

Clara is a gentle soul, prone to solitude and peaceful environments. As small and friendly as Ormston is, it is still a bustling little town and she would regularly become exasperated by its busyness, by the tourists that flock around the place in the summer months, filling the local shops and lining the pavements. She craves the quieter times, the cooler months when everybody has left and their hometown reverts back to its usual placid self. Ormston, the old lady of North Yorkshire. That is how Clara used to refer to their hometown, how she wants it to remain. Not the growing market town it has become. It has grown, becoming too lively for her. This place is more Clara – fewer people. Less noise. Less stress. But of course, there is one thing that is missing form her escape plan. Him. Dominic. He isn't here in the wilds of Scotland. And they are meant to be together. Not apart. Being apart isn't good for either of them. Soon she will see that. He'll make her see it.

A shard of anger is wedged in his throat, slicing at the soft tissue there. Shielding his eyes with a cupped hand, Dominic stares ahead, trying to suppress his growing discomfort. A sudden surge of blood rushes to his head as he turns and squints at the sight ahead. His breath catches in his throat. It's her. Clara. His Clara. A shadow in the distance, a tiny silhouette, but definitely Clara. He would recognise that walk anywhere: her diminutive shape, the curve of her body, the slight dip of her shoulders. She's here, walking towards him, and his fury suddenly dissipates, scattering and disappearing into the warm breeze. Everything in his world is as it should be once again, his out-of-kilter perspective righted, his misery dissipating, replaced by a tide of happiness so large, it almost knocks him off his feet. He had forgotten how light she makes him feel, how giddy and excitable – like an over-eager schoolboy allowed to run free.

Above him, the sun continues to rise, burning at the back of his neck, fingers of yellow spreading over the ground, glazing everything with a welcome layer of heat.

He wants to run to her, to scoop her up in his arms and twirl her round in the air until they are both dizzy but stands instead, arms glued to his sides, his heart flipping about his chest. A drink would be most welcome right now, a tumbler of whiskey to arm him with the courage that he needs, to help him find the right words to say what it is he wants to say. Words that will impress Clara and make her want to come home with him. Words that will make her love him again.

Her figure comes ever closer until he is able to make out her features, to see the creaminess of her skin, the lustrousness of her hair. The grooves in her forehead when she spots him standing there. The darkness that sets into her eyes as she fixes her gaze on his.

His stomach tightens and he knows then that his journey has been in vain. No welcoming embrace. No smiles and kisses. His dream that he would sweep her up in his arms, the two of them clinging onto each other for dear life, falls away, crumbling and turning into ash. It's all been for nothing, this visit. A complete waste of time. No amount of talking is going to persuade her, no number of kind words will win her over. He can beg and plead and cry all he likes but it's obvious that she isn't prepared to listen to him. He can see it from this distance. Before she has even come close to him and opened her mouth, her thoughts are evident, etched deep into her frown, evident in the downward slope of her mouth, the way she holds herself as she approaches him, her spine suddenly rigid as if she is tensing herself for something terrible, for something or somebody unpleasant. Somebody like him.

'Hello, Clara.' He tries to sound jovial, like a meeting of old friends who are looking forward to a reunion, his voice as light as air: not too needy, not too overbearing. The voice of a man who has driven over 300 miles on his day off because he has nothing better to do.

She doesn't reply. She is fortifying herself, trying to work out the correct response. He can still fathom her thought processes – the tiny crinkle between her eyes, the way she bites at her lip – all indicators that she is thinking hard, trying to decide what to say so as to cause minimum upset with maximum impact. Clara isn't one for conflict, preferring instead to deflect and ignore. Or to run away, retreating into her lair until the battle is over. She thought she had run from him, but it wasn't far enough. He's here now, and they have unfinished business, something that cannot be put off any longer. Their relationship is something that requires attention. No more hiding. No more ignoring. The time has come to sort it out once and for all.

'Dominic,' she says softly as she moves closer to him. 'I wasn't expecting you.'

'No, I don't imagine you were.' With growing impatience, he tries to remain calm, to not allow the months of festering anger and unhappiness and resentment to come pouring out. He has to hold it together if he is to gain her trust again. If he is to try to make her love like she used to.

'Have you been and spoken to—'

'No.' He shakes his head as she points over at the home of her grandparents. 'I pulled up here to take in the view of the loch. It's very beautiful.' It's not strictly true. Although the loch is indeed a magnificent sight, he parked farther away so as not be seen. He had envisioned Clara spotting him and hiding away, her grandpa telling him she wasn't available and had taken herself off to Perth or Glasgow for the day and they weren't expecting her back until after midnight, what with the long drive and the roads and the unpredictable weather up here in Rannoch Moor.

'Ah,' she says, a note of weariness all too obvious in her timbre.

They stand together, their hands within touching distance yet so very far apart, the rift between them growing wider by the second. He has to say something, to do something to bridge that gap, to stop her from slipping even further away from him. He needs her, has to have her. He will do anything to get her back. Anything at all.

Gripped by desperation, he steps forward and tries to take her hand. She snatches it away, shoving it into the pocket of her thin, summer jacket and dipping her eyes away from his, her gaze fixed on a point somewhere in the distance. 'Don't, Dominic. Please don't.'

'Don't what?' His voice is an octave higher, a full decibel louder. He struggles to remain calm against the rising tide of exasperation and frustration that is growing in his chest. They are a force to be reckoned with, the emotions that are wrestling inside of him – annoyance at being patronised, the sting of rejection and ultimately, the howling void of desperation at the thought of leaving this place without her. He can't bring himself to think about it, to visualise a life without Clara in it. He won't allow it to happen.

Stepping ever closer, he tries to reach down and stroke her hair, the way he used to when they loved and lived as one, to feel its silken strands as they fall between his fingers, but she jerks away from him, her body twisted at an angle, her feet slipping on the uneven patch of gravel.

He finds himself staring down at her as she falls, her hands grappling for purchase, her backside scrambling backwards, away from him. Dear God, she is acting as if he is a monster. All he wants to do is love her, be with her, be her life partner and make her happy and all she wants to do is escape from him. How did it ever get to this point and how did he miss the signs?

Her hands look tiny against his as he reaches down to help her up.

Resting on his haunches, he tries to pull her up, only to be slapped away, Clara resisting and scrambling back away from him. He doesn't mean to do it. Circumstances conspire against him – her inability to see things from his point of view, her cutting words, the way she glares at him as if he is a complete stranger. It's her face, her features. The hatred there. He can't bear it. It cuts him in two to see it.

'Leave me alone, Dominic. I came here to get away from you. Just go, please.'

He wishes he could remember the chain of events, how it all happened, but he can't. It's a blur. Each movement, each word, fuzzy and distorted as if in a dream. He recalls a struggle, Clara's muffled cries as he clamps his hand over her mouth to stop her screams of protest from escaping, and after that – nothing. Until he finds himself staring down at her lifeless body in the boot of his car, her eyes still wide with horror, her mouth twisted into an ugly, unrecognisable half cry.

Frozen by panic, he slams the boot shut and kicks the gravel back into place, then slips into the driver's seat and starts the engine. In his rear-view mirror, he glances back at the bothy. No movement behind the windows. Nothing to suggest anybody saw him.

Slowly and as quietly as he can, he swings the car around and heads back the way he came, praying nobody sees him.

43

5 P.M., 15 JULY 1978

The house is silent as he lets himself in. He sighs, even manages a small smile. No haranguing, no vitriol waiting for him, his mother's voice commandeering every inch of the house, bouncing off every wall. He can head up into his room, think about what to do next. Because he has to do something. She cannot stay where she is, his dearest Clara, her lifeless body tucked away in the boot of his car.

He will wait until the darkness and then take her out into the woods. Nobody will see him. Nobody will hear or notice him just as nobody noticed him on the journey home. It was an uneventful drive, the roads quiet as he focused on the route, trying to push the thought of what had happened, out of his mind.

It wasn't his fault. It's just how things turned out. She goaded him, doing her best to put even more distance between them both. He had no choice. It was all Clara's fault. If only she had listened to him, not tried to push him away. If only she had relented and come home.

He has heard it said that the first kill is the hardest. After that, it becomes easier, more fluid, less stressful. Perhaps that's how it happened, what came next. Perhaps on the journey home, he became desensitised, or maybe he finally plucked up enough courage to break free of the constant barrage of insults that have been hurled his way for as long as he can remember.

She was lying on the bed as he peeked his head around the door into the murkiness of her room. Curtains drawn against the light, his mother suddenly sat bolt upright, her hands pressed against the sheets, gripping them tightly to her chest.

'I'm not well. I've been here all alone and you left me. You left me here, going gallivanting off to Scotland to see that woman while I laid here suffering.' The venom-loaded words are spat out, her voice a distorted squeak. It makes Dominic think of an animal caught in a trap, its desperate howls sharp enough to shatter glass. Accusations. Blame. He has had enough of them.

He moves into the gloom, dust motes swirling, thousands of them circling in front of her face. Even in the near darkness, he can see that something is wrong. One half of her mouth has dropped. Her left eye is almost closed, the lid drooping over her eyeball, a melting of her skin. Her cheek is hanging loosely, as if it is no longer attached to her face. He steps forward, listening as she starts up again, her speech a warped version of itself, her syllables soft and slushy.

'I know where you've been. You can't fool me, boy. But what about me, eh? When are you going to start taking notice of me and what I need?'

It's a stroke. His mother has had a stroke. He can see that. He has no medical training but can tell by her face what has taken place. He needs to do something, to help her, to stop her pain.

She feels so delicate, so very small and fragile, her resistance barely registering as any sort of movement at all. He pushes her back onto the pillow and places his hand over her mouth and nose. His palm is warm and clammy against her cool dry skin; her eyes cloud over with confusion. He swallows, presses harder. The way she is watching him compels him to turn away, just for the briefest amount of time. He doesn't want to see her die, to watch as the last bit of life ebbs away from her. He just wants the shouting and the abuse and the constant stream of insults to stop.

It doesn't take long. She flails for a short while before her body slumps, her head lolling to one side. It's then that he takes the time to look at her – to really look at her, studying her face with the kind of scrutiny that he hasn't applied in the past, casting an impartial eye over her now flaccid features, using his expertise to assess who she really is. What sort of person she had become.

Now he can see her thin lips and low sloping forehead, things he has never really noticed before, he is able view her in a different light, see what sort of person she truly is – a mean, vindictive woman with no regard for anybody but herself. When he was a child, she would regularly castigate him for the smallest of misdemeanours, his father often joining in, the pair of them leering over him, eyes wide, mouths set in a sneer as he sat on wet bedsheets, cowering and trembling, pleading for them to stop.

Things didn't improve with the passing of time, their constant complaints and criticisms of him chipping away at what little confidence he possessed. He tried to fight back, to defend himself but was never strong enough to bat away their continual volley of abuse.

Dominic stifles a sob. Then laughs. He rubs at his eyes, stands up and stares around the room.

None of it matters anymore now. It's all in the past. Everything is in the past. She is gone. No more insults, no more hurt. Just him, alone in this house.

And Clara.

He has Clara now. She will be here with him. Soon it will be the two of them together. But not just yet.

Snatching up the telephone, he calls the doctor, explaining how his mother took ill and now he can't seem to rouse her and can somebody please, please come out immediately?

Doctor Lindell arrives in a little over five minutes. Dominic stands in the doorway, eyes glazed, lip trembling as the good doctor pronounces his mother dead.

'She took ill this morning. I thought it was perhaps flu but as the day progressed, she seemed to get worse. I went downstairs to make her a warm drink and when I came back, I found her like this.' His voice breaks. He rubs at his face and shakes his head wearily.

They exchange pleasantries, Doctor Lindell asking him about his job, telling him he has always been a good son to his mother, looking out for her after his father passed away. He is a family friend, has known Dominic since he was a small boy, prescribing medicine when he developed measles and suffered from whooping cough. He is practically one of the family.

'I called you first, Doctor Lindell. I didn't want anybody else to see her like this.'

They shake hands and the doctor talks amiably, tells him about the removal of her body and his findings.

'She suffered a mild stroke last year, if you recall.'

Dominic does recall the event. A momentary loss of movement in her left arm, a slight slurring of her speech. It didn't last long. Soon she found her voice, criticising him day and night, her demands and insults wearing him down. But not for any longer. She is gone. A bright new beginning beckons him.

***

He moves Clara after his mother is taken from the house, carrying her into the cellar, wrapping her cold body in plastic sheeting, whispering to her that it's only for a short while, just until the funeral has taken place and everything returns to normal around the house. Then she can join him. Then they can be together once again. Briefly apart, forever reunited.

Apologising, his voice a soft murmur, he slides her into the crawl space using a piece of old rag to cover his face, wiping away his tears as he drags and pulls her into place. The fabric, he realises is one of his mother's old dresses, torn up, used as oily rags by his father whilst working down here as he mended and fixed bits of old machinery.

A pain shoots up Dominic's spine as leans in and throws the bundle of material alongside the body. Salty tears smear his face. He doesn't want to leave her here. It's dark. It's cold, but it's only for the shortest period of time. Then she can live alongside him in the house, the pair of them together once again.

Sleep is fitful, his mind raking over the events of the day, how it all came to this. How his life unravelled so spectacularly in just a matter of hours and became a shabby version of itself, now as threadbare as one of his mother's old dresses.

But not for long. Soon, he will repair it. He will take a needle and thread and stitch together the worn parts, the ragged, tattered parts, meticulously mending them until the splits are no longer visible. He will make them both whole.

*　*　*

The following days are a blur, with distant family and funeral directors milling about the house. The church service and burial are a small affair. Smaller than small, it is tiny, with only a handful of family and friends attending. They each make their way back to their own homes afterwards. No gathering was planned. Nobody asked why. The Roses have always led a private, sheltered existence with few contacts or friends. It suited them, living that way. And now it suits Dominic.

He leaves it for another month before bringing Clara back into the house, cleaning her, dressing her, combing her hair and settling her in bed. The police called the week after she disappeared, listening sympathetically as he told them about spending the day with his mother and her subsequent unexpected death. He shed many tears, telling them that life can be so unutterably cruel. They agreed, patted him on the shoulder and said they would be in touch if they required anything else.

He never heard from them again.

PART IV
THE PRESENT
TWO MONTHS AFTER THE END

44

For once, the weather is kind to them, the sun revealing itself as they drive through the gates of the crematorium, parking the car at the far end next to the new headstone. Alex stares out of the window, a heavy feeling settling in his chest. He isn't sure he likes this place, the expanse of slate and stone, the spread of dead bodies buried beneath them. It doesn't feel right, the thought of it at night, how the darkness will creep in. How alone and cold it will feel.

'Have you got the cards, Kate?' Anthony's voice is soft, comforting and warm.

She nods and scoops the small gathering of white envelopes out of the glove box as he pulls on the handbrake and takes the keys out of the ignition, a sudden silence falling around them.

The air is warm as Alex steps out and heads around to the other side. He pulls open the door and leans in, grinning at the sight before him.

'All right, smart arse. Here, hold this while I clamber out.' Joss gives him her walking stick and shuffles her way off the seat, landing unsteadily on the patch of gravel, stones scattering in all directions, a small explosion of pebbles at her feet.

'It's just over there by the path.' A small, marble cross stands white and incongruous, its newness against the surrounding grey slabs, stark. Kate walks over to it, a sudden purpose in her stride.

Anthony follows, catching her up and placing his arm around her shoulder. Alex's mother appears to shrink a little, leaning into him before taking his hand and clasping it tightly. A small, warm object unfurls in Alex's chest, spreading and settling there, making him slightly giddy. These past two months have seen some real highs and lows in their lives – Granddad dying while Joss was still in hospital, and Grandma admitted to a home with dementia, her mind fragmented, her memory and confidence vanishing into the ether. It's as if a full year's events have elapsed in just eight weeks.

'Slow down! I'm still not able-bodied, you know.' Joss gives Alex a punch on his shoulder and links her arm through his.

'Ah, you'll manage just fine. Anyway,' Alex says with a smile, 'I reckon I should get paid some sort of carer's allowance for looking after you.'

'You love it. It's what you've always wanted: having to wait hand and foot on your little sister.'

It feels good to laugh again, their voices slicing through the calm. Alex wonders if they should keep the noise down, be more respectful, but then thinks that perhaps the deceased have had enough of silence, that this place is in need of some levity and happiness.

Since Joss returned home, their lives have taken a more positive direction. There was a time when they didn't think she would make it out of the hospital at all. There was a time when Alex was convinced that he would end up being convicted of attempted manslaughter and sent to prison. But of course, none of that happened. Once the story emerged, rather than being seen as a criminal, he was hailed as a hero, newspapers writing stories about how he saved the rest of the class from certain death. He isn't so sure it would have gone that far but has enjoyed the sensation of being thought of some sort of modern-day warrior all the same. It bolstered his flagging confidence, giving him a whole new set of friends at school. Dane is still the main man though, the one who protected him, taking a huge risk and saving Alex's life that day.

A magpie swoops down ahead of them, closely followed by another.

They scavenge about in the bushes before hopping about and taking off again, their wings flapping wildly as they disappear into a vast, cloudless sky.

'Two for joy,' Joss murmurs, her eyes pointed upwards. 'That's got to be a good sign, hasn't it?'

45

Everything seems brighter, the layers of grey that have shrouded her life for as long as she can remember lifting to expose a swathe of luxurious, opulent colours beneath. Nina stops and blinks, taking in her immediate surroundings. It's far larger than she remembers. The lapse of time since first viewing the place has expanded the size of each room. She was convinced it was a tiny, makeshift house, somewhere she and Dane would live until they got back on their feet, but actually, now she is here, she can see that this place is damn near perfect. Everything happened so quickly – the separation, her decision to move out and let Rob stay in their soulless mansion, Dane's decision to join her. That fact still gives her a warm, healthy sensation, like a flower unfurling its petals at the first sign of spring.

The incident at school shook him up, re-joining the parts of him that were uncoupled, helping him to think clearly. He views the world through different eyes since that day. He emerged from that situation a fledgling adult, ready to partake in activities that once would have been out of his reach.

'Where'd you want this one to go, Mum?'

It's hard for Nina to not shed any tears of joy as he lugs boxes out of the van, his strong, capable arms lifting each one with all the confidence and ease of a grown man.

'That can go in the dining room, I think. It's got the crockery in it and the big oak dresser is going in there so they can be stacked in that when it arrives.'

He places the box down at his feet and gives her a mock salute. They laugh and she is tempted to step closer and ruffle his hair but knows that there are still boundaries which she has yet to cross, boundaries that given time, she will be able to tentatively tiptoe over to reach her boy. Her newfound son.

Rob has proven to be a better man than she ever thought possible, giving her a healthy monthly allowance until she finds some sort of job. She has no doubts that his womanising will continue but that is no longer her problem. He can sleep with half of Ormston if he so chooses and every town beyond. They are no longer a couple. Even thinking such thoughts sends a thrill of excitement surging though her veins. All it needed was some courage and a crazed teacher to try and kill one of the children at the local school for her to suddenly see how easy it is to start a new life that doesn't include her errant husband.

The thought of Mr Rose makes her stomach dip. She always thought of him as gentlemanly, a true educator – erudite and wise, somebody who had the children's best interests at heart. She wonders what went so wrong in his mind that he turned into a savage man with the propensity to kill. It's hard to comprehend. Maybe something inside him finally snapped. Maybe he hit a low point in his life and everything suddenly untangled, his reasoning and clarity of thought falling away into an endless, dark void.

The papers are full of stories about how he murdered his girlfriend, Clara and kept her body for all these years. Nina finds that hard to believe. How can somebody like that live a normal life, going to work every day and acting as if all is well in their corner of the world when they have a dead body stored in their home? It seems too outlandish to be true. People don't do things like that, do they? Perhaps she is being naïve. Perhaps the world has moved on and left her behind, cocooned in her own tiny, little bubble. A bubble that doesn't involve murder and the storing of corpses as if they are a macabre trophy.

'And this one?' Dane is standing in front of her, waiting for her reply. His smile is broad: a young lad brimming with excitement at having his life returned to him. A new life. A better one than the one he had. Money isn't always the answer. Quite often, it is the problem.

She reads the words printed on the side of the cardboard box in black marker pen and nods at the staircase. 'Up there. That's some of your stuff: your diaries and folders from your computer table.'

He stops and frowns, his breathing suddenly heavy and irregular. 'Right. Well I might have a sort through it all, get rid of a load of stuff. Most of it is stupid kid's things from when I was younger. No point hanging onto any of it, is there?'

She nods and smiles, another wave of gratification warming her. This is her Dane, the one she suspected was always in there yet didn't dare hope. The positive, happy Dane who was too afraid to step forward into the light, He has arrived at along last and she couldn't be happier to see him.

'Do you fancy a meal at the local after we've finished up here? I've heard they do a cracking steak and ale pie.'

'Sounds great. And Mum?'

She inhales, braces herself for whatever is coming next, her body on edge after so many years of unpleasant surprises and turmoil. 'Yes?'

'Thanks,' he says quietly, a cerise web spreading over his neck and creeping up his face. 'For everything.'

46

Dominic wonders how long he will have to stay here, whether he will ever be allowed to leave. He thinks that maybe he will never be a free man ever again but then, what does he know? He has hidden depths, facets to his character that run deep. An unhinged man, a dangerous psychopath. That's all he is now. This is who he has become.

Teams of lawyers and psychologists have been to see him, talking to him, assessing his mental wellbeing, trying to see inside his head and work out his thought processes. His solicitor has advised him to plead guilty. To everything. That way, he will avoid a trial and the media scrum that goes with it. The psychologists are still trying to use the line that he suffered a massive breakdown, brought on by years of hiding his murderous deed. They are wrong. All of them. He has no time for these people who think that life is a series of simple events, one thing leading to another until everything comes toppling down, the weight of it all too much to bear. They think they know everything there is to know.

They don't.

They are ignorant of his life, of the crooked path that led him to this dark and lonely place. Only he has the key to that particular corner of his head, the shadowy, dusty place that contains all of his dirty little secrets. The ones he has hidden away for most of his life.

Doctor Reynolds claims that Clara wasn't even Dominic's girlfriend, that she was an acquaintance, nothing more, nothing less. Just somebody Dominic had become attached to, that their relationship was purely platonic and that she thought of him as a friend, a friend who had feelings for her that weren't reciprocated. It's nonsense. Of course it is. They were lovers, he and Clara, joined at the hip until she left for Scotland and distance drove them apart. If Doctor Reynolds can't see that then maybe he should consider changing his profession, doing something more worthwhile. Something he is good at. He is supposed to be able to work people out, to unpick their snarled and knotted thoughts, the subtleties of their behaviour and come to a logical conclusion, but as far as Dominic can see, he knows nothing about anything and certainly nothing about Dominic and who he really is. Nothing at all.

If he wants answers, then maybe Doctor Reynolds needs to start looking closer to home, casting his net wider and taking a good look at Dominic's childhood and how he developed as a young man, how his parents berated him at every opportunity, how cruel and thoughtless they were with their constant put downs and aggressive words and actions. That's where the problems always begin, isn't it? Home is where the heart is. Or the hurt.

Dominic wants them to ask him how his father died. He has been told that losing a parent at a young age will have impacted upon his personal growth, stunting his emotions, steering him off course. It was tragic of course, him falling off that ladder while working on the roof of the house. Tragic for many – but not for Dominic, not for the young man who shook that ladder then watched his father's body fly through the air, his spine curved into an arc, before it landed with a sickening crack on the rough ground beneath.

His tears were well rehearsed that day as he ran into the living room to tell his mother that an accident had taken place, that he had tried to stop it, done everything he could, but it had proved hopeless and that in the end, there was nothing he could have done to save his father.

They cried together – a fifteen-year-old Dominic, clinging to his mother, listening to her sobs as they merged with his own howls of relief.

He thought it was over that day, the misery and abuse. He thought he had put it all behind him. It was just the beginning.

It was almost instantaneous, his mother's decline into a permanent state of anger and wretchedness, as if being left on her own with her son was too much to bear. Her gripes and moans grew. She more than made up for her husband's absence, berating her son with the voices of two people.

Dominic lowers his head, stares at his shoes, thinking how little they all know – Doctor Reynolds and his team. How little they delve and forage when questioning him. They don't know where to look, how to properly question him, to open and highlight that dusty, unlit corner of his brain that stores his many secrets and lies. He would tell them in a heartbeat, unburden himself of his sins. It's a heavy load to carry, all this weight. All this knowledge.

All those deaths and murders.

He wants rid of it, to shed it all and start again. They just need to start asking the right questions. Then he will tell all. He will tell them everything they want to know.

ACKNOWLEDGEMENTS

There is, as always, so many people to thank once a book has been written that I am in danger of spending as much time compiling this list, as I did writing the actual book. With that in mind, I will try to keep it brief, so here goes.

First and foremost, a huge thank you to everyone at Boldwood Books. Their unwavering faith in me always helps to bolster my flagging confidence. They help authors like myself, who would otherwise struggle to get noticed by the larger publishing houses, into print.

My editor, Emily Ruston is somebody I trust implicitly, her wise words and guidance helping to shape my writing and make it the absolute best it can be. Thank you, Emily. You do a magnificent job!

Who was it once said that if you think writing a book is hard work, wait until you come to try and sell it? Never was a truer word said, so a huge thank you to Jenna Houston, Nia Beynon and the marketing team at Boldwood, who work relentlessly, promoting our books and making sure they get the best coverage possible. Well done, everyone.

I couldn't possibly write this without saying a massive thank you to my family and friends. You never complain when I disappear for weeks at a time, sitting at my laptop typing until my fingers bleed and my brain begins to melt. Thank you, thank you, thank you.

A huge thank you to all the bloggers who help promote my books free of charge. You guys are quite literally diamonds. Keep on shining bright.

And finally, thank you so much to you, dear reader for choosing my book and taking time out of your day to read it. I hope you enjoyed it and if you feel so inclined, a review would be most welcome.

I love chatting to people so please feel free to drop in for a chinwag on any of my social media sites.
Facebook.com/thewriterjude
Twitter.com/thewriterjude
Instagram.com/jabakerauthor
Best wishes,
Judith A Baker

ABOUT THE AUTHOR

J. A. Baker is a successful writer of numerous psychological thrillers. Born and brought up in Middlesbrough, she still lives in the North East, which inspires the settings for her books.

Sign up to J. A. Baker's mailing list here for news, competitions and updates on future books.

Follow J. A. Baker on social media:

facebook.com/thewriterjude
x.com/thewriterjude
instagram.com/jabakerauthor
tiktok.com/@jabaker41
bookbub.com/authors/JABaker

ALSO BY J. A. BAKER

Local Girl Missing

The Last Wife

The Woman at Number 19

The Other Mother

The Toxic Friend

The Retreat

The Woman in the Woods

The Stranger

The Intruder

The Girl In The Water

The Quiet One

The Passenger

Little Boy, Gone

When She Sleeps

The Widower's Lie

The Guilty Teacher

THE *Murder* LIST

THE MURDER LIST IS A NEWSLETTER DEDICATED TO ALL THINGS CRIME AND THRILLER FICTION!

SIGN UP TO MAKE SURE YOU'RE ON OUR HIT LIST FOR GRIPPING PAGE-TURNERS AND HEARTSTOPPING READS.

SIGN UP TO OUR NEWSLETTER

BIT.LY/THEMURDERLISTNEWS

Boldwood

Boldwood Books is an award-winning fiction publishing company seeking out the best stories from around the world.

Find out more at www.boldwoodbooks.com

Join our reader community for brilliant books, competitions and offers!

Follow us
@BoldwoodBooks
@TheBoldBookClub

Sign up to our weekly deals newsletter

https://bit.ly/BoldwoodBNewsletter

Milton Keynes UK
Ingram Content Group UK Ltd.
UKHW040717080724
445163UK00001B/1

9 781835 612569